The Glass House

BOOK 3 - THE MASON JAR SERIES

A NOVEL BY ELI POPE

© US COPYRIGHT 2021 – Steven G Bassett
All rights reserved.

No portion of this book may be reproduced, stored in a retrieval system, or transmitted in any form or means including electronic, mechanical, photocopied, recorded, scanned, or other, with the exception of brief quotations in reviews or articles, without prior written permission of author or publisher.

Scripture quotations are taken from the Holy Bible, NIV®, MSG®, KJV®

This novel is a work of fiction. All names, characters, places, and incidents are either from the imagination of the author or used fictitiously. All characters are fictional, and any similarity to people living or dead is coincidental.

Cover Design – Steven G Bassett
Interior Formatting – Sharon Kizziah-Holmes
Audiobook Narration – Paul McSorley
Audiobook Music Creation – Nikki McSorley – nmcmusiccreative.com

Published by 3dogsBarking Media LLC

ISBN: 978-1-7358159-0-9

DEDICATION

This book is dedicated to my loyal readers and fans that keep pushing me to do better by their faithful comments and reviews. If it weren't for you wonderful people hungry for the story I love to tell, I'd just be writing to satisfy my own whim and mental exercise.

Thank you for letting me write for you.

Eli Pope

ACKNOWLEDGMENTS

There are far too many thanks for me not to accidently leave someone out, but I will attempt to name the ones that have been irreplaceable.

My editor **Julie Luetschwager** has fixed my many mistakes and pointed out changes that make me appear to be a smarter author than I truly am. I say thank you, thank you, and thank you. You've helped keep me inspired to move forward.

Sharon Kizziah-Holmes @ Paperback Press for her formatting. She makes the look!

My partner in the Audible.com side of this series, **Paul J McSorley**, whose professionalism and dedication to his craft helps catapult my written words to an entirely new level.

All the beta readers that stay loyal to my writing, I appreciate you all very much.

My **Springfield Writers Guild** fellow author friends who share ideas, critiques and occasional beers. Thank you.

1

Ethan William Kendrick looked out over the rolling waves as they massaged the beach with each endless trek up and back, washing the shoreline, a breathtaking panorama of beautiful natural peace. It's why he picked this piece of real estate on the forgotten coast of the Florida panhandle to build his beach house. White powdery soft sand with no footprints for as far as the eye could see either way. Sitting while admiring the view, glass of bourbon in hand, brought calm after a day spent in court. It took the edge off conversations he'd shared with others in the past. A perfect setting for the council he dreaded but knew to be necessary. Ethan's quiet and private place to carry on the placatory discussion that could otherwise go south if the setting wasn't just right. "Charley, he's become a gawd damned liability. I think there is only one choice. I think deep within, you know what that choice consists of."

"Ethan, you aren't suggesting what it sounds like—are you?" Charley stared back with caution. He studied Ethan's facial expression and demeanor, down to the tiny palpitations in his forehead that steadily pulsed just under the skin.

"I hesitate to even suggest it, but we have our lives resting on the shoulders of a man who has repeatedly acted out of line with no considerations to you and me." Ethan lifted his highball glass to his mouth and tipped it carefully so the ice wouldn't come crashing to his lips. "I don't believe we have any other viable options."

Charley turned away and watched the waves rolling up the

sandy beach as he swirled the neat bourbon around his glass, giving it several seconds for the alcohol vapor to exit before taking in its oaky scent. "I'm getting apple with a touch of either butterscotch or possibly vanilla bean. Very nice, very nice indeed." He pushed the smooth crystal glass edge to his lips and sipped a portion, letting the liquid roll around his tongue.

"Charley, that's one thing I've always liked about you above Roy. You've got class. You appreciate the finer bourbons instead of just downing whiskey like a high school teen. Cheap whiskeys like Ole Grandad or God forbid, Jack Daniels."

Ethan shook his head remembering just how weeks earlier when Roy came out to confess his stupidity, begging help to clean up his mess, Roy practically guzzled his Blanton's Single Barrel like a teenager shooting Jim Beam with Coca-Cola. "Roy never did carry any stateliness. How can a man, who represents not only our town's law and order but also our towns integrity, be such a damned mutt in a pedigree's position?"

"Ethan, it sounds as if you are taking this beyond protection of ourselves and head-on into personal territory. I'm not sure I want to take the risk you're suggesting if it's not needed and only based on vengeance. Will I be next in your line of imperilment? You're not instilling much confidence in my future endeavors concerning you."

"Look in front of you, Charley—doesn't this view feel majestic? It's a beautiful life I've worked hard to build. Now it's time to sit back and enjoy it…" Ethan drew from his Cuban cigar and let the smoke swirl from his mouth slowly as it billowed above their heads in the light breeze. After a long pause, Ethan continued, "…there's a gawd damn bull in our china shop. A clumsy, arrogant, and dangerous bull." Ethan turned and looked into Charley's eyes with intent. "You too have done very well for yourself. You've worked tirelessly building a standard of trust in our community, a nice respectable lot in life here in Apalachicola as principal of our high school—in charge of our town's finest commodity. I'm certain the superintendent position coming up is on your radar. Lord knows you've enjoyed some wonderful perks on the side!" Ethan held his glass to his mouth and took another sip, swirling it between his cheeks before swallowing and continuing. "You would be willing to risk it all for a bulldog that doesn't watch where he puts his paws? There are piles of his fetid shit he's boldly, or more often, clumsily stepped in—and then tracked all over the place." Ethan lifted his glass for another quick sample. "He's been warned many times to no avail. He's a liability, Charley. A dangerous albatross hovering overhead, and he will dribble that shit all over what you and I have worked so faithfully to build and keep free of debris."

Charley focused his sight on the waves rolling onto shore. He again inhaled the aroma of the Wellers 107 before sipping it, then concentrated on the fruity notes it contained. As he slowly looked over toward Ethan, he asked a question which seemed inconsistent with the conversation they were sharing. "Are the waters out there still brimming with bull sharks and alligators?"

Ethan smiled and then guffawed. "Let's just say the scenery is very beautiful. The water is pristine—but I wouldn't wet my whistle out there to save my soul."

Charley glanced over to Ethan and smiled. "Much like the New Yorker's wife who is opening the new restaurant in town with her husband. She's something to look at, but I'd be terrified to dip my wick in that wax. Tempted though, indeed. But wild as a bitch in heat, I imagine."

The two laughed out loud in mutual agreement.

"She is a shapely and sensual woman, but I concur with you, Charley. She appears to have some questionable baggage. I would be curious to hear her story. Her husband seems very nice, but clueless in how to keep her off the racetrack, if you catch my drift." Ethan sat back with an indulgent smirk across his face. "I imagine the studs are lined up and ready to frisk as soon as a back is turned, and the stall door cracked open."

Charley's thin lips parted into an open smile. "I would be surprized if Roy hasn't already tried using his position to bag her up and rub bones together." He looked at Ethan. "Now when I think of things in this regard—I do believe you may have a valid point in our earlier conversation." Charley gave a stern look of concern. "The man has no appetite for a woman's rejection, nor the patience to oblige it." Charley's head shook back and forth in disgust before returning his restrained attention to Ethan. "I want no knowledge or timeline of it. It must come at me in a total surprise."

The two clinked their crystal glasses together setting off a beautiful tone of agreement, which echoed across the patio. The deal became sealed with a shared conversation over two glasses of Weller Signature Antique 107 bourbon, just like the big boys out east, they imagined.

2

"Mr. Bollard, I do appreciate you taking on this case for us. I believe Jay has been sought out and ridiculed by the sheriff because of some past they share between them." Ben reached over to hold Gina's hand. "As you know, Billy Jay Cader is a partner in our restaurant venture, a very integral part of getting us open and supplied. I don't know the sheriff personally..." Ben turned to acknowledge his wife's presence in the conversation. "...but, without...."

Gina broke into the conversation. "Without Jay, we have no supplies and will also have to scramble to get artwork hung and finishing touches completed. We've already been forced to set the opening back two weeks. We need him!" Gina looked over at Ben and sheepishly smiled. "Mr. Bollard, we have a lot of money invested in this restaurant which means we're invested in this town—and it's going to take every available hand we have to reach the new target opening date. We need to have Jay available to us or we're sunk.

"I understand Mr. and Mrs. Dane. I've got my team looking into Jay's charge and it's quite unprecedented, given the locale of Jay's home opposed to where the complaint took place. The charge is weak. Provocation or incitement of violence is vague at best. The area of the dispute is shared property, a common area—rental property at that." James Bollard shuffled through some pages in a file which sat open in front of him. He peeked up, looking above the rims of his reading glasses. "I plan to have my team delve deeper into some background of Sheriff Burks. I have every confidence they will be able to find something from the past which will help our case. He isn't exactly known for being squeaky clean around here already. In the meantime, I plan to seek both dismissal of the charge and getting Jay released without bail on his own recognizance. I have a good rapport with Judge Williams along with the Franklin County D.A. and I will relay your urgency." Mr. Bollard stood to shake Ben's hand. "We will get this taken care of in short order. Are we handling the son's case also?

"There's been some..." Ben appeared to be rattled. "...I'm sorry, I'm a little thrown by the question. It seems the son's biological heritage has been put in question by Jay. He is claiming Darrell..." Ben appeared confused as he slowly continued. "...well, Jay claims Darrell is actually the child of none other than Roy Burks." Ben paused. "This is an example of Jay's reasoning why Sheriff Burks appears to have singled him out and is attempting to cause him these legal problems. It's a mess Mr. Bollard. No offense, but with all this bubbling up, I'm beginning to question the depth of some of the gene pool in this town."

James Bollard guffawed and couldn't seem to shake the grin from his face. "And that sir, is why I hang my hat in Tallahassee!" Mr. Bollard leaned in close to Ben and Gina. "I shouldn't say this, but you are not the first to put those particular kinds of words together in a shared sentence. There are a lot of surrounding wetland forests—a.k.a. swampy bogs, with a not so heavy dose of outside population. A sharing community, just sayin" He winked.

Ben looked at Gina and tilted his head. "Well, hopefully it has nothing to do with one's tastes in fine cuisine."

They all three chuckled.

***

"Are you okay Gina?" Ben asked as they climbed into the

Cadillac. "You've seemed—kind of off, lately."

Gina glanced over as she slid into the front seat. "I guess I'm just worried about this latest crap in town. We're putting a lot of work into living here and investing most everything we have. I just hope we're doing the right thing. That's all." She smiled. "I've built this town and its people up in my head—I pray the Lord doesn't let it topple down into our laps." She nervously looked away, feeling the sudden re-emergence of guilt over what had happened between Jay and herself. She turned away with some apprehension but then leaned into Ben's shoulder, turning back and whispering, "I hope you know I love you, Benny. You are my everything, no matter what happens. I don't deserve a wonderful person like you." Gina looked up into his eyes and then slid back to her side of the seat.

Ben reached over and touched her shoulder. "It's gonna be alright, sweetheart. No matter what, we have each other. But don't worry. You and I are gonna put this town on the map!" He suddenly burst into laughter, almost uncontrollably for a minute. "Oh my. Did you hear what word I just used—twice? My New York City accent is melting away—are you 'gonna' miss it when it's totally become a swampy southern mess?"

Gina laughed aloud. "Yes, I love you no matter how far south you become. You are just as fine a southern gentleman as you were a Manhattan sophisticate.

***

Gina closed her eyes and leaned her head back away from Ben. The vinyl top on the Caddy sat folded back, letting the warm breeze blow through her short black hair on the hour and a half ride from Tallahassee to home. She hid the tears which began slipping out when Ben laughed at his accent and turned to see her reaction. He looked so happy in the moment. It made her feel even more deplorable.

Why did I let myself get into such a spot with Jay? Am I self-sabotaging like my mother used to accuse me? She always claimed I did it, so I could hurt daddy. Am I trying to hurt Benny too?

Gina beat herself up and questioned why things were happening the way they were. She felt bad but happy to hear about Jay being arrested. She'd thought for a moment it would be the time to step forward and accuse him of raping her. Who would believe him anyway?

But who would believe me? I don't even believe myself. Could it even be called rape? I don't know what the fuck is wrong with me. I finally have everything I want, a wonderful man who loves me with all my fucked-up faults. And I throw it away on a tryst with a likely would-be serial killer. I know that's what he is. It's in his eyes. I saw it. I have no idea what I am, though. I just wish he would have crashed the van with us in it—into the trees at eighty that day. It would have taken care of every problem I've caused at once.

Gina's eyes suddenly opened, but she remained still and continued to stare at the blur of scenery as the world raced past, wishing this moment in life would either change for the good or stop and let her disappear into the background.

3

Kyle was released, after two weeks of listening to CJ taunt him and Darrell.

He wanted to kill Jay.

I could do it. The damned psycho deserves it. He thought to himself.

Kyle walked over to Darrell's cell on his way down the hallway towards freedom. It'd been almost two weeks since he'd seen Darrell eye to eye. They were able to talk but the cement wall between them blocked their sight of each other. He noticed immediately how washed-out Darrell appeared, his eyes sunken dark sockets on his pale face. Darrell's normally combed red hair was thick with oil and slicked back.

Kyle held his hand out to grip Darrell's as he leaned close to the bars. "We will get you out of here. It doesn't end this way."

"Take care of Mitz for me—and—we didn't know…" Darrell's head lowered as he suddenly felt he couldn't face his friend. "…We had no idea...about…being related."

"We know, brother. I'll watch over her and let her know you're thinking about her and worried. Don't worry. We are getting you out and this entire fiasco will sort out."

Kyle glared back toward Jay with a vengeance as the crazy bastard just sat on his cot staring back.

"You get on outta' here little longhair. Run to your mommy's breast and get back to suckling it." Jay's yellowed teeth glowed as he smiled. "I'll take care of this one for you, after all—he's gonna be a—daddy, or uncle, or—something" Jay turned his stare to across the hallway, but Darrell just stood, silently watching Kyle walk away.

Jay began his taunt, "The itsy-bitsy spider climbed down upon my head. Along came the wind and blew him to a shed—the pigs said oh no, you don't belong in here, and the itsy-bitsy spider cried himself a little tear...."

Darrell grabbed the bars of the cell wall and squeezed.

"It's okay, baby-boy. You can let those tears out like that little itty-bitty spider did." Jay climbed off his cot and mimicked Darrell by standing and gripping his cell bars. "I feel your pain. Bet you wish you were my son now. You wouldn't have knocked up your pretty sister then, huh?" He waited to see if his words sank in and sparked an anger inside his cellmate.

Silence. No response.

4

Cat opened the front door to the county jail as she had every other day since her son had been arrested.

The guard smiled politely and stood as she signed in. "It'll be 'bout twenty minutes ma'am. They just been served lunch."

"I'll wait." She returned the smile and walked over to the chair in the corner of the room. As she sat down, the door swung open and the guard said, "Hello, sir."

Sheriff Burks stepped through the doorway and turned to see Catrina sitting in the chair. He suddenly appeared nervous, and he cautiously turned his head away from her.

"Those bruises and stitches look damned painful there, Sheriff. Just what in the world did you get tangled up with, cause it looks like you were kicked in the face by a mule?"

Cat's smile gleamed her pride of the damage Darrell did to the prick who raped her so many years ago. "Karma is a bitch, I hear."

Sheriff Burks took the bait and turned to face her. "Your boy is charged with battery of an officer of the law—that's serious shit. A felony. He'll be leaving to begin his time at Franklin Correctional, just after he's found guilty. Long, hard time is what he's facin' for this."

Cat snapped back immediately. "Don't you mean our son, Roy? Or have you forgotten a particular day nineteen years ago? A glass of lemon-aide in exchange for a ride?" Cat stood up and started toward the sheriff. "Your officers may not have heard the story yet, but they will. The whole damned state is gonna hear it. It may just be you headed to Franklin Correctional! Rape might be a more important word in your vocabulary very soon. A painful word. Repeatedly." Cat guffawed as she turned away to go back to her seat. As she sat down, she couldn't hold back one last comment. "Your tiny little dick didn't hurt at all. We'll see how you take a real man's raping."

***

Darrell's eyes began to swell as he walked out to see his momma. The sheriff ordered not only handcuffs, but also leg irons. Darrell clinked with every hobbled step he took, but it didn't seem to slow him down.

"Ben and Gina have hired Mr. Bollard again. They're working on a plan to get you outta' here, real soon. Don't give up, son. The time is coming."

Darrell raised his head with a look of shame smeared in tears. Cat reached over and wiped them away. "It's okay, sweetie. You got nothin' to be ashamed of. I'm sorry. I shoulda told you years ago." Cat sniffled. "We'll sort through all this once we get you out."

"Momma, they got the bastard in the cell directly 'cross from mine. He torments me all damned day long and into the night. I'm goin' crazy. I miss you, I miss my friends, and..." Darrell looked deep into Cat's watery eyes. "I miss Mitzi. I love her, Momma. What am I supposed to do? I know it ain't right and..." Darrell choked up. "...what do I do? Will you talk to her? It's killing me sitting here, wondering if she hates me or blames me...."

"Darrell, how could she blame or hate you? She was caught off guard just like you were. She's sufferin' the same thoughts and fears about everything, just like you." Cat pulled her boy into her arms as close as she could. "I'll talk to her, to her and her mom. I promise." She rubbed his shoulders as she squeezed him tight. "I'll talk to Ben about trying to have Jay separated from you. It's not right."

The officer walked over and began to pull Darrell back from Cat's grip. "It's time to go back, Darrell."

Cat wouldn't let go as the officer pulled at Darrell while he tried to stand up. Her grip became tighter, and she began to cry out. A second officer stepped in and tugged on Cat's arm. She batted his hand away and bellowed out. "Don't take him—he shouldn't be put back with that son-of-a-bitch!"

Sheriff Burks smiled as he watched the entire event unfold from the protection of reinforced one-way glass.

***

Another week slowly passed with no release of either Jay or Darrell. The two remained in the cells they were first assigned.

Ben kept in constant phone conversations with James T. Bollard.

"We are working on the release of Jay. I assure you Ben. The bastard sheriff is fighting us in every possible way. He should be released by Tuesday afternoon, though."

"Mr. Bollard, I understand, but you said the charge is almost a bogus one!"

"The fact that Jay's interference may have led to the severe beating the boy did on the sheriff is the holdup. The DA is up for election this year and…"

"This is about re-election and politics? Gina and I have invested in this community for God's sake! That should account for something! We need Jay to continue helping, so we can open our business! Now we'll be more than four weeks behind schedule!" Ben became upset and paced the office in their home.

Gina hated seeing Ben so upset. She walked out the back door and stood looking out over the bay and over toward the Big Apple on the Bay building. Their dream was so close to reality yet beginning to feel like an anchor around their necks while treading water.

Ben looked out through the office window and saw his wife alone. "Let me know when we can go pick him up, please, James. I know you're doing your best and I thank you for it."

As soon as Ben hung the receiver up, he shot through the back door to join Gina. She turned in time to feel his hands touch her shoulders. She placed her hands back and on top of his, then nestled back into his chest.

Ben leaned in, his chin resting against the side of her head, his lips close to her left ear. As he squeezed her, he whispered, "I love the most beautiful woman there is. I thank God for you every day, Gina. God brought you to me because of my faith in Him, and for that I am thankful to Him for every minute we share together."

Ben couldn't see the tears of guilt slipping from her eyes, nor would he have understood them if he could have.

The sun continued to shine through the thin clouds and heat their faces with its warmth. Ben unfolded his arms surrounding Gina and let his hands slowly travel downward until they were edging into her front pockets.

Ben pushed forward into her back as he continued to dig his fingers deeper into the crevices of her jeans and whispered again, "Let's go back to bed for a bit and start this day off with a bang." He smiled and touched the tip of his tongue to the opening of her ear.

Gina nervously turned, nonchalantly wiping her face as she met his gaze. "I would love to Benny…" She placed her hands over his as she turned. "…but…" Her voice quivered. "…I don't think my thoughts are in that frame of mind this morning, I'm sorry. Can we revisit this tonight? I have so much tension it wouldn't be what you deserve."

Ben answered her quickly. "What I deserve? I'm not sure I understand what you mean. I do understand you being full of tension, this whole thing happening is causing us both grief and worry. But I don't 'deserve' any better than you do. I just want to pleasure you and show my love." He pulled her into his arms again. "I'll wait though, and hope you'll feel more comfortable this evening. It's okay, sweetie."

Ben slowly backed away and turned to retreat back to his office. He certainly needed to get plenty done.

5

The killer sat caged. No one yet knew the depths to which Jay swam in those dark murky waters of judgments and death. He knew his past wouldn't be understood by anyone. Jay also realized he'd been shaped to judge and punish those he saw fit. Chosen and then formed into the mold; it became a skin which fit so well, it wasn't meant to be shed like a snake's skin. Sorrow or pity of those condemned under his judgment would never be able to penetrate his thickened heart for their punishments. They did indeed deserve what they'd reaped. There was a long trail of what others would call atrocities, but no one had ever put the pieces together or realized the reasoning. But he knew the why, he'd always known, and now he felt called to continue. This "healing" that Ben and Gina introduced to him in the cold of New York, became temporary, or better yet, a farce. Oh, it created some inner turmoil and shook his core briefly, but his true nature yearned for the work to continue. Being back home now in the sweltering heat, it felt like hell was calling, and he stood poised ready to answer.

Jay's mind began to struggle as if fighting to stay afloat, treading in a churning sea. He'd been on the offensive side since Roy got his ass kicked by Darrell and Kyle. He'd watched and taunted that night, playing a manipulative match, but now one of the pawns was freed and the other withdrew from the game refusing to respond in any fashion. This kind of play drove Jay deeper into his own madness. Jay needed to be the one in control.

He now felt as if he were the crumbs left on the empty floor and the rats were on their way to feast. It wasn't a feeling the monster inside found comfort in. Jay didn't have control and without control, his sanity would begin to faulter in time.

Jay's mind began to drift to the past. Cat—the boys—the Sunday night to Friday evening travels that were only his. He enjoyed the solitude and seeing the country. Spending his evenings either locked up in his truck sleeper planning and waiting for the knock of his victim on the cab door or out hunting his prey.

Jay honed his hunting skills with each excursion. He laid back on his cot to mull over some of those past experiences, but before he closed his eyes, Jay stole a quick peek to the other side of the hallway. There was Darrell quietly laying on his side—his back to him. Jay mumbled under his breath, "hmmm—well, he's no help to me. Damn pussy." He then thought to himself. *Well, at least he's not from my loins.*

Jay let his mind travel deeper into his past. Closing his eyes, he could imagine hearing the rumble of his diesel down the highway and feeling the excitement of what would come when he arrived at his destination for the evening.

Jay wasn't asleep. He daydreamed with his eyes closed. The lighting in the jail always a constant soft yellow tone. There were no windows available to them, so there was no real way to know exactly what time of day it was. He surmised it must be getting close to dinner time. "Who gives a shit, the slop they shove under the door ain't fit for a dog," he spoke quietly to himself.

He quickly resorted back to his Bronx ways of carrying on a conversation with himself. Jay pinched his eyes closed even tighter as if to turn off his current thoughts and go back to the ones which excited him. The imaginings that put a thickness in his trousers and a spark in his brain. The young girls he'd stumbled onto in his old way. Young prostitutes and runaways who'd turned to drugs to escape their troubles and parents. They were easy targets. He'd, by

God, been a runaway and never gave in or caved to the weakness of drugs or drink. Hell, he'd seen much harder times than anybody. Poisons to dull one's hurt just put the brain in a fog so you could fuck up even worse. Drugs were a sin; sin which should be harshly reckoned with. He'd even grown to despise Cat and her weak and vile falter to the bottle. The times he'd fought his urge to put his hands around her neck and tighten his grip while they were "doing it." Her in her drunken stupor, allowing him to take her any way he wanted. Weak and mindless is what the bottle did for a person. The prostitutes and druggie gals who would knock on his truck door at the truck stops—made his need to hone hunting skills nearly nil. Once, just for the thrill and to sharpen his prowess—Jay passed on a "turkey" prey and hunted for a more thrilling atonement kill. A target which brought challenge which seemed to bring him more excitement—more "juice and sparks" in his male parts.

Occasionally in his mind-playing game—Ms. Cela would creep into the scene. He'd pinch his eyes together until they began to sting, to make her get the hell outta' his brain. "I don't need you or your preachin' right now, Ms. Cela." He spoke out quietly, but loud enough to stir Darrell across the hallway in his cell. Sure, Ms. Cela tried to help him, showed him plenty of kindness, an oddity in this world. The little old black woman, an enigmatic savior to the homeless masses in the harshness of New York City. *I certainly miss you, but—* "You tried to fill my head with hocus pocus, and it just clouded my thinkin' and robbed me of my purpose!"

Darrell rolled over and stared. "Shut the hell up, you crazy ole bastard."

"Well now, ain't you the pot callin' the kettle black. I had a momma and a daddy and married proper. How 'bout you? Can you say the same?" Jay quickly responded.

Darrell rolled back away, choosing to ignore Jay, knowing how refraining from his argument would get under his skin.

Jay watched Darrell's retreat, which caused the veins in his head to swell. "Just like your Momma, ya scared little bitch." Jay laid back down and for a split second felt in his heart what he'd just spouted. He wondered in a quick reflection, just when he began to hate Cat so much? For the briefest moment in time, she'd shown him what actual love could be. He'd held no idea before the day she sat down beside him on that damned bench. Of course, he'd not fully discovered his purpose by then either. He just now surmised in one exact instant in time—he'd felt mentally molded for his future purpose. Now, he just wanted to push all this old crap from his mind and re-focus on his future. He just needed free from behind these damned bars, which kept him from it.

Jay smirked. He sure played Ben and Gina though. His acting skills were top-notch. He'd played it all the way to Gina's treasure box. Just thinkin' of the day at the dead-end road brought on a "chubby." Again, he smirked. "Chubbs—what a fat piece of work that worthless punk turned out to be..." He spoke in nearly a whisper. "...the sea creatures enjoyed one hellova feast that night, I'll bet."

Darrell's blood boiled. The look on his face when he turned, showed he'd heard what Jay spoke. "How did you do it, you worthless piece of shit? And why? He didn't hurt you. Chubbs was just an innocent kid. He was my best friend, you psycho."

This time Jay did the ignoring. He just laughed to himself as he lay on his cot picturing the blubber and guts spilling out of his fat belly. He remembered moving pretty quick so he himself didn't become an appetizer or an hors d' oeuvre for the sharks or gators. "I hear they found him swimming down by Alligator Harbor. Pretty impressive for a fat boy named Chubbs!"

Darrell turned back onto his side. The tears rolling across his face and onto the sheet. He didn't want to think how Chubb's probably struggled before he died.

6

Sheriff Burks steered clear of the jail house section of the station up until now. He'd just been informed they were gonna need to release Billy Jay. Seems his attorney did some lawyer stunts and convinced the judge to release him for now. Oh well, he grinned while his nose snarled up, moving the mustache hairs to cause a tickle on his nose. He sneezed. I got a little surprise for ole Billy Jay Cader. I'll bet his asshole crawls up in his throat when I spill this on him." He stuck his fingers under his belt and pants and gave a quick tug, bringing his trousers back up under his belly. As he walked by his mirror in his office, he sucked his gut in before looking. "I'm still a damned fine, lookin' officer of the law." He turned to walk out his office door and let the jelly roll flop back over his belt buckle.

"I'm headin' out to lock-up, Mary Lou. Looks like we got to get ready to release Billy Jay Cader. It's a gawd damn shame." He swaggered on by and twisted the lock on the steel door leading to the cell rooms.

The snarky look on Mary Lou's face or her shaking her head back and forth seemed to make her opinion of Sheriff Burks rather clear. Of course, she always sported those looks and actions when Roy wasn't paying attention to her. The phone rang and she reached to pick up the receiver. "Franklin County Sheriff's office, how can I help you?"

***

Sheriff Roy slowly waddled over toward Jay's cell. "Well, well and looky-loo, who we got in here. A couple of Franklin County's finest dirtbags." Roy's eyes were dark little slits still surrounded by dark black and blue bruises beginning to yellow some, the swelling almost gone but his face still appeared sore.

Jay sat up and hollered back, "Hey boy, aren't ya gonna say hello and howdy to your daddy?" He guffawed.

Roy waited no time to answer, "Now this boy looks like somethin' that woulda' squirted outta' your little pecker, Billy Jay. He ain't got the stature of a lawman, but more of a lanky and shifty build of a criminal. And that's right up your alley." Roy sauntered slowly up to Jay's cell and completely avoided Darrell's. "Billy Jay, I got a bit of a surprise for you. Actually—there be two surprises. One is good, and one is not so." He smiled a big turned up grin, like a Cheshire cat. "I'm gonna give you the good one first." He stood and stared at him, taking in Billy Jay's inquisitive demeaner and drawing out the silence to let the moment gain momentum.

"Well, spit it out, Roy boy."

Roy smiled, enjoying the look of impatience on Billy Jay's face. "It seems—Judge Rainey—who will be hearing these cases against you Caders..." Roy stalled again just to get under Billy Jay's skin. "...has been somehow convinced you should be let out on your own recognizance. Of course, you'll be needin' to stay in the area, as much as I personally hate the idea. "Your employers, Ben and Gina begged because they need your sorry ass to get their restaurant ready for the big grand openin'. Lucky for you."

"You bring that fat face over here Sheriff and I may just kiss it. Your food sucks and your hospitality's non-existent."

"Oh, I'm a gonna walk over there to ya, but it ain't for no kiss. It's for private talk. You know, the bad news I got for ya. It's better between just you and I." He winked and flashed a gritty leer. As he got next to the cold steel bars, he motioned with his finger for Jay to come forward. He waited as little sweat droplets collected on his forehead and neck. His armpits already were darkened from perspiration on his uniform.

Jay walked up slow and determined. Once he got up next to the bars, he reached out and grabbed one with each hand. He pulled himself close where he could almost smell the sweat and cigar breath of Sheriff Roy. "So—drop this niblet of shit you're so anxious to tell."

Roy jeered, his lips pursed, and he leaned in close to softly speak his enlightenment. "Seems the occupants of your old farmhouse called Mary Lou to give me a message about some odd things they stumbled onto." Sheriff Roy searched Jay's facial expression, hoping to see fear. "They were workin' out in the garage." Roy stared into Billy Jay's eyes even deeper to see his reaction.

Jay stared back and never flinched. His brows furrowed in question as he tilted his head to the right slightly and then to the left before responding. "And this news is bad for who?"

"It's bad for you, Billy Jay. It's real damned bad…" Roy leaned in closer before he continued, "they found panties and jewelry—several pairs of panties. Look like young girl panties." Roy raised his left eyebrow in question and then let the corners of his mouth turn upward into a dark smile. "And burnt matches? With some alphabet letters written on each one—hmmm."

"I hate to tell you this, Roy, but I don't wear panties and ifn' I did—I wouldn't leave 'em in the garage." Jay leaned back away, but not before Roy noticed his fingers gripped the bars so tightly, each of his knuckles on both hands were white, almost as morning frost. "By the way, Roy boy—I don't smoke—I never acquired the nasty habit." Jay stared.

Roy shook his head and looked down towards his boots before

bringing his sight back up and squaring with Billy Jay's eyes. "After getting' a call from the Bullinger's, the folks that live there, I started doing some research on missing girls around the area and beyond..." He again watched Billy Jay's reactions closely. "...I called Bingers 66 Express trucking to see what routes you drove back three years and before..." He saw a slight quiver in Billy Jay's left eye. "...seems there were young girls disappearing all over in towns you could have passed through. Curious ain't it?"

Jay stood silent as if calculating his answer.

"There's a whole bunch of hookers and runaways missing all throughout the paths you would have been driving weekly. That collection of panties and jewelry the Bullinger's found—well, they want me to come and pick 'em up and to see the little hidey hole where they found 'em. Vertis and Judy Bullinger says' they were in a hidden compartment inside a wall. Sound familiar, Billy Jay?" Sheriff Roy stretched himself up tall as if he'd grinned a grizzly down without a weapon in hand, like Davy Crockett. "I'm bettin' the FBI might want to take a gander into my investigation. Don't you, Billy Jay?" Roy smiled like a proud new father of a baby boy. Well, he looked proud anyway, even though he'd never cared much for babies or bein' a father.

Jay stood tall and walked back up to the bars and clutched them once again. He motioned with his head for Roy to come closer. Jay smiled boldly this time, speaking loud enough Roy could smell the stank from his unbrushed teeth. "You remember way back nineteen year ago or more, when the cute little red-headed high school girl overdosed? A pretty, little thing, very fair-skinned young girl with freckles all over her body. Pretty green eyes. Nice firm titties and a heart shaped ass. She suffered a habit though. I believe it be her momma's Valium and whiskey." Jay watched Roy's eyes to see if he twitched or showed any nervousness, which he did indeed. "Awe, I see I have your attention..." Jay took his turn with curling his mouth into a nasty smile. "I have your fuckin' attention now, don't I?" His yellow stained teeth went ear to ear. "...well, I have a story about her I'd like to tell you after I'm out of here. It's a story I'm certain you'll be interested in. See, we may be at a bit of an impasse here. Somethin' two businessmen of sorts might want to get together and haggle over—maybe come to a deal." Jay continued to watch Roy's disposition shrink. His confidence waned. It appeared to Jay his adversary, Roy, suffered some poor-ass bargaining abilities and weren't quite up to snuff with his own.

"You get out tomorrow, Billy Jay. You best get hold of me in real short time." Roy warned.

"Oh, I'll be a callin', Roy. No need to spoil the air with threats that won't hold water. You got far more to lose than poor white trash like me. You remember I already know what it's like to lose my freedom. How 'bout you?" He grinned a condemning grin as he let his grip loose from the bars and backed up to his cot. "I'll see you tomorrow with the keys to this cage, Roy. Unless of course you'd like to share one of your institution's lovely meals with me in here, might give ya a perspective of a possible future for you?" Jay ended his statement with a grin and guffaw.

Sheriff Roy turned abruptly and scampered out of the cellblock with a deflated persona.

Jay fell back on his cot and tightened his eyes to change the thoughts in his head. He needed juicy thoughts, the kind which brought on the bulge, not these worrisome ponderings which were just discussed. He's certain he held a handle on those. He knew his mission wasn't over just yet. There were those right here in this town which needed adjudication. *And I'll by God be happy to step up to the duty of doling out judgment, verdict, and of course—the punishment. Hell, I might even put together another Mason jar just for the fun of it.*

<u>7</u>

Roy immediately headed to his office to dial up Ethan and he raced past Mary Lou as if a pit bull were chompin' at his ass cheeks. He slammed the door and opened his bottom drawer abruptly. Reaching to the back and behind the files which dangled in green folders on the drawer rails, he found his hidden relief. Beads of sweat rolled down his cheeks as he pulled the tarnished silver colored flask from its spot and quickly unscrewed its cap, holding it to his lips and tipping his head back. *Awe. The sweet burn of relief. Thank you, Mr. Daniels.*

Roy grabbed up the phone and dialed Ethan, then tipped back in his chair as he held the phone receiver to his ear. "Hello, Ms. Addison..." Roy shook his head back and forth as if talking to Addison Charmane, face to face. "...yes, yes Ms. Addison, that's very nice, but..." He pulled the flask back to his mouth and gurgled another swallow as Addison cackled on. "...yes, well I really need to speak with Ethan—it's rather urgent and I have other appointments and yes, yes—I would love to attend the opening of the restaurant with you..." Roy wiped his brow. "...of course, Addi, I can call you that if you'd like. Okay, I'm looking forward to it also and I'll hold."

"Sheriff Burks, what's the pleasure of this call? Sounds like you've stroked the sweet spot on my secretary, just what the hell did you say to her? She's walking around the office like a dog with butter on his ass, head turned backwards to lick it clean!"

"You really need to bed this one down, Ethan. The woman's nether-region gotta' have steam risin' from the smolder down there. But I got news and it ain't that Christmas is around the corner!"

"I suppose you said yes to her invitation the way her voice has risen two or three octaves in excitement." Ethan smiled to himself just picturing Roy and Addi bumping bones together. "Now, what's all this news that is apparently not the best kind that one could receive on this fine June day?"

"Billy-Gawd damn-Jay is being released tomorrow."

There lagged an uncomfortable silence between the two. "You are correct, Roy—it's not the best news to receive on such a promising close to the day."

"The damned New Yorker and his hot little lady-toy begged him out on his own recognizance; the minute Judge Williams took pity on them. Did you know Billy Jay is a partner in their damned restaurant those fuckin' move-ins are opening? They said they needed help to open on time and they've invested everything they have in our town."

"Hmmm, you mean the restaurant you and Addi are attending on the opening night—together?" Ethan forced a snicker out loud even though he wished Sheriff Roy would be out of the picture completely very soon.

"That son-of-a-bitch sounds like he's got somethin' on me, Ethan. Gawd damnit." Roy spouted out rather loudly.

"Where are you at, Roy? Tell me it's private and not at the station." Ethan questioned with a firmness.

"I got my damned door shut—hell, it's solid cypress! Ain't nobody gonna hear me...."

"No, it wouldn't be in Mary Lou's character to have a water glass held against the wall to eavesdrop." Ethan's eyes rolled as he picked up the crystal decanter of bourbon sitting on his leather-topped desk. As he poured, he continued, "Roy—you need to set up a meeting somewhere out of town and very private with Jay to 'talk this problem out' and then let me know the time and place. We'll nip this weed in the bud before it has a chance to take root."

"How?" Roy questioned.

"I'll put some thought to it and take this problem over for you. You don't need to worry a bit, just make sure I have the time and location. Give me some advance notice too, Roy—don't by-God set the damn meeting up tomorrow. I'll need a day or two to figure out a solution before the two of you meet. And tell no one! You hear me? NO ONE." After hanging up the receiver, Ethan sat back in his executive brown leather wingback chair and swirled his bourbon around the snifter before he inhaled its scent through his nose. He then downed the contents in one swallow and carefully placed his glass back on the liquor tray.

8

Ben snuck up behind Gina as she stared out over the bay and gently put his hands on her hips. It startled her and she jumped forward. She let out a scream as she turned back and saw Ben. "Shit! Ben. You almost gave me a heart attack!"

Ben looked at her in shock. "Gina, my God, I just touched you! What the hell is wrong with you these days?" He moved in towards her again. He closely eyed her face for a response. Gina melted as she slowly went to her knees. Ben dropped to her side putting one hand on her cheek and turning her head to meet his gaze. "Gina, sweetie. What's wrong?"

Gina sniffed as the tears began to seep from their ducts and stream down her cheeks. She first dropped her head and then slowly looked back up. "Benny..." Her eyes were pools of fluid, the greenness sparkled but she still wore an overwhelming sadness. "...I—I..." She hesitated and her lips fidgeted as if she wanted to say something but second-guessed herself. "I—don't know what's wrong with me..." Her head dropped back down. A quiet sigh escaped and then another sniffle. "...I'm struggling, Benny. I'm feeling so far down." She looked back up and into Ben's eyes. "It's as if I'm drowning—just below the surface and I can see the world, but it's through the layer of water and I can't get past it..." Gina broke down completely in the moment. Ben reached to hold her tight, not knowing how to react or what to say.

They both sat on the ground in complete silence other than the seagulls circling overhead and the occasional sigh from Gina.

Minutes went by and Gina realized she couldn't hide here in plain sight forever. "Jay is getting out, isn't he? I thought I overheard you talking to Ethan."

"This is a good thing, Gina. We need him to make our deadline. The invitations are out, everything is getting so close, but we need him to hang artwork and do finishing touches. Next Friday will be here before we know it."

Gina wrestled around, changing her position. "I know, I just, something about him bothers me—worries me." She looked back up to see Ben's reaction.

"It's okay. Remember—it was all just a dream. A bad dream months ago with no more repercussions. He's a good guy now." Ben quietly answered. "Tomorrow, when he gets here, we will get so much done with the final preparations. You'll see, it's all gonna work out!" Ben snickered. "There's ma southern talk comin' through 'gin."

Gina cracked a smile and let out a small giggle. Ben squeezed her tight and followed through with a "That's my girl. My tough sassy girl from the Bronx." He smiled at her. "You know—I know a soft breezy place upstairs we could go relax before tomorrow's hectic work rains down on us. You game? I think I'm owed a raincheck!"

Gina used Ben's shoulder to help stand up. "Give me fifteen minutes to change into something more fitting." She smiled. Ben felt it could have been a forced smile, but he accepted it.

9

Gina and Ben hadn't made love since before her episode with Jay on the dead-end road. She'd felt far too dirty with guilt but knew the day would be coming. *Tonight, is the night. I need to bury the day in the past and forget. Benny deserves my giving him my all. Well, all except my loyalty to my vows which I threw away on a killer.*

Gina went through her nightwear drawer and looked at one after the other scant outfit. She felt like a whore preparing for a john with each item she held up to herself while looking in the mirror. She always only danced for her pay. She never sold sex for money. She gave in once or twice for circumstances like help getting out of a jam, but never like a prostitute. Necessity. *I feel more like a whore tonight than I ever did dancing. Why? He's my husband.* She now looked for the least cheap looking nightie she could find. *I want wife and husband sex, not naughty, trashy sex. I want to make love. I want to see if it still really exists.*

She picked up a cream-colored nightie, being the least naughty one she owned. She jumped in the shower to quickly rinse off and rubbed cherry fragrant soap over her entire body as the light drops of warm water spilled down her skin. She knew she couldn't stay in as long as she wanted. She wanted to stay until she disappeared into nothingness. Gina found herself lost in those thoughts when the sound of a light knock on the door brought her back to where she stood and what she needed to do tonight. She rinsed the last of the soap off and then grabbed the thick towel and began drying herself. She looked at the cream nightie on the seat and suddenly walked over to her drawer with it in her hand. She pulled the drawer open grabbing the bright red naughty see through nightie. The crotchless one. *Change of plans. If I've been a cheating whore, I'm going to fuck my husband just like I am one.* "It's the only value I can bring to the table anymore." She uttered quietly to herself.

"What, sweetie? Are you doing okay? You've been in there for almost thirty minutes." Ben asked in a worried tone.

The door flung open and there stood Gina. Ben looked her up and down, appearing as if he never expected her to go from somber to sex-starved. Her hair wet and slicked back close against her head; pulled back behind her ears. It almost looked like a man's cut—but holy shit she looked hot. His eyes spied her bright red lipstick and then down past her neck to where her breasts were exposed through the bright red lace. He then looked below her midriff. Ben's boxer shorts began to grow tighter by the second. "I am the luckiest man in all of Florida. Gina—I don't know what to say? Wow!"

Gina slinked towards him, and he spun around to follow as she walked past, her ass cheeks jiggling under the scant lacy panties. She didn't speak a word until she climbed onto the bed. Gina pulled his shoulders towards herself and then ran her fingers down each arm until she clutched his hands. She pulled them to her hips and took his fingers and maneuvered them under her panties and then leaned up to his ear. Running her tongue around the outer edge of his lobe before poking it deep into his ear canal; Gina softly groaned in a hot sultry breath and then pulled it out. Drawing back to see his face, she noticed how turned on he'd become. It wasn't only the look upon his face, but his body quivered with excitement and his boxers poked out firmly. She leaned into his ear and whispered, "I want you to be rough with me tonight, Benny. I want it hard. I want you to pretend you're paying for this, and you can do anything you crave— anything." She reached down and touched him through his boxers and then began to pull them down past his erection. "I'm bought and paid for. You just tell me what you desire."

Ben appeared shocked. But he looked like a man who just won the lottery and wanted to spend it all tonight.

10

"It's okay Benny. It happens." Gina spoke with a reassuring voice.

Ben turned away with a look of shame. "It's never happened to me before. I don't know what to say or what to do."

Gina ran her fingers across his chest as he lay on his back, head turned facing the window instead of her. Her fingers began to move in small circles and southward. "We can keep trying if you like. We don't have to do it like I started. I'm sorry. I thought you would like it that way."

Ben turned so he could look at her. "I don't know what happened, but it's not you or anything you did. You are incredible in every way. I don't know…" Ben's pale face looked away momentarily and then returned. "…I don't understand why—why my mechanics are stalled, but it's nothing you did. I'm very turned on by you. The only thing missing is a glass of Vavoom Vodka over ice." He stopped suddenly.

Gina's head snapped up to meet his. "I'm sorry, Benny. I am so damned stupid." She lowered her head back down.

"It's not your fault, Gina."

"The hell it isn't. I brought back the whole past you wanted away from without thinking of what it would do to you. The strip club scene, complete with lust and the booze and drugs. I'm a selfish idiot and I am so sorry." She quickly jumped up and covered her body with the sheet as she hurriedly scooted to the bathroom. The door lock clicked with authority.

Ben pulled his boxer shorts on and walked to the bathroom door, softly knocking. "Gina let's talk about this, sweetie. We can't leave tonight sitting like this. I love you."

***

Gina couldn't make herself respond. She sat on her chair in the corner of the bathroom by their walk-in closet, rocking her legs back and forth as her tears suddenly came to an abrupt halt. "What the hell am I?" She quietly asked herself. "I mess up every relationship I attempt to hold. My mom is right—I do self-destruct to either avoid or harm those around me. I'm just a worthless fuck-up…" She looked up to the ceiling as if she were facing Jesus Christ himself. "…why would You even waste Your time with me? I can't be saved and made worthy of what You offer."

Ben quietly knocked again, "Gina, sweetie, what can I do? Please come out and talk."

"You deserve better, Benny." She yelled through the door to him. "I don't deserve a good and perfect man like you—and you definitely don't deserve a fuck-up like me. I can't face you. You're perfect and saved and following God's word and I—I'm just baggage holding you back from—from where you're heading." She sniffled. "I need out. I can't do this. It's not real for me." Her head dropped back down and tuned out everything on the outside of her head. She mentally crawled inside herself and began beating herself up. She knew she should open the door and fess up to what she'd done with Jay, but it would crush Ben and she couldn't do that to him. Not when he seemed to be doing so well. It's like there is no sin that called his name or poked and prodded his brain to fall from grace. *Why can't I do it?* She looked over at the mirror, her lipstick mostly smudged off and her mascara running down her cheeks. She looked like a whore turned into a clown, through her eyes. The sheet fell to the floor, and she sat naked on the chair. *God, you gave me this body thinking it's a gift, but all it is—is a temptation for me to sin. I took it as a blessing my entire life and I used it to get what I wanted by flaunting it. Sure men "want" me. Mostly just to satisfy their own lustful desires.* She knew she'd discovered how she could use her looks very early in life.

Gina shook her head as it dropped back down. *I should have stayed with Meesha and partied that last time with her. I deserve what she got, she didn't. She'd been born into nothingness. Me? I'm the fucking privileged one and not only threw it away—but destroyed my parents without thought or guilt.*

Gina sat at a crossroads. She knew it inside. It wasn't the first pity-party she'd thrown for herself, but this wasn't like those from before. She felt true pain inside. She felt the suffering she'd caused from the beginning until now. Like a movie reel of all her failures inside her brain, looped over and over and it wouldn't stop. Gina knew Benny would overlook it all if she clued him in. He was THAT kind of a man. He would throw his sobriety away if it would help her to survive. She couldn't do that to him. She WOULDN'T do it to him. *If only Jay would have driven the van into a tree like I damn-well dared him. He's surely the devil. He must certainly be enjoying where I've landed because of him and his power.*

How would she face Jay tomorrow without letting Ben see the tension and guilt which would certainly be showing boldly? What would Jay say to him? That killer cares for no one and fears nothing. He's such a fake—an actor—a demon. *But what am I? It takes one to know one is what I've heard all my life. Am I just a different brand of the same demon?*

Knock, knock.

"Gina, come to bed, please. We have so much work tomorrow. I need you. I need to hold you and know you are okay." Ben's voice begged. "You are making this something inside your head which doesn't really exist in our reality. I don't understand why you are upset when I'm not?"

"I can't face you right now, go ahead and go to bed. I'll be out in a little while. I'm okay, I just need to be alone for a bit. Please."

Ben stepped back from the door and turned towards the empty bed with no top sheet. He crawled in and pulled the bedspread over his body and almost immediately fell into a deep exhaustive sleep.

Gina sat in the silence trying to sort out what she should do. She knew if there were a bottle of any alcohol in the house—she would surely consume it all. The fact there wasn't any, caused difficulty for Gina to decide if it were a curse or a gift there would be none to find.

She woke up shivering, wrapped in a sweat soaked sheet lying on the carpeted floor in the walk-in closet. She quietly got up and put sweats on, then gingerly slipped into bed beside Ben. Facing opposite from him.

11

Cat kneeled at the alter and looked up at the cross hanging by wires from the church's ceiling. She glanced around at the beautiful colored shadows cast from the sunlight shining through the bright stained-glass windows. Morning being the time she felt closest to God and especially when she sat all alone. Reverend Gabriel never locked the front door of the church, proclaiming it to be the entrance into God's house and no one should ever be locked out from entering. She knew Gabriel must be an angel chosen by Him to serve His people. She looked around the sanctuary again and took in the abundant silence which surrounded her.

The floorboards or ceiling joists would occasionally creak or moan, likely from the breeze outside blowing mighty against the structure; possibly the sandy ground of Florida letting the hundred-year-old building shift minutely, causing settlement. Cat felt as if it were sounds from the Lord provoking her to speak to Him.

"Lord—You know me more than anybody or anything ever could. You've seen me through the hardest of times and smiled with me in the happiest." Cat returned her eyes to the cross. "I'm hurting more than the physical pain I've endured in my past. Feels like I've gotten both my babies robbed from me." She sniffled as her nose began to run while the tears escaped her eyes. "Oh, Billy James…" Her chest heaved as the ache burst through her body from the sound of speaking his name. The woes of losing her first-born. Suddenly it felt as if she'd lost him this instant. Close to four years of pushing the torment deep down within, instantly exploded into her consciousness and shot out in those three words like lava from a volcano being cast skyward to the heavens. "...my Billy James. I miss my baby, Lord. I know you got your reasons and your plans—but I need him now..." Cat's shoulders shook with each cry as the sobs caused shockwaves throughout her shell. It's what her body felt like these days, an empty shell. Her forehead dropped to the alter rail. "...my Billy, there will never be another like you, son." The air escaped her lungs causing her chest to heave again, searching to draw more oxygen to revive what she'd lost. "My life is a calamity. My husband took my first—and now my second is lost to the law..." Lifting her head back to the cross, she continued, "the devil stole my husband..." She wailed a long painful groan. "...I have nothing to live for...."

The front door quietly squeaked open, and a tall figure stood in the dark shadows against the bright sun behind. The silhouette stood tranquil at the doorway, before stepping forward and releasing the door.

"My husband accused me of adultery, Lord. A sin I never committed. I've lost my entire family over the wickedness of the devil, stealing my husband's soul and another man stealing my promised vows through rape..." Cat's closed fists slammed down on the rail. "...what did I do to deserve this, Jesus? I know I ain't perfect, but I'm a good person! A loyal wife and mother. I used to love helping the less fortunate..." She slammed her fist down hard once more. "...why did you put that gawd damned demon on that bench so long ago in my path? WHY? To give me something beautiful I didn't have—only to let them be ripped from my grip with no reason?"

The large entry door behind her at the back of the church made a solid bang as it seated back into the doorframe and latch. The sound, a huge echo in the still silence between Cat's cries of desperation and demand. She turned with a startle, "I'm sorry for disturb..." She saw the silhouette and immediately recognized the intruder standing in front of the light. And that's what he was in this Holy place. "When did you get out and why are you here of all places?" Her tone mixed with honest perplexity and a pining.

"Is it true, Cat? Someone raped you?" Jay's footsteps rang heavy with each forward step on the antiquated wooden floor. "What son-of-a-bitch did this damned despicable trespass?"

The sanctuary returned to a deafening silence when Jay stopped and stood over Cat at the altar. And then the silence broke abruptly. "Cat! I asked you who in hell did this to you. I deserve to know! I shunned you over it." Jay's voice thundered.

Cat maneuvered herself up to a standing position with one foot on the raised step and one on level ground facing Jay's. She tried to determine internally how to answer his question. She knew there were dangerous implications to her answer. "I think it's best if it's just forgotten—it's been so many years ago and millions of gallons of water have passed under that bridge. Won't do nothin' but harm now if I answer." She looked into her estranged husband's eyes—she saw anger, not compassion.

"I got the right, Cat. A man has judgment coming to him for stealing from me...."

"Stealing from you?" She boldly interrupted him. "I'd give you a mouthful of curse words if we weren't standing here in the Lord's house, Billy Jay Cader. You have a mountain of gall, you son-of-a..." She caught her vile word before it slipped past her tongue all the way. "...You've tortured us with your words and actions most of my life and all of Darrell's. You stuck a hunting knife in our first son's chest, stealing his life and his future from him, his brother and me, and you have the capacity in your selfish mind to think about what's been stolen from you—over me and our boys? The man who raped me, stole from me—not you—you wanted no part of what he took!" Cat spoke with bold veracity. "And what he did hurts far, far less than what you just did to me right now!"

Jay raised his hand in anger, "Don't you scold me in no gawd damned tone like that. I'll…"

"You'll what? Continue to use your devil's anger to brutalize me? How would it be any different than any of the years before now? Judgment, verdict and punishment is all you've ever been concerned about—but not under God's law's or society's view, but only YOURS!" Cat stood bold and firm right to the point Jay began to bring his open hand down. She dodged and when she did, her uneven foot placement caused her to trip to the floor. The back of her head banged the sharp edge of the altar rail as she tumbled down. Her eyes fluttered a moment before rolling back into her head, hiding under her eyelids. She didn't move, she made no sound.

"Cat? You okay?" Jay bent down and talked to her. "I'm sorry, baby-doll. Wake up." He reached his hands to check her head and pulled back fingers covered in warm red blood. He didn't have any idea what to do. He put his ear close to her mouth to see if he could hear her breathing and caught a faint movement of air in a weak exhale. *Good, she's alive, but what the hell do I do now?*

Jay bent down and picked Cat up as if she were a sack of grain or potatoes and threw her over his shoulder like she weighed nothing. He hurried to the door and pushed it open, looking for help outside anywhere.

Reverend Gabriel happened to be walking up the front sidewalk and saw Jay with someone over his shoulder. "Jay? What happened here? Who do you have?" But as soon as he asked, Gabriel recognized the form slumped over Jay's shoulder held firm with his grip.

"We need a doctor, preacher. Quick! She fell and opened up her head from smacking the railing."

Jay followed Gabriel to his car and loaded Cat into the backseat and climbed in after. Gabriel drove faster than he ever did before, taking corners with the tires screeching in pain as if the asphalt were ripping the skin from their tread.

***

Cat's body lie still on the hospital bed, her head bandaged and a fluid bag beside feeding a liquid through a tube into her arm.

Jay held her hand in his with a chair pulled close to Cat. Reverend Gabriel and Gloria sat in the waiting room, unsure if Jay should be in the room alone.

"I don't know what happened, Gloria. I walked up the sidewalk and he came bolting out with Cat over his shoulder—said she fell and hit the altar railing with the back of her head." Gabriel leaned in closer to his wife. "I didn't even know she be in the church, did you?"

"Honey, her life seems so tangled up since that man came back, I don't know what to think about anything. And no, I held no idea, but it sure don't surprise me none." Gloria shook her head slowly back and forth, her eyes appeared to have deep concern reflecting from her dark pupils. "After all the man has put her through, she still seems to hold a love that won't completely wilt. I don't know ifn' its foolishness or a grandness in God's strength He's put upon her."

"For now—I just want to know she'll be alright and then what in the world happened in there between 'em." Gabriel answered. "And I believe it's foolish stubbornness—God surely wouldn't put one of his faithful children to a test such as this."

A nurse walked over to the Watkins'. "Miss Catrina Cader lives with y'all right?"

"Yes ma'am." Gloria answered.

"Well, I have some good news. Doctor Branson asked me to relay Miss Catrina suffered a small intracerebral hematoma, or contusion, which means a bruise to the brain. He doesn't believe there's any serious or long-lasting trauma to the brain. No apparent skull fracture or blood clotting, but he does want to keep her here for a couple of days under observation. She has five sutures on the cut, but no significant blood-loss. In other words, she's a very lucky lady."

"That's the best news ever, Miss. Thank you so much for sharing." Gloria leaned toward the nurse and motioned for her to come closer with her finger. "I'm not sure if her husband will stay or not." She spoke in almost a whisper. "But could an eye be kept on him? They've not lived together in close to four years. He was present when Cat got injured." Gloria eyes showed hopeful agreement towards the nurse.

"Yes ma'am, I'll keep a quiet eye and pass the message to the evening nurses as well."

***

The stillness of the room was filled with soft beeps from the monitor to which Cat was attached by wires. The beeping was steady though. Jay assumed her heartbeat must be being watched. The line on the screen shot upward each time the tone sounded and then went flat again until the next. Jay's eyes began to slowly close, and his thoughts turned to the accusations Cat made—along with the revelation she'd revealed about another man, the apparent father of Darrell and boy he'd provided for and made to believe was his son, but in truth, was the outcome of a rapist's violent seed. The idea caused his stomach to churn. He'd always believed she'd sought pleasure from another and Darrell of course a constant reminder of her unfaithfulness, which he used as his excuse to transact the immoral deeds he'd been guilty of. This caused a deep conflict within. Now made aware of a huge miscalculation or assumption on his part, the wheels of his judgment game were set in motion like a train on rails traveling down a steep hill and could not be reversed after the momentum began to extricate the ability to change course.

His attention drawn by the acceleration of the beep and a light squeeze to his hand. Jay's eyes snapped open as a nurse entered the room. "She appears to be waking up, sir. I'm going to need you to step out of the room for a bit." The nurse said.

"You take real good care of her, ma'am. She's one of God's angels, but we ain't ready to let Him have her just yet." Jay said.

"We'll do our best, sir. I can assure you." The nurse answered.

Jay exited the room still in a daze of his thoughts. He noticed the preacher and his wife sitting across the room. *Awe, shit, I don't wanna talk to them right now. Too late, his wife is motioning me over.*

Jay meandered over to where the preacher and his wife sat. "They chased me out. The beat of the sound on the machine sped up and Cat squeezed my hand. A brown-haired nurse came in and said I needed to leave. I told her to take real good care, 'cause she's one of God's finest angels and we weren't ready to give her back to Him..." Jay turned back towards Cat's room, noticing there was no parade of doctors and nurses headed in. Surely, a good sign. "...She said they were gonna do their best."

Gabriel spoke up, "Sit down here, Jay. I'll get you a cup of coffee and you can rest until they let you back in to see her."

Jay reluctantly sat. "I 'spose a cup of coffee sounds good, thanks, preacher."

"You can call me preacher—or Gabriel or Reverend—whatever you'd like—I answer to 'bout anything. You remember my wife, Gloria, don't you? "

"My mind ain't fully on socializn', bein' kinda busy dodging pellets from your 20-gauge shotgun and all. But I do recognize a pretty face..." Jay moved his attention to Gloria. "...nice seeing you again, ma'am. Circumstances don't seem much better this time than the other."

Gloria tried to muster a smile, "No, Mr. Cader, I reckon not."

Jay grinned at hearing her term of addressing him. "My father weren't no mister, so I reckon he couldn't hand any respect down to me. Just call me Jay. I don't even use my first name, Billy, on account that the son-of-a-bitch shared his name with me. Pardon my language, please, but he be an evil cuss himself and someone who set me on a road of despair for a good-long time."

"Well, Jay, I had no idea. I will remember, and I am sorry for your painful background. Is he still alive?" Gloria asked.

"I got no damned idea, I ran away when I's only fourteen, never really saw the sombitch again after that." Jay answered.

"The Lord can help heal those painful memories that are stubborn to forget. Lay them at the altar and leave them to Him."

Jay's face changed. His eyes sank deeper into his forehead and his lips dropped to a straight line before he responded. "I don't mean to offend—but I've seen what God's altar can bring. Cat knelt at one and now she's in a hospital bed hooked up to all kinda machines. No ma'am, there's been people all my life tryin' ta sell me salvation. I almost bought it hook, line, and sinker from the couple openin' up the new restaurant overlookin' the bay." He shook his head and grinned. "They helped me up from the ground and we gave the good Lord the credit—but it didn't seem to stick with me. That's all I got to say, 'bout that."

Gloria sat quiet, looking for her husband and not knowing the words to answer back, so she remained silent and watched Gabriel round the corner juggling three cups of coffee in his hands.

"Awe—made it without spilling a drop! God's disciple's hands are sure and steady!" Gabriel chuckled as he handed his wife a cup and then Jay.

"Thank ya, preacher." Jay responded.

"Jay began telling me about his struggle with his faith, Gabriel. I thought you two fished nearly every day on the pier. What do you two find to talk about if there isn't time to speak about faith?"

Gloria half scolded her husband.

Jay lifted the cup of luke-warm coffee to his lips and sipped, hiding his smile at Gloria rebuking her husband over the lack of sharing the Almighty's word with him—while fishing.

12

Darrell paced back and forth from wall to wall. It didn't take long to walk the eight feet before turning to walk back the same eight feet. His pace continued to be a frustrated one. He was now the only person in lock-up. That mixed with the fact he hadn't been able to speak to. or hear a single syllable from Mitz, made him feel like the silence killed him bit by bit. It'd been days, in fact, so many he'd lost track of time. His depression began turning into agitation with a short fuse. He was ready to explode like an M-80 shoved down a school toilet. Anyone within the area when the fuse finally reached the tube—it wouldn't matter who you were, you were gonna get covered in shit. He felt like even his mom bailed the kitchen, putting him aside on the back burner.

Darrell re-played the night he attacked the sheriff over and over in his head. He knew it would bring trouble to attack an officer of the law, but what about one who'd done somebody so much wrong? Didn't he have rights to defend his honor and family? Even from a cop whom withheld something so dire, it caused this kind of anguish? "This is bullshit!" He hollered out at which point Darrell kicked his cot and then lifted one side and flipped it over against the wall. It sounded explosive and must have been, because it wasn't ten seconds before the metal door which closed him off from the rest of the building, suddenly flung open.

"What the hell, convict?" The deputy rushed Darrell's cage. "I won't put up with anymore of your shit. Now pick it up and put it straight. You don't want me to grab another officer and open your cell, buddy-boy."

"Kiss my ass, it ain't right keepin' me in here this long. You come in here and you may get what your boss got, maybe even more!" Darrell puffed up like you'd expect a world class boxer to, not a high school senior. But he continued, "It's the way I make my bed, asshole."

Sheriff Roy walked through the door and stood staunch. "What's the problem here, son. You don't like our accommodations?"

Darrell rushed to the bars and stared at the sheriff. "Don't ever call me son, you worthless piece of pig shit. Even Jay made a better father than you could ever be and he beat my ass, damn near drowned me and locked me in a dark damp cellar almost weekly. And I for damned sure could never make his face as fucked up from beatin' it like I made yours look— you donut gorging prick."

"You're really missin' that pretty sister of yours, ain't ya, boy? What's it like anyways? Bumpin' uglies with family members don't seem very natural to me. Fact—seems downright shameful and somethin' even the good Lord might have a difficult time overlookin' and offerin' forgiveness. Why, as both of you kid's daddy, I oughta' open your cell door and spank the shit outta' you, then go over and do the same to little Mitzi." Roy shot the daggers in his eyes at Darrell. He pulled a cigar from his front pocket and a match from his pants pocket. He walked slowly up to Darrell's cage and when he came inches from being face to face, he dragged the match up one of the rusty cage bars until its bright flame flashed. He bit off the tip of the stogie, spitting it on the floor, and then stuck the cigar in his mouth and drew the flame up to the end and puffed. He blew smoke from the side of his mouth into Darrell's face. "You ever have one of these—son?" After blowing another cloud from his mouth, the corners turned up into a shit-eatin' grin. "You seem to be man enough now. If you can apologize to your ole man here for this..." He pointed to his yellowish, black, and blue bruised face while he stared deep into Darrell's eyes. "...and of course, the way you're treatin' my facility along with this nasty conversation—I might just give you one, to kill all the time you still got here with us." The corners of his mouth dropped and the grin disappeared into a straightening of his lips. "I'm tryin' to be hospitable here, son. Turnin' the other cheek and all like the good Lord expects of me." Roy drew another deep puff and held it in his mouth for a few seconds before he released it into Darrell's eyes. "But you are tryin' my patience, boy, to its wits end and my jolly personality has just about run the course to its end." He then winked at him.

Darrell turned his face and resisted rubbing the smoke from his eyes, refusing to show the sheriff any display of weakness. "The only thing I'd like to smoke…" Darrell stepped closer until his chin almost rested between the bars. "…is your fat pork ass when I get outta' here. You think your face felt pained…" Darrell smiled as wide as he could without breaking his mouth apart, his pearly whites shining through the dissipating smoke. "…well, that ain't anything compared to what you'll get—Daddy." Darrell turned, walked a few feet, then dropped his prison pants and popped a squat on the shitter. He didn't need to use it, but he knew it would run him and his crony off quicker. He looked up and grinned. "Your cigar isn't gonna cover the stink your crappy food has runnin' through my ass. Last stinker I dropped, looked a lot like your face, without the bruises though."

Roy took another puff and turned, heading back through the entryway. His deputy stood right behind him and then the steel door slammed closed, the clink of the lock snapping into place was the last sound Darrell heard. Back to silence and being alone. "Well, that brought more fun than stackin' marbles on a slick slope." Darrell spoke aloud while he picked up his cot. It wasn't because of anything Roy said to him. It was because the floor is dirty and he'd seen more than one palmetto bug scamper across it, and those bugs reminded him of home back on the farm. Home when momma laid in bed all day and the living room looked like the inside of a restaurant dumpster. A memory he chose to try and forget.

Darrell laid back down and closed his eyes. The excitement and blood flow in his veins had now ran its course and the slug of boredom took over, nothing to do but lay around and think. And in times like these, it wasn't necessarily a healthy thing to do. It either brought sadness and self-pity—or ways to get revenge when he got out. Vengeance could always lead to another visit back here and he did not want to be an in-and-out regular.

Darrell began making plans just before this happened. Good plans. The kind a woman who loved her man would want. A stable job, a home, and a future together as husband and wife. Darrell wanted a life he'd only seen on shows like the Waltons or Happy Days. Anything but the life he'd grown up in. He owned fears he kept pushed deep down. Fears one day the devil would pass from his poppa to him. A gift he didn't want or ask for, but one he became afraid he might not be able to say no to. He didn't feel any demons inside him though, not yet anyway. Maybe the monster would die inside Jay's evil carcass. It became a prayer and thought he kept regular tabs on. He didn't want the devil to just sneak in because he wasn't watchin' the door to his soul close enough. He knew if he stayed with Mitz, he could fight anything that came at him. She gave him the kind of confidence in himself he needed. But now—now the power lay in limbo. Maybe it was always the devil's plan to sneak in through an unguarded door—through the temptations of a girl. A wolf in sheep's clothing, but really a tool of his to use with deceit. Could Mitzi be that tool? Had he already fallen into the trap?

Darrell's eyes grew heavy and he felt the tension in his shoulders and neck release. His muscles sank down into the cot. Gravity finally won over the anxiety which held him bound in knots.

In the dim lit cell with nothing to break the silence other than a soft sigh or a slight snore of a boy trying to be a man; lay a teen coming of age in a world which seemed hellbent to wreak havoc for him.

A large palmetto bug quietly scampered from under the cot, searching for crumbs to sustain its life in a place where life slipped away. Minute by minute, but feeling like hours upon days.

13

Mitzi tried to avoid everyone at school, except her friends Vio and Kyle, now that he'd finally been released and returned. Kyle never said a word about Darrell until Mitzi asked. Not sure how she felt about Darrell at this point, he didn't want to cause her any more pain than she'd already dealt with. But then, she asked about him.

"Mitz, he misses you. He is like you; he doesn't know what to do but his feelings haven't changed. He's in shock over the entire deal. He wanted me to tell you when he gets out, he wants to see you first thing."

"Vio, what would you do in my place? My mom is telling me I don't have to have the baby. The thought makes me want to throw up." Mitzi began to tear up. "I can't do it, Vio. But if we're related there most likely will be problems, you know, health and stuff. Let alone how people around here will treat him or her after it's born." She wiped her eyes and sniffed. "People are so mean, and they won't understand we didn't have any idea. We'll be the freaks of Florida. I need to talk to Darrell. I need to know what in hell to do." Suddenly her stomach flopped, and she knew she could puke any moment. She abruptly ran for the restroom and disappeared around the corner.

Five minutes later Vio went into the restroom looking for her best friend. She found her by the sound of sniffles behind the last bathroom stall door. "Mitz? It's me…" Vio stood quietly beside the door and waited patiently for Mitzi to respond. "I'm here for you, girl. You do know that don't you? We're thick. Too thick to let anything get us down." She spoke with the assurance only a true friend could.

"I know Vio, and I'm so glad I have you." The sound of the latch sliding out of the slot let Vio know she'd either come out—or invite her in. She waited several seconds to see which it would be. The door slowly swung open, and she soon saw Mitzi sitting on the lid, her head down, face in her hands which muffled the sobs. She raised her head and tried to smile through the stream which poured down her face. "I wasn't thinking about all of this when we were falling in love. I followed my heart and what it wanted—not my brains. I'm being punished for it, Vio."

"No, you're not! I don't believe God works like that and I'm pretty certain Reverend Gabriel and Gloria would agree that isn't how it works." She wedged her way in closer so she could touch Mitzi's shoulders. I think Gloria would be a great one to talk to about the whole thing, from the beginning to now. She's smart, loving and about the most non-judgmental person I know. She's helped me out after listening to me 'til the wee hours into the night."

"My mom wants me to think serious about terminating the pregnancy." Mitzi stared intently into Vio's eyes as if her friend held some magical powers which could heal her quandary. "I can't do that—can I? Could you if you were in my place?" Her eyes begged for an answer.

Vio took a deep breath. She could see the desperation in Mitzi's face. "Mitzi." She paused. "I wish I could snap my fingers and give you the answer that would solve this and take away all of your pain and worry, but…" Vio felt a tear of her own slip from her left eye. It seemed to always be her left eye which gave into her emotions first and betrayed her wall of strength. "…Mitzi—only you know what your heart will allow you to do. I can't make that decision or imagine what I would do. I don't think anybody could truly put themselves in your place and know an exact response. I'd doubt their answer if they could. I know I don't look like a girl who has any faith. Lord knows I don't wear it on my sleeve where it should be easily seen..." Vio's eyes both now betrayed her strong façade and began to let a stream gently slide down both cheeks. "...but the truth is, I do have faith in God. I believe he opens doors for us and will lead us to the right answers and to healing..." She reached over to hug Mitzi and pulled her close to her chest. "...but you gotta pick which door to go through on your own. You have Kyle and me and we will be there beside you, but nobody should choose your path except you, girl. Free will is what faith in a loving God is all about. Hard choices and wrong ones will happen along the journey. The good news though, is He is beside you through it all."

Mitzi squeezed Vio tightly and then pulled away so she could look at her. "How did you turn into my grandma? You're not old enough to have her wisdom." Mitzi let out a slight snicker and after a second, they both broke into giggles. "I guess I'm the comedian smartass and you are the Mother Teresa. What a pair we make!" Mitzi suddenly felt like she could make her own decision but would want to think hard about it before she did. A day later she heard on the news Mother Teresa suffered a heart attack while she visited St. Paul II in Rome. She would recover though and go on in her walk and two years later would receive the Medal of Freedom, the highest award a civilian could receive. Upon hearing of her recovery and moving on with her work, Mitzi believed it to be an answer reassuring her life for herself would move on and she would survive. She wondered at the time, *does God talk to us through circumstance of others like that?"*

14

Saturday morning came when Joyce heard movement and thumps through the walls from Jay's apartment. She stopped in her tracks and quietly walked closer to the wall which divided the two spaces. Mitzi rounded the corner and started to holler to her mom when she saw her standing with a glass between her ear and the wall.

"Mom? What's going on? CJ ain't back is he? He's in jail!" Mitzi questioned with a stunned look on her face.

Joyce brought her finger to her mouth as if to shoosh her daughter.

The stomping sound grew louder. Joyce could hear rambling through the cup which magnified it but didn't help the clarity. Joyce stepped away and put the glass down. "I'm gonna call Ethan. This isn't gonna work out anymore—living next to a crazy man who's not afraid to come over and start trouble like he did." She reached for the phone and dialed.

***

"But Ethan..." Joyce's voice cracked, and she pounded on her kitchen cabinet to accentuate her frustration. "...the crazy bastard walked into my home uninvited and caused the ruckus my daughter's boyfriend is now sitting in jail for! And he can still live—literally the other side of the wall from us?" Her blood boiled more with each answer she got from Ethan. "This isn't right, why did he get released from jail? Why weren't we informed—why, why, why...."

Ethan attempted to calm her but to no avail. "Unfortunately, the law in this case is on his side. His home just happens to be where it is and yours is unfortunately on the other side of the wall. You have two separate entrances and Jay's been informed he shall use only his entrance which contains its own stairwell...."

"But we share a common outside deck area that lies between us visible to both of those entrances! My daughter and I will have to look for another place to live because a psychopath happens to live next door! It's bullshit!" Joyce slammed the receiver down on the phone cradle before she thought about the fact that her boss was on the other end of the line. She looked at her daughter, "Well, that probably wasn't the wisest move I've ever made." Seconds later her phone ringer broke the silence in the room. Joyce reluctantly picked it up and held it to her ear, "Hello...."

"Please don't hang up, Joyce. I have a temporary solution." Ethan paused, instinctively waiting to hear dial tone in his ear before proceeding with the conversation. Silence. "Joyce? Are you still on the line and agreeable to listen without anger clouding your judgment?" The line remained blank with no tone for several seconds. "Joyce?"

Joyce finally cleared her throat into the receiver before she began to answer, "I'm sorry. Mitzi and I are edgy over all that's happened. I didn't mean to take it out on you, but we're gonna need to move. I can't leave Mitzi here alone."

"Settle down, Joyce. I have an offer which may be a temporary fix, but it'll be better than staying there. Problems with people like him usually resolve themselves in one way or another but take time. I'd be surprised if he wants to stick around here for much longer the way he's making enemies." Ethan said.

"What's your idea? I've settled down enough to listen," answered Joyce.

"You've been out to my beach house..." Ethan's tone sounded different than normal, almost coming across to her like he may have hidden motives. "...there is lots of extra room which could accommodate you and your daughter for as long as it takes...."

Joyce interrupted, "My Lord, Ethan. You've already given me employment, put me up in a fabulous expensive beach hotel, given me an executive style office as if I were actually a board-certified attorney instead of just the paralegal that I am..." She sighed. "...and now you're offering for my daughter and myself to invade and overtake your home and retreat from the tensions of your job? We can't do that. We'll just find another way to get by. I'll talk to the landlord and maybe get out of the lease—stay in a motel until we can get things worked out..." Joyce talked with her hands even though Ethan couldn't see. She abruptly stopped mid-sentence, then with a tone of humor, she continued, "...unless of course you know a guy who knows a guy who can persuade Jay to..." She laughed with a half-serious, half-joking smirk. "...you know, I'm just playing—I think...."

Ethan chuckled. "It'll all work out, Joyce. This much I'm confident to say. I tell you what. If you don't want to take me up on my house option, although quite frankly I can't imagine choosing a rinky-dink motel over a scenic beach offer..." He sighed and then smiled to himself. "...I'll at least pay the cost of your temporary relocation there. I wouldn't feel right having you add an extra cost on top of your rent. I know it must be difficult raising a daughter with all the expenses on a single salary."

Joyce interjected, "I appreciate both offers and I'll think about them over the weekend—okay?"

"Certainly, how about the three of us have some dinner tomorrow evening? We could have it out here at my home and just let Mitzi look around to see what kind of feeling she gets. Say, come a little early so you two can walk the beach and make a day and evening of it? Ethan asked in a persuading tone.

"It's a wonderful offer, again, I feel like you are being way too kind. Hang on while I talk to Mitzi and check her plans." Joyce set the receiver on the counter and walked around the corner to Mitzi's room and tapped on her door before slowly opening it. "Hey, Mitzi." She proceeded to tell her about Ethan's offer.

"Sounds to me like somebody's hot for teacher, is what I think, but sure, you deserve an evening. I'll go. I kinda' wanna watch this guy in action!" Mitzi smiled a naughty kind of smile. "Who knows—maybe we can stay there until crazy Jay disappears from our lives." She smiled again. "Book it with your boyfriend, I'm all in."

Joyce made her way back to the phone hoping like the dickens Ethan hadn't been able to hear any of their conversation. "Ethan? You still hanging on?"

"Yes indeed. And I'm hoping I somehow used some of my persuasive attorney wrangling-talk to get the answer I'm hoping for!" He chuckled again.

"We will both be there tomorrow at whatever time you'll have us—just for the day and dinner though, we aren't bringing our bags just yet!"

Ethan laughed. "You remember how to get here don't you? And is there anything special Mitzi likes to eat or drink?"

"Yes, I can find it. Mitzi will be fine with whatever you have planned. Should we bring swimsuits?" Joyce asked.

"I would love to say yes…" Ethan hesitated, remembering just how he'd described his beautiful spot of beach to Charley just awhile back when his friend asked him if there were still bull sharks…" Remembering the conversation took his mind briefly to the reason he'd called Charley to see him.

"Ethan? Swimsuits, yes or no?" Joyce asked quietly.

Ethan snapped back to the present conversation. "I'm sorry, something crossed my mind to which I needed to make a note. I wish I could say yes about the swimsuits, but as beautiful as the beach area is..." He glanced out to observe the beauty while he reached for the decanter to pour another glass of bourbon. "...there is a reef area or collection of rocks just under the surface. There are cave-like formations and it's what makes the waves sound and look so beautiful I'm told. But anyway, it also entices sharks to the area. I definitely don't want you or Mitzi to bump in to one of those."

"Oh my! Thank you for telling me. Mitzi loves the ocean and swimming in it. I'll be sure to relay a warning to her. I'll need to handle it in a special way because the boy they just found last month by Alligator Harbor used to be one of her very best friends. She's still having a hard time getting over it and then what she's going through now on top—I keep expecting her to wanna move back home."

A moment of silence between them caused Joyce to wonder if the line was broken and then Ethan began talking again. "What a sad outcome this poor boy must have gone through, but on the other note, we surely can't have you moving away! I just got you here, and you are quite the addition to my firm!" Ethan laughed light-heartedly.

"Well, I don't know about that, but I am loving it here, other than the crazy psychopath who lives next door." Joyce quickly rebutted.

"I'll plan on seeing you two by nine or ten in the morning? We can have brunch and then scout the beach area out and I can have a chance to get to know you both even better. Call me any time if you have any problems at all."

"Thank you, Ethan—for everything. Really, I mean it from the bottom of my heart. You've been such a fantastic boss and good friend. I'm lucky to know you and want you to know how I feel."

"You're an incredible woman, Joyce. I'm looking forward to getting to know you and your daughter much more."

***

The medium caramel-colored liquid glistened in the sunlight when held up to inspect. Lightly swirling the glass to draw the notes from the bottom, Ethan raised the snifter to his nose, inhaling its sweet yet peaty aroma. He closed his eyes to explore and decipher the bourbon's make-up more in-depth. The decanter held his favorite stock of now disappearing special reserve. It held a combination of a fourteen-year extra-aged Kentucky rye bourbon combined with an eight-year aged bourbon and then finished in cognac barrels, plus another eight months in wine casks. A limited supply and another run would never be produced again. Ethan felt fortunate to have stumbled onto it and he'd been very selfish with whom he'd share it. Priced ridiculously, but when savored properly—the finish, was almost comparable to making love the first time with a beautiful young woman—breath-taking.

Ethan swallowed and lowered the glass to his lap, then allowed his mind to travel back in time to the woman he compared his rare and valuable bourbon to. *The experience will never be reproduced to me again, a limited run.* Like slowly taking in the bourbon's aroma, he leisurely let his memory soak in every detail of a long-ago day. One from his distant past. He'd felt something very different from the usual sex he'd enjoyed before. *She brought so much more than just animal lust to me.* The years which went by after she disappeared seemed empty. He could never get Roy to tell him where she'd gone or what happened other than they divorced. The mystery within Roy had never been spoken of. His demeanor would become agitated whenever asked, as if it involved some sort of pain, yet he never spoke of any nor let it show.

But now, she's finally back in my life and although Roy showed no desire to have her back, it's obviously an itch in his craw she now works for me.

A smile washed across Ethan's face as he sat in his favorite outdoor chair, captivated by his memories. He clutched his glass of exclusive bourbon in his aging hand, swirling it again, a habit by now. Poised on his back deck, facing his private elevated view of the coast, the smile swept slowly across his face, mirroring a distant wave on the horizon, slowly rolling into shore. It quietly swept his frown into a pleasure-filled glowing beam. It had taken years to track her down. He'd used every means possible, from friend's debts to him being forgiven, to favors called in from private investigators he'd used for his clients. There'd been boundless personal finances consumed, but now the reward would soon be reaped for his endeavors.

He'd move very slowly, like necessity demanded. She still remained a thing of beauty which begged his craving to obtain. Not just as an object of pleasure alone, but one he could share what he'd built by remaining alone all his life. He didn't want to scare her off, lose her again to obscurity. She must never know they'd already been together intimately in the way they were. She'd obviously retained no memory of their tryst, but Ethan had never forgotten. Keeping it a secret to this day became another reason he'd kept it to himself when he'd discussed Roy's risk to his and Charley's positions in life now.

The "roofie" Roy mixed in Joyce's drink on that particular "Sunday afternoon drive" those nineteen years ago, turned out to be successful. She'd entered Ethan's house so uninhibited that long past afternoon.

Playful and sexy. He'd handed it to Roy, one the few plans he'd headed up which came to such sweet fruition. A serendipity which became a curse for much of Ethan's life later. He'd spent fortunes searching for her after she became his obsession before disappearing.

Ethan's mind kept drifting to the moment she "spilled" through his doorway, Roy behind her helping her up the steps and playfully grabbing at her backside. *I became instantly jealous of Roy's hands touching her body in the insidious way his finger moved between her cheeks when he turned and winked at me. I couldn't justify having those feelings, she was after all, his wife.* But Ethan wanted her for himself, immediately upon sight. Roy after all brought her to the beach house to share with him. He remembered how he'd hoped Charley wouldn't show up. After all, it wasn't one of the scheduled get-togethers. There were going to be no high school girls today. A three-some, while Ethan didn't really want it this way, would be acceptable this one time. But a four-some seemed very objectionable, so he slipped to his office to call Charley last minute and say the afternoon needed to be postponed to another day because of work.

Roy obviously held a head start on drinking. Ethan appreciated this a lot. In fact, he'd brought out his lesser expensive Jack Daniels and cans of Coke for Roy to plow through. Roy always liked to drink like a high school boy, even if he was a grown man, and a police officer at that.

Once they got started on manipulating Joyce into the "playroom," the room with the round bed and assorted toys, he turned the stereo system up and Herb Albert played on the radio, "A Taste of Honey" just beginning. He dimmed the lights down. The jazzy song must have been a favorite of Joyce's because in her state of drug-induced seduction, she began removing her clothes and slinking over to him. Drinks in both their hands, she clinked her shot glass to his and then lifted it to her mouth and downed the entire contents. She ran her tongue around the rim of the glass and then plunged it in as she coyly eyed Ethan, a man she'd never met before. He looked over to Roy as Joyce dropped her glass to the floor, missing the tabletop, and then reached for his pants and began unzipping them. Roy winked as he slipped his clothes off. "She's a wildcat on this stuff, but frigid as a popsicle without it."

The two of them had done this kind of thing many, many times. They'd shared other men's wives and young girls from the high school, and included Charley Bingham, a teacher at the time. Charley, a high school friend of theirs from way back in the day, became involved because of his uncanny ability to convince his tight-bodied female high school students to participate in getting high and hanging out with him. Back then, the girls seemed to crave him and willingly came to participate, sometimes five or six at a time. But this rendezvous became different. It felt awkward and dirty. He remembered how much he did not want Roy in the room. In fact, he didn't want to have Joyce in that room even if they were alone. He longed to take her to his bedroom in private where he could focus pleasuring her in the ways he now daydreamed. Ethan craved to make her the center of attention instead of him, which was always his usual intent.

If I could have killed Roy with no threat of being caught and not have been forced to share her for this first time before he passed out drunk—I would have done it. I wish I could erase him from my memory now. But soon....

15

The day looked beautiful outside. The bay water glimmered in the morning sun as Joyce opened her windows to air out the stuffiness. She felt the morning breeze blowing in along with the smell of the salty sea. She'd quickly grown to love these attributes of Apalachicola and living so close to the water. She'd hated having to close everything up at night, but with Jay back home, she wasn't taking any chances of making it easy for him to get in. She didn't trust him anymore. She held Roy, her ex, Mitzi's estranged no-account father, on the same plane as Jay. Two snakes in the weeds is where they stood—or more appropriately, slithered. They should be exterminated and taken away with no mercy or pity given, like dangerous coral snakes. She hated men who treated women as playthings or took for granted their value as living breathing human beings. She vowed never to fall for another who took advantage of her. Never.

Joyce didn't want to waste any more time on thoughts of male losers when she was undoubtedly being courted by a man who was not only respected and well established in life, but a true gentleman also. *Why couldn't I have met Ethan before I settled for a dick like Roy?* She knew why though. It was of course, Mitzi. She wouldn't have Mitzi if she'd met Ethan first. Mitzi, the one thing the worthless prick ever did that turned out good but too ignorant and stuck on himself to see it.

Joyce lightly tapped on her daughter's door, "Mitzi, are you thinking about getting up and getting ready?"

"I'm awake, Mom. There's a beach at his house, right?" Mitzi asked as she finished making her bed.

"Yes, ma'am, there is. It's beautiful and private." She answered.

"So, I can put my swimsuit on underneath my clothes?" Mitzi asked as she dug through her drawers and pulled it out. She looked down and the tears began to flow.

"Honey, you won't need the suit—Ethan says the waters there have rocks or something that attract sharks. We can walk in the waves as they rush up, but we won't be getting in past our knees! I know, it sucks, right?"

Mitzi didn't hear a word her mom said after she'd seen the swimsuit in her hand. The suit she'd worn the day "they" were in the middle of the driftwood together now held her attention. Darrell slipped the suit off her body just moments before he kissed and caressed her sun-drenched skin. They'd made love right there on their beach towels, hidden from anyone who may pass by. Her crying must have grown to an audible level past the privacy of her door because it opened, and her mom came in and held her.

"What's wrong, sweetheart? Why are you crying baby doll?" Joyce asked as she pulled her tear-filled daughter into her arms.

Mitzi held her swimsuit which she'd buried her face into, to absorb the wetness of her eyes. "I know you don't wanna hear details..." She looked into her mom's eyes knowing it didn't matter what she'd tell her if it wasn't the truth. She knew her momma knew her well enough to see through any lies. "...this is what...what...I wore before we...when we...made love on the beach. The one you and I went to. You know...the first day after we...after we moved here. It was...probably when...when Darrell and I made our..." Her head dropped back down, and she looked at her tummy. "...our baby." Mitzi buried her face into her mom's chest and broke down completely. Bawling loudly and hard. Her entire body shook as if a hundred continuous earthquakes were erupting throughout her insides.

Joyce ran her hands over her baby's back and her fingers through her hair, attempting to comfort her girl. She'd never seen her so crushed and broken.

Suddenly the moment became shattered by three loud bangs on the wall from the other side, followed by a loud, "Shut the fuck up! Is that Darrell over there crying like a pussy with a broken fingernail?"

"Honey,..." Joyce pulled away from her daughter and looked into her eyes with a seriousness she'd never shown her daughter before. "...pack your bags with everything you'll need for several days, we're leaving and we won't be back here without Ethan with us to get anything else we need. We're leaving as quick as we can." Joyce asked if she needed help before she packed her own bag.

"Are we staying at Ethan's house?" Mitzi asked.

"I don't know, honey, but we aren't staying here another moment more than we need to." Her mom's eyes held a dead firm sobriety to them.

"Go pack, Mom. I can get my stuff together in less than ten or fifteen minutes, tops."

***

Joyce and Mitzi made it out to the Volvo in just under twenty minutes. Both looked at each other while tossing their bags in the back and then hurriedly climbed in, shutting their doors in unison. "Oh my God, Mom—this must be some kind of record for us!" Mitzi stated and then looked over and grinned before continuing, "I would have never laid around in bed snoozing my alarm five times straight on a school day if crazy friggin' Jay did this every day!"

Joyce looked over at her daughter, her face still wearing

concern while she twisted the key forward to start the car. She nervously cracked a matching grin and simply said, "no shit, babygirl—no shit!" She turned the key and the car attempted to start before stopping dead. "Oh, come on you piece of...." And she turned the key back and then forward again. It did nothing but click and chatter. Joyce banged both hands on the steering wheel. "This can't be frigging happening!" She looked at Mitzi who stared back at her. She tried again and the click slowed down to a quiet buzz and then stopped making a sound at all. She suddenly felt like a fish who beached itself and flopped for the final time trying to swim back into the sea. Hopeless.

"Um, Mom..." Mitzi's eye caught movement from the upper right corner of her field of vision. Before she could focus on the moving figure, she knew exactly what, and then who he was. "...Mom, he's headed this way! He's almost to our steps!"

Joyce instinctively turned and then tried twisting the key back and forth as if multiple attempts would surely do the trick. But of course, it did not. "Lock the doors, Mitz!" and she twisted to her left slapping her hands on the lock knobs front and back, then looked over at Mitzi and yelled, "Mitzi! Lock your damn doors! Front and back!"

Mitzi turned toward her mom. "They are! What do we do now?"

16

The nurse hurriedly walked over to where Jay, Gabriel, and his wife, Gloria were seated.

"Mr. Cader, sir." The nurse touched his shoulder, "your wife suffered some complications. She's awake and she's trying to talk, there may not be much time, Doc says you can come in for at least a minute to two…" The concern and immediacy showed on her face. "She may go into convulsions and then you gotta leave."

Jay dropped his half-full cup of coffee to the floor, the sound of it shattering echoed across the porcelain tiled waiting room, causing faces to turn and stare. He quickly got up and followed the nurse. Reverend Gabriel hollered, "If you need me, son, I'm here prayin' along with Gloria! Just call out to me or send a nurse." Gabriel looked over at his wife and grabbed her hands, both bowed their heads like muscle-memory in silent prayer together.

When the door opened, Jay rushed to the bedside and put his hand on Cat's. Her eyes were wide open showing fear mixed with a confused look. "J…Jay? Is it you?"

"I'm here Cat, baby-doll. I ain't goin' nowhere." His eyes were moist, a sight which seemed to confuse Cat. Jay quickly wiped his face with his sleeve, not wanting anyone to see tears in his eyes. "I'm sorry, baby. Stay with us…" He turned to search the room for the doctor, and he saw him and a nurse looking at some monitors and talking. He looked back at his estranged wife who seemed to be calming down, but the beeping sound he'd noticed earlier seemed to be sounding faster, but less steady. He needed to know. The question still burning as if it were branded in his brain, he leaned closer to Cat's ear. "Who raped you back then, Cat? I gotta' know."

The beep sped up and he asked again, a little louder than he meant. "Cat —who in hell raped you? You gotta' tell me!"

Cat's eyes opened wider, and a look appeared across her face which made Jay feel distraught. He wondered if she sensed a limited time to her life. She barely bumped her head. How can she be so bad off? *I gotta' know who the son-of-a-bitch is, so I can make him pay.*

Only seconds later Cat struggled to give the perpetrator up to him. In a very soft voice she spoke his name, "Ro...Roy—B...ur...ks...."

Jay leaned in and spoke to her, "I didn't catch it, can you say it again?"

In a louder and unbroken sentence this time, she repeated the name plainly, "Roy..." She took a shallow breath, then swallowed. "...Burks...it's Ro...Roy." Cat's neck muscles untensed and she visibly sank back down into the bed and closed her eyes.

Jay quickly responded without thinking of the repercussions his words might bring, "Cat—baby-doll—I'll take care of him. I'll condemn that motherfucker to death by my own hands. No matter what, your suffering will be vindicated, I promise!"

The doctor and nurse turned and witnessed the entire conversation and stood shocked as Jay walked toward them.

"Doc—take care of my Cat, do whatever you can to save her, but please keep her outta' any pain. I got business to tend to." Jay turned and moved swiftly through the door, pushing his way past Ethan who had just arrived to check on his client. The word was already out amongst the small town's people of her accident.

Ethan knocked on the door and the nurse rushed over while the Doctor made his way to Cat's bed. "You can't come in here, sir.

You gotsta' wait in the waitin' room wit' the others." As Ethan backed away, his eyes attempted to scan the room before the nurse closed the door. He wanted to take a mental snapshot of all present in the room. Some may need contacted for questions at a later date. Mental notes were always in Ethan's thoughts, brain muscle-memory from years of being an excellent attorney.

17

When Joyce and Mitzi failed to meet at Ethan's beach house for brunch as arranged, he'd called her phone several times to no avail. He raced into town to her apartment which connected to Jay's and found Jay working on Joyce's stalled vehicle. She and her daughter were safe but were terrified earlier he would harm them. When Ethan arrived, Jay left the two ladies in Ethan's charge and took off in his van.

Joyce and Mitzi ordered drinks at the Coffee Caper while Ethan ran up to his office next door where he found a message about Cat's accident.

"I need to run by the hospital Joyce. One of my clients was involved in an accident." Ethan said.

"Oh, 'Mitzi and I will come with you." Joyce said.

"No, it's okay. I'll run over and check on her and you two go ahead and relax after your excitement filled morning. I'll only be a matter of minutes."

Joyce smiled. "I'm sorry, we'll wait here, and you take whatever time you need."

Ethan walked to Cat's doorway after checking at the front desk. Just as he'd began to enter her room he overheard Jay's question about rape and his statement to Cat about killing Roy, as did Cat's doctor and nurse.

Ethan suddenly realized he now only needed to perform some minor orchestration instead of following through with an earlier plan of removing Roy from the picture. A phone call here and a tweak there—violá! Problem solved all the way around. With luck and fine-tuning—Roy could be murdered, and Jay instead of just being set up for the killing, would actually do the killing himself. Jay would then end up doing life in the big house and out of Joyce and Mitzi's lives along with making whatever blackmail he held over Roy—mute. He could even volunteer to be Jay's defense attorney pro-bono, insuring his verdict of guilt, without anyone holding him responsible. There were witnesses who'd heard the viable threats from circumstances of passion and of course any evidence left at the scene wherever this takes place. He just needed to get a handgun into Jay's hands. He knew Jay swung the balls to complete the rest but lacked the common sense to think a plan through. Jay had, by God, made himself the perfect fall guy.

Ethan walked into the Coffee Caper and over to where Joyce and Mitzi sat waiting for him. "Sorry, ladies but I need to run back up to the office and take care of some quick business before we head out to the house."

"Certainly, but is there anything I can do to help you?" Joyce asked.

Ethan looked over at her as he answered in a humble tone, "Not on this one, Joyce, this particular case contains some delicate matters the client won't want openly shared. It's a no-brainer anyway, you're far too valuable on a couple of cases coming up. It'll be something we can discuss tomorrow after exploring the beach."

***

"Hello, Jimmy. I need to talk to you about some changes in that special case we've been working on...."

"Yes sir, Mr. Kendrick, I believe we can get those changes worked up quickly. I have some thoughts which could be beneficial to both of us...."

The phone line ended in a quick dial tone before Ethan placed the receiver in the cradle. He'd waited to listen for any extra clicks. He always became a bit paranoid when working out details on this type of matter. In his career, he'd seen how the state and federal government could operate.

***

"I'm done ladies. It didn't take too long did it? Did you grab a bite to eat?" Ethan smiled as he pulled a chair out across from them.

Joyce returned the smile and answered, "We decided to just get a coffee and a Coke while we waited for you. This way we could all eat supper together."

"You didn't need to wait for me—but I must admit, I'm glad you did, I'm famished." Ethan pulled up a menu and opened it. "I just wish it were next Saturday evening!" He stated.

"Why? Are you wishing your time away from us already?" Mitzi questioned.

"Mitzi! It's not nice to joke around with someone you've barely met. He isn't aware of your brand of humor just yet." Joyce turned to Ethan. "I love her quirky comedic side—but only because I know when its sarcastic comedy."

"It's okay. I figured she drew her sword only to spar and not trying to stick the blade in just yet!" Ethan chuckled. "And no young lady, I am most assuredly not wishing our time away. It seems as if this day sports a mind of doing just that, though. I'd been looking forward to our Saturday together and now it's almost gone before it started." Ethan shook his head. "I looked at this menu, and while I love to eat my lunches here or order take-out after work, nothing really sounds like a nice dinner out with two lovely ladies. How will I impress you, Mitzi, if I just feed you a burger or a BLT and coleslaw?" He looked at his watch. "How does a juicy steak sound or some fresh caught red snapper? I know a little out-of-the-way place over at Port St. Joe. A quaint little spot which sits just off the beach with great steaks or fresh seafood. It's only a thirty-minute drive and I could call ahead and get us seated. Sound interesting?"

Joyce looked at Mitzi and got the wink of approval. "It sounds delicious to me, but I hate to make you drive an hour round trip for dinner."

"I insist ladies. It's still Saturday night! Let me see if I can borrow Sue's phone and call ahead. Be right back." He got up and headed over to the phone on the counter.

Joyce leaned in closer to Mitzi as they both watched Ethan walk away. "He's cute, mom. Seems a far cry from the bozo you slept with to make me!" Mitzi winked and laughed probably too loudly.

"Mitzi B, I swear! Where did your mischievous humor come from? Sometimes I think I still need a bar of soap to clean your mouth out." Joyce shook her head. "I think maybe you've become a little too buddy-buddy with me and forgotten I'm your mother! One that's obviously failed in holding the reins on you tight enough." She gave her daughter a sideways look, but it broke quickly into a cracked smile.

"I love you, mom. You're the best of the east all the way to the west, north to south."

***

Mitzi tried to listen to her mom and Ethan's conversation up front, but the back seat felt so luxurious she just sank back into the supple leather and stared out the window. The sky became dark with pink and blue on the horizon quickly disappearing into yellow then black. She'd managed to distract herself from her troubles most the day. Of course, Jay gave her a head-start by quickly turning her self-pity into stark fear. She just knew when Jay came bouncing down the outside stairs towards the car after pounding on the wall and cursing at them earlier, he seemed at the time able to kill them. But he didn't, instead he'd helped with mom's car. Now her fears were quelled, and nerves settled, old worries began to settle back in. A baby in her tummy. The father to the baby, also her brother, she didn't know existed—and a love which now became innocently an abomination, yet still lay unsettled and unsolved between them. She felt emotional again. Mitzi felt vulnerable and breakable. She felt glad they were still going to stay a night or two at Ethan's so she could walk the beach and soul search with no distractions. Ethan convinced her mom that Jay could still be a possible if not probable dangerous and unhinged threat.

Mitzi, by happenstance looked to the front of the vehicle and caught Ethan's eyes peering back at her in the rear-view mirror. It made her briefly feel studied. Not in a creepy way really, and maybe it's all just a coincidental moment of time that their eyes met; she didn't know if he'd been staring, or they were a glimpse like two strangers passing on the sidewalk. She felt certain he knew her circumstances and suddenly felt scrutinized or visually grilled. The feeling quickly passed, and her mind re-entered her yearning for Darrell. She missed his touch. *Will he ever be able to touch me in the ways he did before?*

Ethan's southern aristocratic voice broke her daydream. "We are close to arriving at Poppy's Net and Pasture! I think you two will enjoy this place. Don't judge it by its appearance! It appears to be a bit of a dive, but Poppy knows how to prepare a steak from a cow or one from a Red Snapper!" He leaned towards Joyce's ear, "and he serves some sublime bourbons. Do you ever enjoy a good whiskey, Joyce?" He winked. "Maybe a shot or two to take the edge off?" He grinned.

"I suppose I'm not opposed!" She coyly reached and rubbed his leg, glimpsing back at Mitzi, hoping she hadn't noticed her action, but by her expression, she did.

Mitzi caught a quick thought as she climbed out of the black BMW. *I do come by my flamboyance naturally—from my mom.* She felt the pull of her wide smile then shut the Beemer's door with a quiet thud. She quickly caught up and grabbed her mom's hand before Ethan could open the door to the "dive."

Mitzi scanned the room as they walked in. She conceded the inside did not mirror the outside as far as appearance. It appeared cozy and most of the clientele seemed average with several suited men coupled with women wearing nice pant suits and dresses. There were lit candles on each table with black folded napkins sitting like statues at each place setting. The stark contrast to the outside which appeared shabby with the neon sign brightly lighting Poppy's in red, the net shining sky blue while the pasture glowed bright lime green. The place held more of a small-town bar appearance where she'd half expected to see gnarly old sea-salts sitting bar-side with mugs of ale and stinky cigars docked in the ash trays. Their thick smoke creating a dark seedy ambiance she'd seen in movies.

As they were taken to a table and seated, Mitzi became amazed at the bank of expansive windows which ran the entire back of the restaurant, giving a beautiful view of a lit pier jutting out into the ocean for what appeared longer than her school's football field. It looked to be filled with people night fishing from its elevated position much like the one near her home.

Mitzi glanced at her mother. Joyce seemed enthralled by Ethan. The two looked like a new couple slipping into the grips of love for the first time, but still not aware or comfortable with the notion of the other. Yet, their eyes appeared mesmerized to the others, like moths drawn into the flame. She felt almost jealous, but also happy her mom finally met someone electric and engrossed in her. Mitzi's gleamy smile appeared unnoticed as if she weren't even sitting at their table. She felt totally oblivious to them and faded into the blur of the background scenery.

Ethan appeared older than her mom, maybe by ten or fifteen, even twenty years difference, but he didn't carry himself as if he were an older man. He looked very handsome, well-mannered, and sophisticated. She noticed immediately his reddish-brown hair had some silver creeping in, mostly apparent in his goatee and mustache. His profile in the candlelight as he looked at her mom and smiled made her feel warm and comfortable. His greyish eyes were haunting yet inviting. Mitzi could understand why her mom felt attracted to him. *I wish they'd met years ago, and he'd been my father. Our worlds would be much different.*

"Hey young lady... Ethan softly spoke. "You should look at the menu! And I bet they'd serve you a cocktail if you like?"

Mitzi looked up from the menu, "I won't be having one but thank you. I really can't."

"Nobody here will tell..." Ethan winked.

"I'm kinda' pregnant, so I'd probably better not." She forced a pleasant smile. A moment of awkward silence crept in, but the waitress stepped up and asked if she could take a drink order.

Ethan, about to order for Joyce became aware of the thirty something woman suddenly showing a spark of recollection. "Mr. Kendrick? Is that you?" She asked.

Ethan re-directed his attention back to the blonde-haired woman. "Why yes, yes I am. How are you Miss..."

"It's Cali...Cali Lea Jenkins. I haven't seen you in forever. Last time could have been at the...."

Ethan cut in. "Yes, I remember, you were with Charley, I believe. It's been quite a long time. Christmas party maybe?" He turned to Joyce and quickly introduced her and Mitzi.

"Well, I should take your drink orders and give you good folks a chance to decide from our menu. The smoked red snapper Special just caught today, and Poppy prepared a new seasoning he's added, it's getting many kudos. Just an idea to think about." She smiled.

"The lady will have an old-fashioned and Mitzi, do you want an iced tea or soda?

"Sweet tea with lemon please." She replied.

"And I'll have..." Ethan began.

"I'll bet a fine bourbon neat on the rocks." She whimsically smiled.

"Why Cali Jenkins, you do have a good memory. It's been what..." Ethan pulled his hand up to his chin and rubbed his goatee a second. "...ten, fifteen years?

"I'd say you are in the ballpark, sir. Is WL Wellers 107 okay for you tonight?"

"Sounds fine and please make this beautiful lady's old-fashioned with Wellers also." He winked and then turned to Joyce and placed his hand over hers for a moment. A gentleman's code to let a woman know he is already with someone. Joyce smiled, but it carried a flair of jealousy.

"I'll get those drinks and be right back to take your entre order." She turned and headed over to the bar by the kitchen entrance.

Mitzi jumped right on Ethan with a question. "Old friend? Fifteen years past and she remembers you like yesterday, even your drink."

Ethan looked as if he were slightly annoyed by the question. "Just an acquaintance. A friend of a friend kind of association. I would never have recognized her. I do hope I didn't hurt the lady's feelings."

Mitzi decided not to press the conversation and instead let it go. She would, however, be much more observant of him. She'd felt he didn't much care to be scrutinized by her. She turned her gaze to her mother and smiled, then looked down at the menu. She looked back up and around the room. "Do you like to play games Mr. Kendrick?"

Her mother looked over at her with shock, shooting her "the look."

"My mom and I like to look around at the different tables of the other patrons and try to guess what their conversations are about, along with what their jobs might be." She smiled at her mom. "Sometimes she will play the part of one and I'll play the part of the other." Her smile grew bigger before she looked back at Ethan. "So—have you ever played it? We call it 'role the play and make them say.'"

Ethan chuckled. "I must admit it sounds very interesting. Very interesting indeed." He winked at Joyce. "I'm in—if your mom is?" Tilting his head down her way his forehead wrinkled when he looked over the top of the reading glasses perched low on his nose. He closed his menu, "Who picks the table and patrons?"

Joyce held a look of doubt as she cocked her head at Ethan first and then Mitzi. "I think Ethan should be able to pick since he's never played. This way he can pick one he feels comfortable with."

Ethan studied the room as he rubbed his chin with his right hand. A beautiful golden ring with some unfamiliar symbol shined in the candlelight. "Hmmmm—okay. Now don't both turn at the same time, but I've found my choice."

"Ethan, really? I mean, we have both played this game our entire lives. Do you really think we'd get caught by someone the first time playing with you—in a new but strange setting?" Mitzi snickered. "Excuse me, I know this is your home field advantage, but you're still the damned rookie in this game." Her smile remained animated and there was a staunchness in her face, but also painted with a brushstroke of defiance.

"I realize it. I spoke foolishly, please blame it on the fact I am an attorney, whose represented many clients that needed babysitting and directed to the Nth degree." He gave a grin which matched Mitzi's. "It's habit."

Joyce broke into the conversation, "Before we start this 'game' and the waitress comes back, I need to visit the powder-room." She turned to her daughter and gave her an evil-eye. "Mitzi, care to come with me?"

Mitzi looked at her mom and then turned to Ethan and leaned over the table closer to him as she stood up. "Will you represent me if this gets outta' hand? I believe I'm being drawn into a forced interrogation, and I should probably have representation, but you're not dressed like a lady so...." She smiled and Ethan laughed aloud.

"I'm not certain I've practiced enough family law to keep you out of lock-up, miss. But I do beg mercy from the prosecuting attorney." They both laughed—Joyce however did not. "Go gentle on her Joyce, she's just playing—and looking out for her precious mother. This is not a bad trait in the defendant I may soon represent!"

18

Jay experienced a furious anger. He'd been driving around since he'd left the hospital, his blood boiling angrier with each second. "You son-of-a-bitch, you're gonna pay, Roy boy. You ruined our lives! God may find forgiveness for you, but no way in hell will I." He pounded on the steering wheel with his hand in a fist as he yelled aloud. "Should I beat you to death bare handed? Or should I find some sorta' weapon. The ole tire iron to the head works well on a fat one, which fits you too, Chubby Roy!"

He couldn't believe he hadn't stumbled onto Roy in this two-stoplight town. His patrol car wasn't at the station or on any of the streets he'd driven. It's as if the damned rapist got tipped off and now hid out on the lam. "What you don't know, you bastard, is I won't ever give up looking—I'll find you and when I do—my virtue will be my wrath!"

***

Jimmy Wayne picked up the tools he needed to complete the job. He knew what Jay looked like and the possibility he'd be in a plain white dodge work van. He held a paper with an address and the only thing left to do was to find him quickly and hope the appointment would go down like clockwork. These off-the-cuff projects were difficult, but he was the guy who could make things work like magic. Ethan knew it. Ethan paid very well when things went flawless. It gave him incentive and Jimmy worked well with the fact he'd received bonuses many times before, for jobs well done. He loved well-paying projects which kept him from being the major player with his balls out on the line. Jimmy felt comfortable being merely the instigator and tool supplier on this one. With this particular engagement, his balls would be left intact and not hung out there waiting to be smacked with a bat. He grinned as he drove around in the banged up green impala which easily blended well in this little shithole of a tourist trap fishing town.

Out of the corner of his eye, Jimmy saw one hot short-haired bombshell walking down the street away from him. "What a sweetheart-shaped ass, I could spend fifty bucks on that." He said to himself as he slowed down, pushing the button to lower the passenger window the rest of the way. His car slowed to a crawl as he crept up closer. "Hey sweet-pea, you need a ride tonight. I'm headed right where you're goin' I bet." He stopped beside her while his mufflers rumbled and made it difficult for him to hear what she answered. "What you say, honey? Climb on in and I'll give you the ride you won't forget!" He spoke louder.

Gina turned, never slowing her pace, "I said—fuck off, loser!"

"That ain't no way for a pretty-little thang like you to talk, do you kiss your momma with your dirty shit-mouth? You can sure as hell kiss mine, I like it dirty, real dirty, all the way down."

Gina walked over toward the window and Jimmy slowed to a stop. Gina gripped the top of the door in the window opening and leaned in slightly. "You really think you got something in those pants, lady-pleaser?" Gina reached in the side of her shorts and pulled out a stiletto that Ben gave her in New York to carry for protection. She held it up and pushed the button. A five-inch blade instantly shot straight out of the handle with a click. "You're welcome to hop out and show it to me, mister—but if it's as tiny as I imagine…" She hit the button and the blade retracted, pushed the button and it snapped back out. "...I'll cut that shriveled little fishing worm of yours and use it for bait to catch a pinfish—you know, so I can use the big fish to catch an even bigger one. One large enough to fill a pretty girl's appetite and not leave her wondering if it's on her line or not. You willing to bet what size a worm I like to fish with? Because I'm betting your bait could fall off the hook really easily, and no pretty girl would even feel it." She pushed the knife's button several times for effect, causing the blade to dance in and out, closer to his face than he looked like he wanted.

"You're a real uppity bitch and you can fuckin' walk...." Jimmy mashed the gas pedal to the floor and squealed off in a cloud of black and grey smoke. Gina disappeared in the cloud as the impala sped away. Jimmy looked in his rear-view mirror and laughed at the woman then looked ahead to continue his search. A block up the street, he saw a white work van almost to the four-way stop up ahead. In the light of the streetlamp when they both pulled up facing each other, he saw what he'd been looking for. "Bingo, Jay, you made my day."

Jay began to turn left and cross into Jimmy's side of the lane and Jimmy slowly pulled out causing the two vehicles to collide with the sound of a thud and glass breaking.

They both stopped and the doors of each automobile flew open.

"Gawd damnit, you ran the stop sign and hit me!" Jay screamed.

Jimmy answered back. "I'm sorry, you're right, bro. I got shook-up by a broad I just tried to pick up and my foot slipped off my brake." He began to walk around to where the damage would be. "Awe, shit." He said when he saw the van's bumper pushed in and his impala's headlight busted. "I ain't got fuckin' insurance, my ole' lady is gonna kill me." Jimmy dropped his head.

Jay studied the damage and determined he could probably pull the bumper of the van out on his own, it didn't get into the paint. "I'm gonna need some cash for this to try and fix it myself. We can keep the cops outta' this mishap of yours. I gotta fix it though, or my boss will blow a gasket." Jimmy leaned in and looked around. "I got fifty bucks I could slip ya." He looked at Jay with his brows burrowed in hopeful question.

"I don't know if that's gonna do it," replied Jay.

"Hey bro…" Jimmy's expression appeared as if he thought of another way. "… can you keep cool, 'cause I got somethin' else you might could sell for the rest."

"What's that?" Jay asked.

Jimmy lifted his t-shirt and the butt of a revolver appeared to be tucked in his pants. "It's a 38-caliber snub-nose Smith and Wesson. Clean as a whistle and fires great. I could give you this and fifty bucks."

Jay's eyes sparkled as if a miracle came his way again. "Ask and ye shall receive, is what I say. Got any rounds for it?"

"You betcha', bro. Got a pocket full right here." He reached in and pulled out about six or so bullets. "It's got one in each cylinder too."

"You know what? Keep your money so the ole lady don't rip your ass and hand over the gun and bullets. We'll just pretend this never happened." He smiled as if he were doing the guy a solid when in truth it couldn't be farther from the truth.

"You're an angel, bro. He dumped the bullets into Jay's hand and gave him the revolver. "I gotta' git, thanks for bein' understandin'.'"

"Watch where you're goin', the next guy may not be so negotiable, and you never saw my van or my face."

"Right-on, brother, I got you." Jimmy responded and smiled.

The two climbed in their vehicles and went their separate ways.

***

Gina stood about thirty or forty feet away in the shadows but couldn't hear what they said. She thought she saw something being passed from one to the other but shook her head and watched Jay drive off. "I'd hoped you would hit a tree at eighty, not some loser at only five miles per hour." She continued to walk, attempting to clear her head.

As she walked, she kept wondering what in the hell would Jay be doing driving around in Ben's business van on a Saturday night? Would he confess the minor fender-bender to either of them? *I'm glad it wasn't Jay who saw me and instead the slimy creep.* Gina snickered to herself. *Other than Ben—I've always seemed to be a creep magnet.*

Gina felt lucky Ben gave her the stiletto for protection. The creep's wide-open eyes as her blade shot in and out was priceless. She wanted to tell Ben about it, but her thoughts drifted away from what just happened and back to her dilemma between he and her. Benny deserved so much more than what she'd done and how she handled their last time together in attempted intimacy. Gina scoffed at her thought. "Yea, intimacy, right!" she said aloud as she kicked some gravel with the toe of her shoe. "He wanted love and I brought him a sleezy dancer and caused him to question his manhood..." Gina shook her head in self-disgust. "...maybe I'm just not cut out for Florida and a decent man able to provide a life for me..." Her eyes became watery at the memory wearing the trashy nightgown instead of the one she'd first chosen. *And now the damned tears rain on cue to try and muddy my self-anger into pity. I don't deserve the self-compassion.*

She felt like hurting herself in some way to receive the penance she deserved for her poor choices. Roads she chose and were now always pointing in the direction of hurting the only man she truly ever loved. *I am such a twisted fucked up human being. Worthless, except for tasteless entertainment to loser men.* She turned and continued down the path to the pier entrance. The pier made no sounds except for the slaps of water against its wooden supports holding it firm. There didn't appear to be a soul the entire way out to the end, so she slowly meandered along occasionally looking to the stars overhead. Some twinkled in the darkness as if attempting to communicate in a language she may understand. Gina slowly continued down the warped and weathered planking until she reached the railing separating her from the coal-black vastness of the ocean.

Dark thoughts began to enter her head. She thought, *I could climb the railing and jump,* but she knew from recent experience and reflection of her past that in times like these, you are most vulnerable to the clutches of self-doubt and self-persecution. *I should think this decision through, there would be no turning back past a certain point.* She knew it but controlling the voices in her head taunting her with those thoughts—sounded like a whole other battle, a battle she wasn't prepared to proceed with.

Gina's new faith held strong at first when she realized she'd experienced miracles from God with Ben and Jay. There were no other explanations other than coincidence and she'd never bought into this line of thought. The three of them discussed in length, deciding it wasn't possible to be a happenstance. It most definitely seemed to be a gift from God. A miracle. Coincidence became a concept she quickly regurgitated from her thought. A miracle from the creator came to be much easier to swallow and keep intact within her psyche. A coincidence, which she found impossible to exist without God's hand, meant it linked directly back to Him. Therefore, making it truly a miracle. She did however question why God would put the effort into creating such a Godsend and instantly save three lost souls, only to let two of them wither and fade separately after such a gift. *I feel almost like a pawn in some great supernatural experiment. But I can't believe this is why He gave Jesus, His son, to suffer and die on a cross.* Gina now sat on the deck at the end of the pier with her legs dangling under the railing and out over the bay. She continued her thoughts. *It just doesn't ring true to how I felt back then and up to the point when Jay and I....*

The last thought which flowed through her intellect seemed to ring a note of recollective truth. *Free choice. He'd promised the gift of Grace but only through free choice.* Ben, Jay, and she rigorously discussed this meaning and how it pertained to the Bible. Free choice to either accept and follow Jesus and receive His gift of everlasting life—or the freedom to choose to deny Him—deny belief that He is your sole creator and forfeiting His interacting presence in your life. He would be there to receive you back into His flock at any time, but He would never force it.

Gina remembered scripture about sin pushing you farther away from His presence by free choice. Something about using your freedom to choose helping someone humbly instead of the indulgence of the flesh. Her shoulders dropped. Indulgence of the flesh held her entire life. She'd given it up for only a short period before turning and traveling back to her old familiar life of sexual gratification. She now felt unworthy beyond redemption, choosing the easier path of hiding from her Father instead of confessing to Him. Gina believed while the spiritual high was new; only to let it fade into the background of her life as time passed. Now temptation stepped in and gripped her once more into an adulterous lie now swinging over her head like a pendulum.

Gina looked up to the sky, but quickly looked down to the earthly darkened waters, not wanting Jesus to see her sin filled soul. There is no new miracle for a lust-filled temptress and adulterer who performed pleasure on Jay, just as she lured sin-filled men on stage in her past. *I had my chance and saw it took too much effort and work to keep it, so I threw it away on a murderer and demon.* The devil who tempted her so easily, now reigned victorious in convincing her to let shame keep her from forgiveness.

Gina reached behind and retrieved the knife Ben gave her.

Unlike her earlier need for protection—the reason now became the polar-opposite. She held the handle and pushed the button several times, watching the blade flash each precise movement, as with each clicking sound it opened and closed. Then holding it steady, close to her face, Gina studied the blade's thin sharp edges as they shined brightly in the glimmer of the moon's light. She remembered from science class from a teacher who taught the light of the moon "in truth" reflected from the sun on the opposite side of the world. It was as if the moon were the devil tonight, close enough to feel she could reach out and touch him. He enticed her to commit a gruesome act, one which would end her pain. Then she pictured the sun being God, so distant from her touch, she believed He would never see the desperate ugly act she now contemplated committing.

She couldn't even shed a tear. Her broken shell of a soul could easily, in this moment, walk up to the gallows pole without faltering, because of the guilt she could not deny. Gina touched the button several more times, watching the blade dance in the darkness, flickering in the light each moment it escaped its sheath. Pushing the button again retracted the blade and Gina positioned it just left of center on her chest. She knew all she would have to do is push the button sending the blade plunging into her heart. It would surely do the same carnage as hitting a tree at eighty miles per hour in a van.

19

The Watkins rushed to the nurse's station after seeing Jay leave the room and then practically run to the exit. They witnessed a rush of nurses into Cat's room along with another doctor and nurse pushing a crash cart.

"Please ma'am—can you tell us Catrina Cader's condition? We're family." Gloria asked.

The nurse looked up from a monitor and after a brief look at them, she answered in a doubtful tone. "Um, y'all are black as me and she be whiter'n snow. I'm sorry but the doc is in the room, and I can't give out patient info like this, less you be immediate family."

Gloria leaned over the counter, "She don't have no other family but us. She and her youngest son have lived in our home for over three years. She's family, miss."

"Ma'am, I'm sorry but I got no time to argue, I got patients in bout' every room. I'll let the doctor know your concern when he comes outta' Ms. Catrina's room."

Gabriel grabbed his wife's arm before she did or said anything. He knew to do so by the look he saw on her face. It started by the twitch in the corner of her eye. He knew his wife as a God-fearing Christian down to the bone. He also knew her to be capable of vocalizin' hell's fury if she felt it need be done. "Gloria, there ain't no purpose to go ballistic. Won't solve nothin' and no preacher's wife supposed to act out from bein' upset. I know what the young girl said sounded snarky, but she got her job to do." He pulled her arm and walked her back to the chairs. "We'll wait 'til the doctor comes out."

"Gabriel..." Gloria patted her husband's hand. "...God knew His work when He led you to that ice-cream social all those years ago. I'd be anythin' but a preacher's wife if you'd not picked me out to take care of and steer me against my own grain." Gloria shook her head back and forth as she lowered into the chair. "No sir, I'd probably be cuttin' weeds along the highway with the prison guard eatin' my lunch."

They both looked at each other and snickered, shaking their heads in mutual agreement.

"It's 'bout time to pray again, Gloria." And they bowed their heads in unison once more.

Twenty minutes later the two were nestled together and napping peacefully.

A nurse walked over from the nurse's station and looked at the cozy Watkins' couple sleeping. She smiled. "Mr. and Mrs. Watkins? I have some good news for you." The couple's eyes opened quickly.

"Yes? Yes, please tell us." Gloria answered.

"Indeed, we been prayin' hard, Cat's such a wonderful young lady." Added Reverend Gabriel.

"The doctor took care of a blood clot which developed and got a serious bleed stopped. He believes with some rest and a watchful eye; she should heal and be just fine." The nurse said.

"Does he think there is any brain damage?" Reverend Gabriel asked with concern.

"It's too early to know for certain, but he is ninety percent positive her brain functions will recoup with no or very little residual effects." The nurse smiled and as Gabriel held out his hand, she reached out and clasped his. "In other words, your Ms. Catrina is a very lucky lady she'd been brought in so quickly and

Dr. Patel happens to be one of our best in head trauma injuries."

"Oh, thank you, Jesus!" Gloria praised with exuberance. "Can we go in and see her?"

"She's under mild sedation and will be for several hours, but I think you two can go stand beside her quietly." Said the nurse and she led them to Cat's room.

Gloria and Gabriel walked softly to Cat's bedside, Gloria reaching to touch her hand. Cat's head bandaged down to her blackened eyes made her appear a dark broken soul. She wore oxygen tubes in her nostrils and both of her arms held needles leading up to bags hanging beside. She lay still as pond water, silent as the clouds.

Gloria looked her over and then turned to her husband. "I think we almost lost her, Gabe." A nick name she rarely used these days. Big tears rolled down her cheeks. "She's my daughter we were never able to conceive. I love her like she be mine."

"I know, baby. She is our daughter." Gabriel stuttered. "And Darrell is our grandson. I'd never really thought about them in this way until today. God brought 'em to us and laid their needy souls in our hands to help heal and comfort." A tear rolled down Gabriel's face. "We loved 'em up good and kept 'em in prayer. God is good, all the time…."

"All the time, God is good." Replied Gloria.

Gloria felt an ever so slight squeeze in her hand. She knew her baby girl either sensed or heard them talking by her side.

20

Kyle and Vio were cruising in his Chevy, windows wide open and traveling down US 98 highway across the East Bay Bridge. The radio loudly blared Bruce Springsteen's "Dancing in the Dark" as they headed back to town, moon shining brightly in a dark night sky. They'd been at their favorite beach spot all day on St. George Island. The two found the secluded hideaway in the middle of a pile of driftwood where they'd spotted Darrell and Mitzi the last time they were all together. They made love together on their blankets spread out, then spent the afternoon talking about the future. They didn't swim today, instead enjoyed each other's warm bodies and conversing together. They hadn't wanted to leave but they felt they needed to get back and find Mitzi. She'd desired the closeness of friends since the horrible night which stole Darrell away from her—in more ways than one.

Kyle sped excessively, but the bridge was free of traffic. He loved hearing the roar of his big block 454ci motor which produced almost 400 horsepower ricocheting back and forth between the embankments. The low roar snarled throaty like an angry lion growling at an advancing opponent. The sound gave him a boost of hormones and charged his sexual desires again. He glanced over at Vio to see the smile on her face and wind in her long blonde hair. The day finished fantastic, even though they'd failed to get hold of Mitzi. It did, however, give them the chance to fool around again.

Vio looked at Kyle with eyes of satisfaction. She glowed and she knew Kyle could read it all over her, head to toe. Mad love. Overwhelmed and drowning in it.

Kyle returned Vio's smile, and the car drifted a bit to the right, closer to the cement rail bridge side. He turned his gaze back forward and realigned the Chevy with the divider line. Hormones and adrenaline raging through his veins with each hard pump of his heart. Is this what love felt like, he wondered. He snuck another peak at Vio. *Yep, this is what love is supposed to be.* He felt another fervent surge charge through his body, and he mashed the gas pedal down to the floor. He looked at the speedometer—115mph and the needle kept moving to the right.

Vio reached over and grabbed his leg. "Slow down, baby, I'm getting scared."

Kyle let up on the gas and the car instantly swerved, crossing the centerline and headed for the guardrail. He turned the wheel back to the right, but over-corrected and bumped into the concrete side barrier shooting sparks and tiny bits of debris down the side of the car and into Vio's open window. Kyle held the wheel and the car swerved back to the left, crossed the center line and smacked into the opposite barrier sending more debris and sparks. Back and forth from barrier to barrier the Chevy ricocheted mimicking the steel ball under the glass of a pinball machine. The sound to the outside world was probably deafening with scrapes and bangs and whirs cutting through the air from debris. But inside all Kyle heard, became silent when the car quickly turned sideways busting out the windshield sending fragments of glass moving in slow motion, Vio's arms and legs flinging through the air. Her face showing shock and terror. Suddenly everything turned black and violent.

The car rolled end over end mashing the top into the cab as it rolled and twisted like a fumbled football down the field. Pieces and parts were flying in the air and scattering behind the trail of sparks. When the carnage finally came to a halt and the dust settled, an eerie calm fell over the scene. Only the faint sound of water below slapping against the bridge pylons could be heard. No movement or sounds came from the two left inside the twisted wreckage. The moon remained shining brightly until a cloud slowly blew across and briefly obscured its beam as it drifted on its path. Silent.

***

Bloody fingers twitched as the hand lay in a puddle of moisture on what used to be the car's top. The Chevy lay perched upside down with fuel spilling from the tank. The roof of the vehicle kept the motionless bodies from lying in the fluids dripping down making trails and puddles as it spilled.

A pair of faint headlights and a red flash which seemed to spin in circles came speeding toward them in the distance. Kyle attempted to conceive what just happened. "Vio!" He called out in as loud a voice as he could muster but left his lips barely above a raspy whisper. "Vio…."

Twisted below the back seat that hovered barely attached to the floorboard, lay Vio. Her arm tightly pinned between the smashed roof and back dashboard where the back window once remained. The appendage dripped blood steadily into a pool beside her head. She didn't move or respond to Kyle's voice as he choked and called her name again and again, each time growing weaker and even more raspy.

Kyle blinked his eyes attempting to clear his blurred vision, making it hard for him to comprehend where he lay. He knew he'd been with Vio, but where was she now? As he tried to squirm around, he found himself unable to move. Kyle reached around and brushed his hands over something that felt fleshy, but he couldn't make out what it could be with the combination of darkness and water in his eyes. He rubbed and squeezed on it thinking it may be Vio, but the object didn't move. He tried wiping away the moistness in his eyes so he could see. It looked like a fleshy leg, which caused him to panic. He pulled back using his hands and arms, his torso tightly wedged, and his legs were numb, he couldn't feel them or see how they were pinned. "Vio! Where are you, babe?"

He began to sense pain in his upper body and head. He felt nauseous. He lifted his head back up again and strained to look completely to his left and then to his right, scanning for Vio. As he twisted as far to the right looking behind him, he thought he saw her. She looked like she was faced down. He didn't remember her swimsuit being covered with a dark t-shirt. He'd remembered her just having her bikini on. He strained with all his ability to reach back behind him and touch her. It wasn't a t-shirt she wore. It felt dark and wet and when he pulled his fingers down, they left smudge tracks. "Are you bleeding, babe? Answer me if you can...." His memory began to come back. He'd been driving. *Did I wreck? Who will find us?* And then it all hit him. He'd been speeding. The memory of seeing the speedometer at 110 mph. *My God, did I kill her?* He screamed one more time with all he could, "Wake up, Vio—I love you! I love you, babe, I...lov...love you...." Everything went dark again. Silent.

21

Sheriff Burks got the radio call from operations:

"Sheriff Burks. Please respond, immediately. We have a 10-50 mid-way on the US 98 East Bay Bridge. Definite PI, need immediate 10-52. Repeat 10-50 US 98 East Bay Bridge, could be multiple PI, need immediate 10-52 dispatched—10-4?"

Sheriff Roy went out to Ethan Hendrick's beach house and was unable to find him. Roy had just driven almost back to the station having just been on the bridge not ten or fifteen minutes earlier. It appeared completely barren at the time. He thought it odd for a Saturday night at this early evening hour.

He quickly spun the car around in front of the station and hit the gas. A block or two away he flipped his rooftops on, lighting a red glow around his vehicle. He wouldn't flip the siren on unless he encountered traffic. He hated the loud high pitch sound as much as he hated responding to car wrecks. He wasn't squeamish of blood, but he hated the responsibility of being first on scene and trying to pull people from vehicles or God forbid having to perform CPR. He would more than likely be first on scene. East Point patrol were always slow to respond to accidents. Maybe a Florida highway patrol had a car nearby, he pondered? *Nah, they never lower themselves to come out this far into swampyville, too boring for 'em.* Roy smirked and gave his head a quick nod back and forth in disgust. *They're always concentratin' on catchin' dope-runners, 'cause that's what the television folks want to talk about. More glory in catchin' cartel dope-movers than saving citizens lives. Not as newsworthy. Not as much glory in it.*

As he drove onto the bridge, the flashing red lights bounced back and forth between the bridge embankments on either side of the roadway. It brightened the area around him almost like driving in a tunnel. He looked down and saw his speedometer read eighty-five. Judging the midway point, he began to slow his vehicle, looking ahead for the crash site. Listening to the radio chatter he heard the relay the citizen who drove by and reported, "the accident looked horrendous, debris scattered all over the road on both sides, and the car lay flipped upside down, mashed and twisted. No visible occupants. He didn't stop because he knew he needed to get to a phone in town to call for help."

Roy knew immediately it wasn't a good sign when he heard the broadcast. They could be trapped inside, and the vehicle could be on fire by now or about to ignite—or they could have been thrown free of the vehicle. If that were the case and the passerby hadn't seen any bodies, they could have been launched over the bridge embankment into the bay. No scenario on this one sounded like a good ending to anyone's evening.

***

Jay's anger grew deeper with violence as he failed to find the son-of-a-bitch cop who raped his wife. "The waste of life got away with it for almost twenty years while I raised his bastard son—and watched my wife fall into the whiskey bottle." Jay raged. his eyes dark islands of madness surrounded by pools of stark white glowing in the darkness of the van. "I've judged the defendant, his victim naming him, sentenced his guilt with the death penalty; now I'm gonna execute the fuckin' vermin upon sight." Jay bellowed loudly to himself in a tone filled with uncontrolled resentment and fury. Irrational indignation all but burst through his skin. The grip he held on the van's steering wheel began to cramp his hands. He awoke the numbness by clenching his fist and beating the door, roof, or console. Taking turns between hands, his knuckles now oozing blood through the ripped and open wounds.

Jay began his second circle around the police station when the hairs on his neck immediately prickled. It looked like Roy boy's squad car pulling up to the station's front parking lot.

Jay eased up on the gas and slowed, pulling over in the shadows of some trees near the roadside. He didn't want to execute him right in front of the station. Even though the thought of his deputies finding his fat-ass carcass layin' at their doorstep would be funnier than goose turds sprinkled with sequins. *What a decoration he'd make!* Jay knew it would be foolish. Too many possible witnesses with the fire station next door. Too close to traffic too. He wasn't done with his list of defendants just yet. No need to act stupid and get locked up right away before he retired his missions. He knew the time certainly came closer with the clock ticking, but it would by-God be on his time. After all, he believed he was the judge, juror, and executioner. "I'll wait and see where the prick goes, no need to rush it now when I have him on the hook. I can slowly reel him in with pleasure, let him dangle on the line before swooping in with the net and smacking his fat head on the cutting board." Jay almost enjoyed the rush through his body, knowing the retribution to come. He'd never shot anybody before, always opting to do his killing in a more hands-on approach. Squeezing their throats, crushing their airway, watching the life drain away as they flailed like a fish outta' water. This would be different, killing from a distance. Missing the personal connection as the gleam in their eyes fade. Oh well, he'd enjoy firing multiple rounds into him before delivering the kill shot.

Roy's squad car quickly turned as if reacting to a visual sighting of Jay. *Did the fucker know my plan and now ran scared? Or is he answering some sorta' police call?* Jay decided to follow from a distance, just in case it wasn't him he was runnin' from. If he was—well, that could be fun too.

The squad car quickly accelerated past the speed limit out Highway 98 towards the bay. "What the hell Roy boy? There ain't shit out this way. What are you up to?" Jay questioned as Roy's red spinning lights suddenly lit up.

Jay's palms began to perspire and feel warm as it became apparent the time now drew near. He reached with his right hand to his waistband checking to make sure his revolver still lay tucked there and hadn't slipped out. "Awe, I got ya right here baby, ready to get me some redemption! Be patient now," Jay said as he patted the grip of his new faithful companion. "That's right, be patient." He repeated.

Earlier he'd spun the cylinder and removed and replaced the bullets several times familiarizing himself with the way it felt in his grip. It's operation and function. Hell, point and shoot. Couldn't be much easier than that.

Like the fourth or fifth date with Cat on the park bench, he began feeling more comfortable touching and holding her, getting to know her intricacies. "I'm damn-well ready Roy boy, ready to draw a fuckin' bead on your forehead. I'm ready to make you so ugly even your momma won't recognize that smug-shit face of yours." Jay squirmed and cackled as he followed Roy boy's squad car. "You're on a call alright, Roy. Your own last rites death call! Yee-fuckin' haw!" Jay's mind now careened over the wrong edge of insanity. He'd lost all humanity he'd ever owned, if it were ever inside him at all.

***

Sheriff Roy saw the carnage before him, about forty to fifty feet ahead. There seemed to be no movement at the scene he could see. He quickly pulled closer and parked, opened his door and trotted around back to his trunk, grabbing his pry-bar. The car appeared mashed together and he doubted the doors would open. As he approached the mangled mess, he smelled gasoline and saw the puddles surrounding the car and trailing away toward the edge of the concrete rail. Turning on his flashlight he leaned down and yelled, "Anybody able to talk in there? Can you move?" He quickly saw a male figure which appeared unpinned. He put his ear to the kid's chest to listen for a heartbeat. He caught a weak palpitation and held the glass front of his flashlight to the victim's mouth and nose for several seconds before pulling it back and looking for humidity which would form on the glass from a breath. "Bingo, he's alive! Hang on buddy, I'm gonna get you outta' this mess. Anybody else with you?" He leaned further in feeling the fuel soak into the knees of his trousers. He knew if something ignited, he would burn up along with the driver and anyone else inside the twisted carnage, but his inner hero kicked in. Shining the light to the back he saw skin of another person. Looked to be a young female. Her arm looked pinched between metal where the rear window once was. Dried blood appeared to have fresh blood flowing down alongside it. The girl's face pointed down where he couldn't see her. He reached in further trying to find a spot to check her pulse. He crawled deeper inside the car and never heard or saw Jay's van as he parked it maybe twenty feet back and walked up on him.

***

Jay immediately recognized the bright red car and knew who it belonged to. Kyle and more than likely Violet. *Gotta be already dead.* By the parts and wreckage strewn as far back as he could see behind the car, Jay figured they were doing close to a hundred when the crash began. *Ain't no way they could survive after this, I mighta' guessed this would be in that punk's future.* He could see concrete chunks knocked out from one side to the other across two lanes of traffic as far back as the streetlights allowed him to focus. He redirected his mental regard to the task at hand.

Old Roy boy began gruntin' and groanin' as his big ole pork-ass moved back and forth. He caught himself smilin' and about to laugh out loud from the sight. He'd have felt bad about the kid in the car, if it hadn't a been the long-haired smart-ass, Kyle. *Little rich prick pretty-boy deserved it, not knowin' how to drive and be carryin' on at such high speeds.* Jay surmised he'd better act quick; there were more cops surely on their way.

"Why hey there, Roy boy! Somebody got himself in a bit of a pickle, huh?" He watched the fat sheriff try to wiggle out backwards. "You don't wanna move too quick without empty-n' the pistol outta' your holster and tossin' it out careful this way."

Roy strained to turn his head back to look at the voice talkin' to him. "Is that you Billy Jay?"

"Sure-nuff is, outta' your cell and back in hell! Now how about your pistol getting' tossed out here?" Jay repeated.

"Jay, I need some help here. Got two non-responsive kids in here and there's spilt fuel everywhere. Can you help me get 'em out before we have a fire ignite? The girl's arm looks pinned pretty good. I gotta' pry-bar just outside the door here. These kid's lives are dependin' on us."

"I'd love to help, but I'm kinda' short on time 'cause of—what I got to do here, with you, and all." Jay pulled his revolver up and pointed it at Roy as he wiggled out enough and began to reach for his sidearm.

"I'm getting' my gun out to give ya, Jay, but gawd damn I need some help with these badly injured kids." His clumsy fingers pulled out his gun and he tossed it behind him onto the road. Jay kicked it away with his boot.

"I gotta' talk to you 'bout a story I just heard. It's a real doozy." Jay said in a raspy slow slurry way.

"We got no time for this, Jay. I need to get these kids out. They're barely breathin' you selfish som'bitch! Be a hero and help!"

"Get the—hell out—of the damned car, Roy. Them damn kids are done. There for, there ain't no time to save 'em, if they're even alive. Hell, they wouldn't make it to the hospital breathin'. And you as a fuckin' rapist couldn't care less 'bout those two anyway! Hell, that pretty young girl ain't in a position health or comfort-wise for you to rape her—rape her like you did my wife 'bout twenty years ago. It's time to pay your debt now. You enjoyed your fun and lived free and clear, leavin' me your damn seed in my wife, so I could feed and raise him as my own, like your own personal damned fool." Jay spit on the road as Roy backed on out and plopped in a seated position, legs sprawled out in front of him—soaking up more fuel. His balding head sweatin' a river down every spot of his head. "Did you know—you drove my—my sweet, sweet Cat to seek refuge inside a gawd damned bottle a whiskey? 'Bout thirteen or fourteen years of leavin' her babies to fend for themselves while she lay stoned-ass medicated. Self-medicated on medicinal tonic called Jack "fuckin" Daniels, Thank you very much." He lifted his revolver and pointed it at Roy's left leg. "We're gonna start the reconciliation part of this here hearing. I got five shots loaded into this revolver meant for you. I got 'bout ten more in my pocket, but I doubt I got time to reload. So, I think I'll pop one in each leg and that'll leave me three more to work my way up to your ugly, damned, rapin' motherfuckin' face."

"I'm sorry Jay. I confess. I did take advantage of your sweet wife. I've regretted it every single day since it happened."

"So, I'm guessin' you've told her you're really sorry, right?" Jay asked.

"I'm sorry Jay, I avoided her, hopin' the problem would just fade away in time." He dropped his head and moved his legs. They were beginning to burn from the soaked-up fuel against his skin.

"Can you forgive me long enough to get these innocent kids away from this dangerous scene? You shoot your gun at my legs and your very likely gonna spark and set this pool of gasoline off. It'll burn us all alive, if they still are."

Jay thought a minute. "You know, I hadn't even thought of that scenario. Hell, them kids are already goners. But you..." BAM. Jay fired a round into Roy's knee, and he screamed out in pain. "You've been judged, sentenced to death for the rape of my wife Catrina Anne Cader, a beautiful creature of God before she got tarnished by your self-serving deviant sex act..." BAM, BAM. He fired two more rounds into Roy's stomach. "This is about to conclude the final part of this trial, the carrying out of the sentence. He raised the revolver and aimed it at the center of Roy's face. Deadeye aimed at his nose. Roy's face cantered to the side. Finger on the trigger ready to pull. "I'll see you in hell, Roy Burks, convicted rapist, and then—I'll kill your sorry ass again." BAM.

Roy's body slid down to the ground, face turned, lying in a pool of blood and gasoline. Eyes open as if he were still alive, but they were hollow, no gleam.

Jay Cader heard a faint sound of sirens and looked back towards Apalachicola. Distant flashing red lights were speeding his way. He leaned down and shoved Roy's bloody dead body enough from the opening so he could peek inside. "Helps a comin' kids, hang tight, you'll be alright." And he got up and walked towards his van slowly at first, thinking about firing his last round into the fuel puddle to burn up the evidence. He pictured sweet young Violet. Such a pretty thing. He then revealed a meager form of grace by turning his back and heading towards the van. He gave her a chance to be saved by the help coming, if she still breathed life. Jay broke into a jog and climbed in, starting the van immediately. He left the headlights off and pulled up to the wrecked barely recognizable 1970 Chevy 454. He yelled out through his open window, "What a waste of horsepower, Kyle...."

Jay smiled with a feeling of accomplishment as he wove the van back and forth dodging debris until he drove past and came on clear road again. He sped up, looked in the rear-view mirror to make sure no one followed and headed to East Point to catch Highway 65 North to Hosford and then Highway 20 to Blountstown. There he'd turn back south on 71 all the way back down to Port St. Joe where he'd pick up 98 and drive southeast back home to Apalachicola. A nice hundred and sixty some mile round trip. About three hours of thinkin' time, to let it all soak in and gel. He reveled in his completed masterpiece. He wanted to get back and tell Cat how he'd avenged her. "This'll help clear my conscience of what I let happen. Kyle, also on my defendant list, now received a pardon for his crimes and sins." Jay doubted he'd live long enough to enjoy it anyway. He did feel some compassion for Violet; she just got caught up with the wrong feller. "God rest her soul." Jay carried on his conversation as he steered the van homeward the long way. "I think I'll soon be okay for the devil to take me back home to the glass house where I can live my final days bein' fed and cared for—and of course rehabilitated." Jay let out a much more subdued laugh as the gravity of his evening began to settle into his brain. He knew he'd have some strugglin' on the drive home.

Ms. Cela would sure 'nuff be preachin' from the Book to me tonight. She owned 'bout three long hours of me driving through the darkness. She'll sure 'nough try her hand at drawing out the devil from the bright silver moon above, and then work at makin' it shine into my ice-cold heart. Jay laughed out loud. *Tryin' to warm it up to a lovin' Christian carin' ticker, with pretty words of comfort and kindness—like I ever knew such a thing.*

22

Ethan, Joyce, and Mitzi ordered their meals from "Miss Cali Lea Jenkins" who popped in and away from their table more than any other waitress since the introduction of restaurant servitude! Mitzi seemed to become more, and more protective of her mother and less and less trustful of "Mr. Ethan William Kendrick." The way the two thought they were sneaking looks back and forth got under Mitzi's skin. *I'm not blind and I'm certainly not stupid Mr. Coyboy.* A nickname she'd just coined. Mitzi had become top in her class already and she'd just moved here. *Those two, Ethan and Cali, are cozier than a pair of wet-nosed puppies cuddled together in a tightly wrapped blanket.* How could her mom not see it? She mocked the annoying squeaky hillbilly accent that the bitch spoke in, inside her own mind as she attempted to be pleasant at the table. *"I bet you'll have a fine bourbon, neat on the rocks?"* Ew, the little bitche's tone and all-knowing eyes. *There's more to the story between these two!*

"So, now we've all ordered—what about this game?" Ethan questioned. "Role the play and make them say—right?"

Joyce looked at her daughter and then over to Ethan. "I think it's best if we tuck it back for another time." She took a sip of her old fashion before continuing. "I think I'd rather just share some 'friendly' conversation instead."

Mitzi sank in her chair a bit, knowing her mother's continued way of reprimanding her even more than their "powder room" conversation just ten minutes earlier. She forced the smile more than likely recognizable as such. "Sooo, how about those Miami Dolphins this upcoming season...."

Ethan choked on his drink with the snicker which shot from his mouth along with likely a half-teaspoon of WL Wellers. He quickly grabbed his napkin from his lap and wiped his mouth. He then checked the front of his shirt. "Joyce—no worries, I like your daughter's brand of humor. I think we'll get along just fine!"

Cali came back with their entrées and again just a little too cozy for a girl who hadn't seen Ethan in over fifteen years. *I call bullshit on this situation.* Something far deeper between the two of them existed besides some trashy looking restaurant on the outside which camouflaged an above average clientele on the inside. She quickly thought the analogy of this dining place fit her description of Mr. Kendrick and Ms. Jenkins, and somehow, she would get to the bottom of it. *I have a mission, maybe this will help alleviate my constant yearning for Darrell.*

Mitzi enjoyed her red snapper with lobster cream sauce even though she felt designated to concentrate very intently eavesdropping on Ethan's and her mom's quiet whispers—for her mom's protection. Private conversations spoken at the table as if she wasn't even present, is considered rude. Her mom would have vocally reprimanded her if she'd done such a thing. Joyce taught her daughter to be proper around others, especially around the meal table.

Mitzi just wanted to get to his beach house so she could wander the shore as the tide rolled up and cool her feet. She owned thoughts to mentally unpack and the bright silver moon outside the car window begged for her to be there already. As much as she tried to stay awake and listen on the ride home, she let her eyes slide closed for just a minute or two and slipped into a restful nap. The deepest sleep she'd been able to have in weeks.

Ethan and Joyce were holding hands as he steered the BMW

homeward. They just began to cross the East Bay Bridge when Joyce moved closer and laid her head on his shoulder, clutching Ethan's free hand in both of hers. Her eyes felt heavy from the recent drama she'd been through. She nestled in and felt safe lying against Ethan, head on his shoulder. She instantly succumbed to sleep as the steady bump of the bridges section joints began, the steady rhythm lulling her to dreamland. Ta-tunk.   Ta-tunk. Ta-tunk.

***

Ethan slowed when he saw the tow trucks and road crew cleaning up what appeared to be a horrid accident. A bright red muscle car being dragged up onto a vehicle transport as state trooper cars were everywhere, and in the middle of it all sat Roy's squad car. Troopers crawled around inside and out of it. Flashlight beams crisscrossing on the road as if they were searching for something in particular. He didn't see Roy anywhere as he intentionally slowed to a snail's pace to observe. A trooper motioned Ethan to keep moving forward but he slowed even more and pushed the button to lower his side window. As he approached the trooper he briefly stopped.

"I need you to keep moving sir." The trooper motioned with his hand.

Ethan spoke as he let his car idle. "Is Sheriff Roy Burks on the scene? I noticed his patrol car parked back there amongst the wreckage site. I'm an attorney and also a close personal friend of his."

The trooper leaned closer to the window and glanced inside his car noticing a sleeping female in the front along with a younger napping female in the backseat. "Your name sir?" He asked.

"Ethan Kendrick, I'm a defense attorney in Apalachicola...."

"I know who you are sir, I shouldn't be telling you this, so it's off the record, you understand what I'm saying, sir." The trooper stepped back to motion to the car coming up behind to stop and then turned back to Ethan and leaned in closer to speak softly. "He's deceased sir, that's all I can say at this time."

"What?" Ethan asked in a louder tone. Joyce began to rouse enough to ask what was going on. "It's okay Joyce, there's been an accident and I just finished talking to the trooper."

"Sir, this is all the detail I can inform you." The trooper answered. "You have traffic behind you sir, please pull forward carefully and continue safely on your way."

Ethan looked at the scene once more and quickly tried to determine what happened here. *Did Jimmy orchestrate this, or could this be coincidence?* He would be keeping an eye on the local news when they got home to his beach house. He looked down at Joyce, asleep again and snuggled in tighter to his side. His car began to edge forward, and he turned to face the road ahead, which placed his ear close to Joyce's lips. He could feel her warm breath and he felt a long-waited comfort inside. It felt nice, a feeling he'd longed for but never expected it to be in his cards. He glimpsed in the rear-view mirror and noticed Mitzi slid to the left and rested her head, eyes closed, against the window. Ethan dropped his view down and to his right to Joyce. Her top gaped open and he spied cleavage. Her black lacy bra enhanced her white chest, making the dark valley between her breasts showcase what he had only imagined to see once more. It had been so long since their bodies were this close together. The only other time in their past had been nothing like now. Back then it began tawdry, drug-induced, and loveless. He almost wished his memory mirrored hers, non-existent. But now the awful reminiscence of that night could be gone forever; his secret dead and buried with Roy. He moved his legs to adjust for the sudden warm thickness in his lap. Ethan wanted to lie beside Joyce tonight in his bedroom, their bare skin rubbing against each other's, one gifting the other goosebumps; hoping to convince her how he felt. He'd craved her for nearly twenty years, with her never being aware he even existed. But with the news he'd just gotten, he would forego offering drinks when they got home and show the ladies to their rooms, suggesting to turn in early. Then he'd grab his decanter and watch the local channel for breaking news on what the hell happened on the bridge tonight. Ethan took seeing the accident and hearing about Roy as a sign to take things slow and steady. *She's here in my home, I don't want to rush and lose her again.* Slow, nice, and easy—like his favorite exclusive bourbon sliding across his taste buds taking in the nose and enjoying the satisfying finish. *It'll be worth the wait.*

***

Joyce tucked Mitzi in and now Ethan came to her room to say good night. She tried to persuade him she wasn't tired, but he convinced her tomorrow would be much more enjoyable being well-rested. When he turned to leave her room, she reached and grabbed his hand, spinning him back towards her as she stepped forward. Reeling herself closer to him, she dropped his hand and moved hers to his cheeks. Looking wantonly into his eyes, she drew close enough he could feel her breath on his lips. She pulled him in even closer until their bodies met. She ran her tongue softly around his mouth and then plunged it in slowly, first touching the tips of his teeth before exploring a little deeper. She felt heat within, it radiated.

Joyce felt Ethan fight his urges. She could feel his body begin to tense. She knew he wanted to take her in his arms and rip off her clothes, ravaging her wildly. Her instincts felt it. She however wanted to make sure to leave him wanting her even more. *Take your time, move slow, reel him in steady but not too fast, he'll be worth the wait....*"

Joyce withdrew her tongue methodically and opened her eyes to see him. "I can hardly wait until sleep comes tonight; I have a feeling we may see each other in our dreams."

Ethan smiled. "I don't doubt it a second. Good-night sweet Joyce." Their hands reached down, each grabbing the other's hand into a light grip which slowly broke free as Ethan exited the door and walked to his room.

Joyce peeked out as he walked away, waiting to see if he'd turn and change his mind—but he didn't, and she slowly closed her door.

Lying in bed, listening to the ocean waves rolling up the shoreline, she thought about her reactions tonight. She'd never been like this before. Sex as a teen began awkward for her the first time she experienced it. Sex with Roy felt unenjoyable every time. Wham bam thank you ma'am. Never any passion or love with Roy. He held the "I got mine, you get yours" philosophy. *Where were all these memories coming from?* She wondered.

23

The state police sought a search warrant for Sheriff Burk's home. They found no clues left behind at the scene of the accident. The area made no sense of why the sheriff would be gunned down. Did he stumble onto some sort of trouble or drug deal going down? One would think there would be signs of another vehicle, but on the pavement there were no other questionable tread tracks left behind. It appeared the only other victims were the two kids pulled from the overturned Chevy and taken to the hospital ER. No evidence of anyone else being in the Chevy. It became a perplexing crime scene with no evidence pointing at anything other than answering a traffic accident call.

Judge Calvert awoke by phone around 11:45pm and after hearing a probable cause to search the sheriff's home, granted the warrant. By 12:15am, Roy's home was entered, and investigators began searching every nook and cranny for something to tie his death to tonight's accident. A couple of minutes into the search, one of the investigators, Sam Hayden, called out from a back room. "Tony—you're gonna' wanna' come see this, I think we may have a lead to research."

Sgt. Tony Rawling entered the back room and saw a desk with a computer and monitor, behind it the wall held dozens of posted notes and maps. An open box sat on a black two-drawer vertical file and as Tony walked up, he could see what looked to be clothing inside.

"Interesting home office, huh Tony?" Sam looked at Tony and pointed to the box. "Take a look at what's inside there. Either Roy owned some hidden quirks—or they were the belongings of whoever he apparently had been looking into?" Sam pointed to the wall of paper.

Tony walked over and with his gloved hand carefully reached into the box and pulled out a garment. "Women's panties?" He carefully poked around with his flashlight pointed inside the box. "Several women's panties..." Then something caught his eye. He brought the pair he held in his hands closer to his face to observe. "Now this is strange, there's a burnt wooden matchstick attached to the waistband?" He studied the object up closer and focused his light on the matchstick. "Sam, take a look at this—there seems to be a letter etched or carved onto the side of the stick. Hmmm..." He dropped the pair he held in his gloved hand and looked inside the box, pulling up another pair and turning them around as he studied them. "Now isn't this odd? This pair contains a burnt matchstick also—and it's got an etched letter also, but different." Tony took the first pair and laid them out on the desktop. He flattened them out smooth and then laid the other pair out in the same fashion. As he followed through, placing one pair over top of the first pair, they completely covered the first pair up—by a sizable amount. Looking back to Sam, he made a statement. "These obviously don't—or didn't belong to the same female."

Tony paused as if thinking about the find they'd just begun to study. "We need to bag everything up in this office, every paper, picture—everything, along with the box of panties and take plenty of pictures of the wall art. I want nothing but gloved and careful hands touching anything in this room, and I want to be able to reassemble those notes exactly like they are here, down to the tenth of an inch." He put the two pair of underwear back in the box and folded the flaps to where they locked together. "This is a very interesting find, Sam." Tony shook his head. "Very interesting indeed. My first inclination is maybe this town's sheriff became mixed up with something he shouldn't have been. Or—he had a beef with somebody, and he found evidence of something either quirky—or possibly insidious." Tony looked over at the forensics officer. "Dust this entire place, I want every fingerprint and semen sample there is."

Sam agreed. "I wonder what the matchsticks represent?"

Tony eyed his partner, "I don't know, but I'd bet my grandma's favorite puppy every pair of undies inside that box contains one with a letter etched on its wooden stick." Tony stuck out his hand towards Sam. "Wanna take the wager? Cost you a Benjamin Franklin!" He laughed knowing his partner wouldn't take stupid odds like that. "Let's get to the police station and check out this sheriff's office and files to see what cases or incarcerated civilians he's got or held lately."

"I'm thinking just the same, Tony." Sam agreed. "And I wouldn't touch that long-shot with a nail-shrouded nightstick." They both chuckled.

As the two left the office, Tony called out to the next in charge. "Bobby, I want this place carefully bagged, tagged and photographed until the walls are burnt by the flashbulbs. Be prudent. There's evidence all over this house, but the office in the other room is crucial. Fingerprint the shit out of this place. I wanna' know who's been in here, who's pissed in the can, and every act of sex that's gone on here, down to which damned neighborhood cat saw the action!"

24

Sunday morning, 8am.

Darrell roused when he heard the snap of the lock on the jail room door. He reached up still discombobulated and wiped the sleep from his eyes. With no windows, he didn't have any idea what time it could be, day or night. By this time, he'd also lost track of what day of the week. It felt like maybe a Sunday, but he wouldn't bet money.

Jailer Pete stammered on his hobbled leg, keys a janglin' over towards his cell. Darrell stretched and swung his legs around 'til his heels rested on the cool concrete floor. "Feels early for dinner or late for breakfast? I give up. What time of day is it, Pete?

Pete was the only regular thing in the place. He seemed to also be the only person who treated Darrell with any kindness. Darrell liked Pete. He'd been hurt in a war somewhere on some foreign shore and he mumbled some of the story to him at one point recently.

Pete said, "Sunday, Mr. Darrell, it be Sunday mornin' 8am sharp. You be gettin' outta' here ta-day. Sure 'nuff."

"What? Released on a Sunday? The sheriff ain't even here to give me warnings and scream threats in my face!" Darrell replied.

"Be some big news ta-day, but backed up with a whole lotta questions!" Pete shook his head and jingled his keys as he looked through the ring which held several.

"You're shittin' me ain't ya Pete?" Darrell quizzed. "I mean, don't get me wrong, I want the hell outta' here. I couldn't even tell you how long I been in?" Darrell hopped off his cot and started pacing in front of the door. "I just figured there'd be more fanfare or somethin' before they let me out." He looked at Pete with a confused expression. "Sheriff sleepin' in and just lettin' a Cader go without goin' through some sorta initiation or nothin'?"

"Not sure I should be the one sayin', but I guess it won't hurt, bein' how it's all over the news and all. You be hearin' it on your own soon 'nuff." Answered Pete.

"What in hell are you jabberin' about? What's on the news?" Darrell gripped the cell's bars on the door as Pete mumbled and fidgeted with the lock, trying to open it.

"Sheriff Burks be dead. Found 'em dead with bullet holes in him out on the bay bridge last night. There be some big wreck and a couple a young high-school kids are in the hospital. Don't nobody know if they's gonna make it or not. They's still unconscious and on machines to breathe for 'em. Both were in surgery through a good portion of the night. They flew in a brain trauma specialist from Jacksonville and some other kind a special surgeon drove straight here through the night from Wewahitchka. He be on some kinda' vacation or something."

Darrell stood puzzled as the door lock finally clicked and started to open. "Sheriff Burks is dead, from a gunshot? Who did it? They catch 'em yet?"

"Nope. Don't have no clue yet. They ain't named those kids either 'til the parents know. The report just on again 'bout fifteen minute 'go." Pete answered. "I just got told by Mary Lou the state police says you been held 'bout a week and a half past time you shoulda' been freed." Pete shrugged. "Hell, they don't tell me much 'bout nothin' here, but lucky for you, I 'spose."

Mary Lou got your belongin's in a bag out at her desk. I reckon she'll tell ya what else ya need to know on the way out."

As Darrell picked up the baggy holding his wallet and coins he'd held in his pockets along with his belt and shoestrings, he walked to the door. "So just like that, I'm walking out of here?"

Mary Lou looked up from her desk and in a snarky tone answered, "Yep, just like that."

25

Mitzi pulled the drapes to find her window to actually be a double French door leading outside to a deck. She quietly opened it and walked outside. The night air felt slightly cool with a breeze. The large silvery moon shined on the waves rolling into shore, making the white curls appear as long cotton balls rolling across a dark abyss. The sky shone completely full of stars. She immediately noticed the difference from the sky in town. The brightness of the small town's illuminations from streetlights and business signs drowned out all the lesser glowing stars that beamed so brightly here. The sky here seemed mesmerizing. Mitzi immediately walked down the stairs to the ground level. One step off the stairway from the deck and she felt sand. She kicked her sandals off at the foot of the stairs and began walking towards the glimmering water.

Swoosh. Swoosh. Swoosh.

What an incredible sound, each set of waves rolling in. She remembered her and her mom's first trip to the beach when they arrived. St. George Island, the first time she put her feet in ocean water. The memory took her back to how she stood calling in the waves as if she were queen of the sea, directing them in with her hands like a conductor of a band. "Hum-ah-na, hum-ah-na, hummmm—she laughed at the thought of what she probably looked like to a local. They probably thought of her as just another crazy foolish tourist. But now—she was the local. So many things happening which should scare her away from wanting to stay here and call it home. But—she sighed. "Oh, sweet Darrell, I would have never met you if I'd not stayed and gone to school that first day..." She spoke his name aloud and then brought both hands to run her fingers over the belly she now looked down at. "...a baby we made. From scared, to happy, to shock. So many emotions in such a short time." She looked up to the moon and the heavens. "Jesus? If you're not too busy and you're up there listening..." Her eyes began to lightly water. "...I really, really need to ask you—no, I need to beg you please, please let Darrell and I not be related. Please let it all be a mistake. I love him. I don't want to live without him, and I can't be a momma by myself." She began walking towards the water again. "I know you still perform miracles. I believe in you. I put my life in your hands to do with as you choose." The sand changed consistency, wet but firm. As she continued talking to Jesus, the leading edge of a wave slowly flowed over her toes and then grew higher than above her shins. Swoosh. It felt cool and refreshing.

Her thoughts changed as the water receded back into the abyss. "Ethan. What's the real story with him, Jesus? I feel strange around him. I want to like him, and I think I could be thankful for him—for my mom." She turned and began walking away from the house and farther down the beach, engrossed in her conversation. "My mom's done everything for me. She's not been with a man really for—well, since I can remember. Everything's been for me and her parents before they died. She's so beautiful and such a waste she's not been able to experience what Darrell and I have..." She replayed the statement in her head. "...or what we had anyway. You know Jesus, the gift of lovemaking is really incredible. I don't ever want to share this with anyone else other than Darrell. He's my one and only forever if he'll still have me." Tears dripped down her cheeks. "If he'll ever have me again. It's not like we are really brother and sister. We didn't know each other, had no idea. It's not fair, we didn't grow up together like a brother and sister, we don't have the same mom!" Mitzi's voice grew louder. "Please! It's not our fault! We didn't even grow up in the same town or even State!" Her head dropped back down, and she looked at her tummy again. "I'm keeping this life inside me, God. He or she is a gift you've given me, I won't let anyone take this baby from me, no matter what." Mitzi suddenly felt weak, drained. The late hour, the drama, the not knowing and now all the emotions flooding her. She needed to sit before she fainted. She plopped onto the sand. She looked back towards Ethan's house and noticed not only her light on but saw another that hadn't been on when she left.

***

Joyce couldn't sleep. She'd tossed and turned trying, but to no avail. She couldn't believe how quickly things meshed with Ethan and her. Their new relationship felt new but comfortable like an old favorite pair of shoes. She felt like she'd known him in a past life. She also felt a sexual side of her awaken she thought long dead and buried. *But it's not. I want passion and to roll under the sheets naked with him.* She sighed with a hunger. He'd kissed as if he also hungered. *Could he possibly be as passion-filled as me, or just being kind and regretting what started happening between us?* All the sudden she wondered if he was in bed asleep. How would he react if she knocked on his door? *What would he do if I just slipped into his bed with him?*

Joyce held so much sympathy and concern with her daughter's revelation after watching their relationship grow so quickly, she'd put her oddly ripening courtship to the side. She never reacted on sexual feelings quickly. She'd been burnt so bad by Roy. He'd just wanted sex and when he found out she'd become pregnant, he ran like a scalded dog, ignoring her and later his daughter as if she'd never existed. She vowed to never let another man fool her for sex ever again. She'd felt like tainted goods not worthy of being placed on the shelf again, instead concentrating on her baby girl and her needs.

But Ethan made her feel womanly again. She felt like her lady parts were again operational and ready for re-entry into the possibilities of desiring a man and fulfilling him. Joyce tossed in the bed and her hand accidently brushed the front of her panties as she turned. Chills shot through her body and her mind plunged instantly into daydreaming it were Ethan's fingers lightly caressing her there. She sighed quietly and pulled her hand away in shame. She instantly remembered her daughter's confession to her and how she'd heard Jay talk nasty while he watched her through the window. Afterall, *I'm much too mature to do those things to myself. What would Ethan think if I lost control and he walked in on me?*

The fact being, she is laying in a state of mind in a strange bed, and she would not be able to sleep. Not without a drink. She remembered seeing the bar when they came in. Could she find it in the dark though?

***

Ethan couldn't believe the newsflash he'd just seen. The horror of the shocking accident. The reporter said it had to be a miracle the car hadn't caught fire and exploded with the amount of fuel surrounding the area. The two kids were miraculously still alive when the ambulance and EMTs' arrived. And Roy gunned down like a wild dog—he almost felt regret. The two were friends for so many years and been through so much during high school and after. He wondered how it all went down. *Could Jimmy really be the one who did this? How?* He never really pictured Jimmy being so gruesome. *Why the wreck and the kids? Were they just collateral damage?*

Ethan wanted to call Jimmy and confirm, but he surely would have already called by now to let him know the job had been complete if this happened to be his doing. Ethan never asked him to help with this kind of operation before, especially not one involving innocent bystanders. Sure, he'd hired him to threaten witnesses before, even caused a mild accident or two, but this is not what he expected. If this could be his work, he felt uncertain it would be bonus worthy, but then again, he also didn't want to be on Jimmy's bad side if he was capable of such heinous acts.

Now for his other quandary. When and how would he tell Joyce and her daughter he'd known Roy, Mitzi's father, was killed tonight?

26

Ethan heard a noise in the other room. He quietly got up from his chair and turned the television off before opening his door to listen for sounds, as he grabbed his handgun. He hoped Jimmy wasn't here, he'd told him never to just show up at his home.

Joyce must not have been as quiet as she thought. Ethan watched her from behind as she filled a highball glass from a bottle of bourbon found low on the bottom cabinet shelf.

Ethan stood in the shadows watching Joyce's beautiful body maneuvering around his bar, bending over and searching for what looked appealing to drink. Her gown gapped open, and the wispy fabric left nearly nothing to his imagination. She still owned a twenty-year old college girl's body even though by now she must be closer to forty. Ethan became very aroused by what he stood in the shadows watching.

Joyce bent back down straight legged to stow the bottle where she found it.

"Can't sleep?" Ethan asked in a low raspy voice.

She almost dropped the bottle from her hand and turned around. "Oh, Ethan you scared me to death! I'm sorry if I woke you. I hope it's okay I poured a glass of whiskey. Can I pour you one also?" She smiled. "And no, I couldn't calm down enough to even close my eyes.

"So, do you have a real taste for fine bourbon's? I haven't seen you order a bourbon and Coke, so it does titillate my thoughts. I must admit, I've developed quite a taste over the years and have become a bit of a whiskey snob." He quietly let out a short chuckle. "If you do appreciate the different notes in the finer whiskeys, I have a special reserve of my one-of-a-kind I'd love to share with you. Should I pour you one?" Ethan moved from the shadow of the hallway towards her. "Speaking of finer things in taste—Joyce, you look incredible. Like a beautiful gift ready to be unwrapped." He coyly smiled.

"I'd love to try your special reserve. I'm in the mood to try something I've never tried before." Joyce smiled a rather devious grin in return.

The sexual innuendo sparring, cued Ethan's heart to pound harder. He'd searched to no avail for almost twenty years, only to finally find her living less than six hours almost straight north, in the adjoining crimson tide state of Alabama. His heart yearned to be with her all those years he couldn't find her until he almost reached the point of abandoning the pursuit, although he'd never been a quitter at anything. But now, here she stood, standing less than ten feet from him, and playing an arousing game of cat and mouse. She'd become his employee, the new addition to his single council firm and there in front of him with barely a stitch of clothing, she stood within view in his dimly lit study. He felt stimulated and hearing her last statement, he grew emboldened. "I love your sleep attire, Joyce. Did you wear it wondering or hoping I would see you in it during your stay?" Joyce took her time in answering him, making him wonder if he'd pushed too hard. He started feeling instant regret. A feeling he wasn't used to having with the ladies. The biggest part of his life other than building his firm, consisted of searching for the woman who now stood in front of him. One he'd encountered in a way he wished he hadn't—from day one. But she's finally here to behold and he feared he'd pushed too hard. *Did I just make the most emotionally expensive mistake of my life?*

"You know Ethan, it hasn't been too many months ago I didn't even know your name or who you were. Why would a renowned defense attorney be querying me? I'm just a paralegal. Honestly, I researched you trying to find an excuse to turn your offer down, feeling it too suspiciously generous. I thought there certainly must be a reason other than my work for you to want me to make this move. I'm good at what I do, but not outstanding." She lifted the highball glass to her mouth and breathed in the aroma through her nose, before tipping the glass and taking a sip. She moved toward him and asked if he wanted her to pour him a glass and sit down somewhere for a minute or two.

Ethan reached above the liquor cabinet and brought down two shot glasses. He reached to the upper cabinet to the right and brought down a crystal decanter. "I would love to do just that. This is a special barrel I don't share with many. When it's gone, it's gone, never to be replenished again. It's what makes it so special. I have to savor each taste as if I won't be able to savor it tomorrow." He winked at her as he carefully filled each glass a quarter inch from the rim. "Would you like to sit outside on my bedroom deck? The silver moon is almost full. It will begin waning now. I love a full moon myself, but a waning crescent, although filled with the sadness of losing reflective light, is much more beautiful to me."

Ethan picked up the two shot glasses, Joyce reached for Ethan's arm, "Yes, let's sit outside your bedroom on your deck. Nothing could sound more enjoyable."

Ethan led her down the hallway and into his bedroom.

Joyce scanned the spacious room taking everything in. The large pieces of artwork she imagined were one-of-a-kind paintings. The bold and bright splashes of color which danced on the canvases enhanced the bold dark wood armoire, nightstands, and magnificent headboard. "I love this room! Very impressive. Aggressive bright walls balanced by the calming dark woods. Did you pick these paintings out yourself?"

"Yes, I love the contrast of bright almost brash colors conflicting with the warmth of dark woods in a shaker style furnishing." Ethan opened the double French doors, letting the ocean's sounds and smells enter. The cool breeze rustled the long sheer drapes and the light of the moon and stars beckoned Joyce to step outside and take in the magnificent view.

"Oh, Ethan—it's spectacular. She pulled his arm in close to her side. Either her excitement or the cool breeze hardened her nipples and goosebumps scattered across her entire body suddenly forcing her to hastily shiver which ended in a sigh. She quivered again, ever so slight.

"Is it too brisk out here? We can go back in. Or I can light the gas fire pedestal?"

"Oh no, Ethan, not at all, I just need a sip of a shot and I'm certain to warm up." She smiled.

They both sat down in an overstuffed outdoor couch and when Joyce became situated, Ethan handed her the shot glass.

"This is something to savor and sip, even though it's in a shot glass." He tipped his glass to his nose and inhaled the aroma, taking it in and enjoying it as if he'd never experienced the scent before.

Joyce watched and mimicked him. "It smells slightly sweet but oaky, it's got a finish of something I can't quite decipher."

Ethan smiled. "Yes, it's a mixture of two ryes one aged twelve years the other eight and then finished in cognac barrels. The scent you can't place is a hint of the rye." He then lifted the glass and sipped, letting it sit on his tongue to savor. Joyce followed suit.

She lowered the glass to her lap as she continued to taste the liquid in her mouth. "It's very good, it's so smooth and delicate." Ethan smiled and then Joyce smiled in response. She continued, "Now, back to what we were talking about." She eyed Ethan's response and he displayed a perked attention. "I took careful considerations in my decision to uproot and move before accepting your offer. It's not just me who would give up things from Hoover." She fidgeted. "Mitzi held lifetime friendships she'd built since one can remember such things. I thought very carefully about taking those solid staples in her life away from her. She's never held any kind of relationship with her father, Roy. He never wanted to see his daughter or me for that matter. He just dumped us like unwanted puppies. So she took solace in me and her grandparents until they passed, and then her lifelong friends." Joyce again lifted the glass and took a brief sip. "But here we are now, both under your roof tonight. It's crazy what a few months can bring a person, don't you think?"

Ethan held his thoughts and response, instead he took his time and swallowed more than a sip of his glass. He let it roll around his tongue and release the different notes. He swallowed and felt some tension release from his shoulders as he enjoyed the long finish this bourbon gave.

"You know Joyce, for some it can be amazing what life brings in just a couple of months." Ethan paused and finished swallowing the rest of his glass, not taking his usual time of enjoying it. "But for others in life—it seems like a lifetime can pass, in slow-motion before you attain what you've sought for so long. And this is if you are fortunate enough to ever obtain it." He looked into her eyes, never giving in to a blink or turning away.

To Ethan, this felt like a moment between only two card players alone, the others at the table, already calling the game quits and folded. It came down to all or nothing, looking at your investment in a pile before you. The risk and the rewards compared internally by both players. "I can understand with the drastic change in your environments—yours and Mitzi's, I can understand how things have rolled quickly to you. Both having to react on the cuff and make drastic changes which could cause difficulties in your lives—or on the flip side of the coin, the slim possibility the gamble could pay off a hundred-fold." He still stared into her brilliant dark brown eyes, the moon's sparkle contained within them. "I've held my cards almost my entire life with my eye on winning one particular pot I knew would be the win of a lifetime. I've let many games go by, folding up front and walking away safe and unhurt, unscathed but nothing risked. It's truly been most of my life spent searching and waiting even praying—hoping that one game for all the chips—the whole enchilada, would be found by me. Something I felt so confident about I would be willing to risk going all-in with everything I've ever obtained by playing cautious—and by doing so—missing out on the spoils of life."

A pause which seemed to last infinitely, caused Joyce to look nervous. So nervous she took the glass and downed the remainder in one swallow. She never broke contact with Ethan's eyes. Never blinked. "It appears by your beautiful home with the most magnificent views I've ever seen that you've played the game to your advantage and have basically won that pot."

"It does 'appear' that way on the outside doesn't it? But you know how the saying goes…" Ethan broke their eye-to-eye contact, looking out across the dark horizon and then slowly back to Joyce. "Money and things don't fill a man's heart and soul—they merely camouflage what he's missing in life temporarily. What he yearns for deep within." Ethan considered risking the pot in an all or nothing with Joyce. Something which held so much value to him he used other circumstances to convince Charley that Roy needed to go. He wasn't worried about the past. He wanted rid of a bad memory. One which could crash the dream he'd chased, and now about to swallow him whole if he didn't follow through. He'd risked murder for the chance to woo her and win her heart.

"I guess what this boils down to tonight—is it's come time for me to risk it all and to call what the other player is holding—so, here goes Joyce—what's in your heart tonight? I ask because I know what's in mine."

***

Joyce's heart suddenly pounded hard, a feeling like fire pumping through her veins as never before. Sensing everything rode on the words ready to spill from her mouth in this instant. Joyce knew her feelings inside. This slice in time scared her to hell and back. Hoping he too looked for the answer she wanted to share. But could he be bluffing? Common sense said to fold and safely walk away. She sat thinking, her brain buzzing and colliding inside with the alcohol attempting to calm the quagmire within. Joyce closed her eyes and demanded that all thoughts seized at once. Her face turned flush but she swore she could feel the heat turn cold and flow from her head down towards her toes. She opened her eyes and looked out at the beach, scanning from left to right.

That's when she caught the glimpse of movement in the distant shoreline. Her daughter Mitzi walking the shore, her feet in the waves, hands talking with motion. She couldn't tell if her daughter was walking towards her or away, but by the stance, the steps taken, the flailing arms, it was her life's love. It had been just her and Mitzi, all these years. She wouldn't trade them for all the gold in California, but could she be ready to share herself again? She looked up again at Ethan, sitting staunch and calm like a true poker player wearing his poker face. *No tells within his eyes or actions giving what he held, away to her in hints; dead calm and waiting to see if I, the player across the table from him, calls his final bet or folds and walks away—hurt but not completely wiped out.*

In an instant she knew her answer. It wasn't necessarily an answer she'd been prepared for, but she began her game speech and when the words left her mouth, she'd be past the point of no turning back. One way or the other, this hand would play out. All or nothing.

"Ethan." Joyce began. "I lost the urges and the hunger to place myself back into the game years ago. I barely remember a winning hand because I probably never held one before. The last time I even played I fell for the bluff, and I bought in, thinking I'd won." She looked into Ethan's eyes, not able to see the brilliant greyish green they were because of the night darkness. "I moved here not knowing if I'd be doing the right thing. You've given to me beyond my value and in doing so, shown me not everyone who pulls up a chair and wants in, is a cheat or marauder." Joyce blinked several times, thinking she should stop, but continued. "You've given me the desire to want to enjoy my body again and share it with someone I want to trust will never hurt me." Joyce lifted her hands and twisted around in the couch, so she squarely faced Ethan. She took her hands and moved them towards him as if she were pushing all her poker-chips she owned—to cover his bet. She smiled as she put her hands on each side of his face and said those three words which gave Ethan the feeling he craved. Her mouth formed a smile she could barely contain, and she spoke, "I'm all in!" With a quick chuckle, she followed with another three important ones. "I'm in love."

Ethan stood up and reached for her hand, pulling her up and into his arms. "I've searched for you my entire adult life, Joyce. I love you." In one move he dipped her down and then up into his arms and carried her through the open French doors and onto his bed where they quickly landed nearly naked into a shared romantic and long- awaited bliss.

***

Outside Mitzi made her way back to the house just in time to witness the final moments before Ethan carried her mom through the door into what she assumed would be a night filled with the passion mirroring the moments she and Darrell shared. Part of her felt happy for her mother—the other was scared as hell of what she could be getting herself into.

When Mitzi got inside her room, she lay on her bed running her fingers back and forth across her tummy and quietly talked to her baby. She would occasionally hear her mother softly moaning with sounds of pleasure as she lay there alone not knowing what to think and feel. Tears rolled down her face and onto her pillow. "I'm going to be to you, my baby, what my mom's been for me. The best possible momma ever." She smiled with a new comfort.

They were all so engulfed in their very different personal worlds to ever notice a white Dodge van parked in a dead-end road just before the entrance of Tate's Hell Swamp. Those words were chiseled into the face of a large stone which sat dimly lit, about 500 feet up the driveway from the beach house Ethan called home.

"Things are about to get interesting." Jay said under his breath. "Ethan William Kendrick, you're about to be judged." He curled his lips into a Cheshire cat grin. "And you ladies are just pleasurable collateral damage. Hmmm, you two are gonna feel good. A mother and daughter shouldn't be here alone with this one—or me neither I guess." He snarled a nasty chuckle as he put a leather work glove on each hand.

Jay climbed out of the van and walked into the wooded area, heading toward the house. Smith and Wesson in hand.

When Jay reached the house, he slowly walked the perimeter looking at every window and point of entrance. He cautiously prowled like a black panther blending into the background, quietly stalking his prey's lair. As he rounded the corner and entered the backside of the house which sat perched on large stilts and wooden framework not visible from the front—he first heard a sound which didn't fit the picture. Jay's movement stopped, but his eyes continued to scan until he saw movement.

It was Mitzi. Apparently, she walked back from the beach, footsteps silent in the sand until she reached the creaky wooden stairs. When her legs disappeared up the stairs from his sight, he stealthily moved under the wooden framework supporting the underneath of the house. He could see the silhouette of her body moving upward through the plank seams.

Jay's body felt electric. This is the kind of activity he previously self-trained for, with many opportunities in his past to perfect his prowess. He moved like a well skilled predator. He lived as a well-trained huntsman at one time.

The door clicked quietly closed above his head and the silence again made every step on a twig or kick of a rock echo. He continued in the hollow cover underneath Ethan's home. He noticed and made mental note of everything that would make his entrance easy and unnoticed, he also took mental snapshots of anything which might hinder his speedy escape if need be.

As Jay rounded the back of the house and strode up the opposite side from which he'd come, he heard unmistakable sounds. Sounds of a woman being pleasured. The moment gave him a quick flashback sitting huddled in Ben's closet while he ravaged a dancer. Later he began his judgment of Ben. Gina then uninvitedly walked through his door. *Oh Gina, the two of us did share a special moment, didn't we?* Jay's eyes rolled back under his lids. He listened to Joyce's moaning. He imagined her beautiful naked body thrown back in passion as the selfish, sinning bastard who was called Ethan Kendrick, deceivingly raped her again. That's what it is when girls are drugged and helpless. That little red-headed teen Jay found on the roadside all those years back had told him things about Roy and Ethan, and that damned teacher at the high school. And little Ms. Joyce's dead prick of a husband had brought her here and participated in the debauchery back then. *Deviant sicko. Karma may not always be fast, but it does seem to eventually be a bitch. Don't it, Roy? You certainly got your judgment and just reward, and now yours is a comin' Mr. Ethan William Kendrick. Soon, very soon.*

27

The beauty of a small town like Apalachicola is that everything is close. It only took Darrell minutes to reach Mitzi's house from the jail. The bright sunlight blinded him when he first walked through the police station door and into freedom. A temporary pain he could get through. His heart pounded the closer he got to his destination.

He barreled up the stairs two and three at a time and immediately knocked on the door. His patience wasn't at its best this morning. He knocked again only louder. Could she be at church today? He pounded this time, wary the sound may also wake the neighbor. He hoped not. He'd seen all he wanted of that demon. Darrell side-stepped to the window and peeked through the curtains as best he could. Nothing visible, no movement. He walked around the deck checking each window until he came to one of Jay's. He hesitated but leaned in noticing the blinds were slightly open. Both places appeared to be empty, no one home at either. He looked at his watch, 9:15 am, he could make it to the church by service time. Joyce's car sat in the drive, and this perplexed him. Jay's van however was not. This bothered him greatly causing his skin to prickle.

***

Ethan's eyes opened, he looked to his side, his thoughts

immediately replayed last night, his sense's renewed. She lay quietly beside him, her bottom nestled tightly against him. *Could it really be true? Is this the feeling love could bring to a person?*

Ethan, a natural early riser with the sun, turned and spooned with his newfound enchantment. Joyce stirred but felt very comfortable tucked into Ethan's heated body. The morning breeze blew through the drapes and the sound of the waves washing up to shore were lulling both her and Ethan back into a comfortable slumber.

***

Mitzi woke wide awake at 5am. She ventured out on her own down the opposite side of the shore than she'd walked last night. Sunrise across the horizon shined with beauty. The sound of rhythmic waves calmed her woes. Mitzi stomped and splashed as she continued farther down the beach, not caring nor paying any attention to the distance she put between her and Ethan's house. *They'll sleep late from their late night and probably wake up and repeat. They won't even miss me.* She wondered just how long her mom and she would stay now? *She'll probably never wanna leave. I'm not moving in here though!* With just a bit of anger mixed with frustration, she tromped on down the beach.

***

"Good morning, Joyce." Ethan ran his finger over her shoulder then down her back, watching the goosebumps form. He leaned into her ear and gave it a soft kiss. "We can't sleep forever, although I would love to spend this Sunday in bed with you all day long. Remember, we promised your daughter an exploration of the area today."

Joyce slowly turned as she tried to make some sort of

assemblance to her hair which became wildly twisted in her arm and pillow through the night. "I must look a mess." She stated as their eyes met.

"The picture of perfection." He replied. "I'm going to get up and attempt a stab at a breakfast, hopefully one which won't make the two of you too scared to keep staying!" He grinned a cautious grin. "You—will stay, won't you?"

Joyce rolled all the way over where the two were on their sides, heads propped by arms and hands, "If we work together—and play together—and have my almost grown daughter, along with me, living with you—how long before you grow tired of us? You've been a single man coming and going where you please. You're surely not ready to have two women running around and sharing a bathroom and kitchen. Sure, you think it's sounds great now, but what about a week from now when you look over to the passenger seat on your way to work? And there I sit, again?

"We could start with some boundaries if this would make you feel more comfortable? I suppose you could have your own room and space—we would be roomies! With visitations occasionally?" He mischievously smiled.

Joyce sat up in bed, the sheet falling to her hips, her breasts visible until she reached and quickly pulled the sheet back up to cover herself. "I don't want to be any man's occasional, Ethan. I know I'm being wishy-washy, but I don't want to move so quickly it all comes crashing down into my lap."

"Is this our first disagreement already?" Ethan reached to touch her shoulder. "Make-up sex can be grand I hear." He gingerly laughed. "I'm teasing you, Joyce. I love you and I don't want you to go, even for an instant, I'm at your mercy, under your spell."

***

Jay decided, after hearing the bedroom sounds, that last night wasn't the proper time. He'd rather deal with momma Joyce and her little girl at different times so—he could enjoy them more. Their judgments should be less harsh than Ethan's. He knew how jaded Ethan's life had been. He'd been told. It's amazing the secrets one can learn if they only open their eyes and ears to receive them. Poor little red-headed girl's momma knew so much about this town's dirty little secrets and the naughty puppets that performed such debauchery. She'd just been too scared to do anything about it or expose them. Ethan and his friends were a treasure trove of naughtiness, and it went way back. Way, way back in the past. "I'm just the one to start breakin' eggs around here and cookin' up restitution instead of breakfast for the sinner's victims of this little Peyton Place." Jay grinned the most insanely devilish smile as he steered the van into his driveway. In the middle of the madness, Jay's mind couldn't stop the echo in his head of Ms. Cela calling out for him to listen to the Word. I AM is your peace and salvation, child, like a nursery rhyme stuck in his head.

28

The sound of a vehicle pulling into the drive caused Darrell to run to the other side of the deck. His heart pounded hoping it would be Mitzi! He rounded the corner and came to a screeching halt. His heart still pounding but suddenly for another reason.

Jay. His white van pulled into the parking area. The last person in the world Darrell wanted to run into or share words with. He wondered if Jay saw him. Maybe he could go back around the apartments and avoid Jay going into his place? Darrell squinted down to the windshield from the cover of the building corner.

As Jay climbed out of the van, he looked around as if he were checking for someone or nearby neighbors. Darrell thought his movements were awkward until Jay reached in the van, his head below the window by the seat. He pulled out a revolver and lifted his shirt to tuck it under his pants. *When the hell did Jay get that? Why? Are Mitzi and her mom okay?* Darrell noticed Jay looked like hell, as if he hadn't slept for days. He appeared as if his demons were active, the whites of his eyes were totally visible. He thought he heard him mumbling also. The hairs on Darrell's neck lifted and a slight buzz charged just underneath his skin. *Something isn't right here. I have to find Mitzi.*

Jay locked his van door and walked toward Mitzi's stairwell. When he got to the base, Darrell could hear him whistling some odd and broken tune. The steps creaked and moaned with each step he'd made. *I don't remember them being so loud.* Darrell didn't move until he heard Jay's voice. "Awe, the pretty little lady's place, all empty and lonely. Lucky Mr. Ethan Williams Kendrick, until the sinner's time to pay." Jay said in a creepy psychopath's voice. "The peace and quiet like before. Before the two noisy bitch's moved in. Thank you, Jesus? I guess that's incorrect! Thank you, myself!" Jay paused. "I hope poor Cat's recovered."

Darrell stood bewildered by what Jay just said, and then he heard the door slam. *What the fu....* He caught himself. He'd heard the very word come from Jay's evil mouth and the last time he heard it in jail, he'd thought what an ugly and vicious meaning it held. He would try to erase it from his vocabulary. But, he became petrified with the thought of what Jay may have done. *The concealed gun, Mitzi and Joyce missing, Ethan Kendrick's name mentioned and something about Jay thanking himself? And my mom hopefully recovered? What does it all mean?*

Darrell prudently made his way down the wooden steps careful not to make a sound; when he cleared the bottom step, he took off down the street toward the church like a rocket chasing' the moon.

***

Joyce came out from the hallway into the kitchen. "Have you seen Mitzi this morning? She's not in her room."

Ethan looked up from the stove and answered, "Did you check the bathrooms or the study? She can't be too far away."

"She's not inside, I'm going out to look on the beach, she was out there last night when we were on the deck." Joyce wasn't frantic, but she'd hopped onto the train that was well on the road to panic-ville.

"Let me shut the stovetop off and I'll go with you." Ethan pulled off his chef's apron and they headed out the back stairs.

Joyce kicked off her shoes at the bottom step and put her bare feet onto the sand. "Wow! This is soft sand. It's beautiful out here."

Ethan reached for her hand with his open to catch hers, she quickly reciprocated, and they walked more briskly than normal, feet sliding and painting the freshly windblown beach. "Look Joyce, there are footprints leading off to the left. They head out toward the peninsula. If she keeps going it takes a left to the entrance of Boggy Jordan Bayou. She really can't go back to the left of there." Ethan gave her a squeeze on her hand for assurance. "My bet is we'll see her on the way back."

***

Mitzi sat with her legs crossed watching the waves roll in. She hadn't seen a soul all morning and it fit the mood she felt comfortable in. Alone. Not too many weeks back, she'd been happy and content, in love and her only problem was how to tell her mom and Darrell about her pregnancy. Now her world flipped upside down and twisted into something she couldn't even comprehend. It became like holding this great beautiful shiny precious object in her hands. She'd just gotten used to looking at it and understanding it when all of a sudden from nowhere a hammer came down and smashed it into sharp shards she could no longer hold without slicing her skin. It turned ugly and scary—and there was no one anywhere who could help her. No one could understand what fears were swallowing her up. She felt even God had abandoned his care over her and the baby within her tummy.

The waves continued as if nothing could break their pattern or upset it. Rain, darkness, or bitter heat, the surf continued in a steady reliable pattern. *If only life could be like this for me. I don't even know if Darrell still loves or cares for me? All of my steadiness just got smashed into pieces and swallowed up in one huge gulp.* Mitzi's teary eyes just stared and watched the ocean react as if nothing ever changed. She lowered her head and prayed.

"Please God, if you are out there? You gave me Darrell. You gave us this life inside of me, growing and counting on me. I can't do it alone. Please...."

29

Cat lie resting in bed. She held one thing on her mind. Darrell. She didn't remember why she'd been lying here, or who all the people buzzing around her were. Just Darrell. She remembered he meant the world to her. He was her only son. And she missed him. She owned no memory of the last time she'd seen him and no idea when she would see him again. Only knowing he was all she had, she lay trapped in a reality she held no control over.

***

He paced around his living room. Jay's brain felt wired from no sleep and tired of hearing the voices in his head arguing back and forth. Ms. Cela's sweet broken sentences in her preachy old black woman's tone worked on mellowing him down, but the demon's voice kept gnawing away at him. *Judge or servant?* Which voice could be louder? He looked over at his readin' chair in the corner, the good Book on the table beside. "I hear ya, Ms. Cela!" Jay yelled. He walked in small circles pulling at his hair, not knowing what to do or which conversation to listen to and act upon. The demon won last night, unless releasing God's justice was truly called upon the man who'd raped his wife and sullied many others with his perversions of malfeasance.

Remembering how Roy stared at him with nothing to say about sparing his own life, not one word of pleading or begging, only showing concern for the safety of those two damned injured kids. Roy portrayed himself as if he were some sort of noble angel of God.

"Bullshit! You got what you deserved, Roy-boy! You got no rights to present your case to me now with your gawd damned chivalrous gallantry! Case closed! Punishment rendered! Jay's eyes exploded full of white anger, as he hoofed in circles of rebuke. His veins were thickening with blood full of consternation. His mood swinging from left to right like the pendulum of the old grandfather clock which stood in Lila Pasternack's living room. Tick. Tock. Tick. Tock, as if each sound stole another increment of oxygen from the air.

Jay's head began to feel light. The circles he paced became slower and tighter. He stopped briefly and looked toward his chair, spying Ms. Cela's Book. The gospel which stared back at him as if unnerved by his erratic behavior. "You would still show mercy for me?" His eyes began to quiver in their sockets. Jay quickly squinted as if the light in the room became brighter. He blocked his face with both hands in either protection or shame. His right hand stretched skyward as if to reach for another hand which wasn't there. Jay suddenly toppled forward into his chair, knocking it and the table over before rolling to the floor onto his back, arms stretched out and silent. Ms. Cela's Book of wisdom, rule and guidance lay open face-up just inches away from his reach. Eyes closed, his fists relaxed. Jay lay motionless with only the faint sound of struggled breath.

It felt again as if Ms. Cela's attempt to warm his heart came seconds too late. James 4 was displayed on the open page of her Bible lying next to his hand.

4 What causes fights and quarrels among you? Don't they come from your desires which battle within you? [2] You desire but do not have, so you kill. You covet but you cannot get what you want, so you quarrel and fight. You do not have because you do not ask

God. ³ When you ask, you do not receive, because you ask with wrong motives, that you may spend what you get on your pleasures.

⁴ You adulterous people, don't you know that friendship with the world means enmity against God? Therefore, anyone who chooses to be a friend of the world becomes an enemy of God. ⁵ Or do you think Scripture says without reason that he jealously longs for the spirit he has caused to dwell in us? ⁶ But he gives us more grace. That is why Scripture says:

"God opposes the proud but shows favor to the humble."

⁷ Submit yourselves, then, to God. Resist the devil, and he will flee from you. ⁸ Come near to God and he will come near to you. Wash your hands, you sinners, and purify your hearts, you double-minded. ⁹ Grieve, mourn and wail. Change your laughter to mourning and your joy to gloom. ¹⁰ Humble yourselves before the Lord, and he will lift you up.

¹¹ Brothers and sisters shall not slander one another. Anyone who speaks against a brother or sister or judges them speaks against the law and judges it. When you judge the law, you are not keeping it, but sitting in judgment on it. ¹² There is only one Lawgiver and Judge, the one who is able to save and destroy. But you—who are you to judge your neighbor? (James 4:1-12, New International Version)

30

"Ethan, there she is! There on the sand." Joyce began running awkwardly as the sand shifted underfoot with each step until she reached the wet lightly packed terrain. "Mitzi!" Joyce hollered as she waved her hand, slowing to a jog.

Mitzi climbed to her feet before Joyce reached her and began to move toward her mother. Ethan continued his pace, just a silhouette in the background, the sun behind him. As Joyce reached her she took Mitzi in her arms as only a mother could give comfort for a pain she hadn't seen but felt intuitively. The embrace between the two culminated into a loving connection, which obviously conquered the summit of tension between them at this moment.

Ethan slowed his advancement and stood back not wanting to intrude on their moment together. He turned his gaze oceanside, the breeze blowing his loose white collared shirt in ripples like the sheets of a small sailing vessel changing directions into the wind during a tack. His silvery and reddish-black strands of hair whisked across his face and goatee before he turned and faced the incoming breeze. Mitzi looked over her mother's shoulder at him as if to say, *"I will do anything to protect this woman."*

Several minutes later, Joyce and Mitzi eased up beside Ethan. They all shared a glimpse of each other followed by an assuring smile showing an "everything will be okay" look. The three all watched the waves roll in from the horizon on their journey to the shore before turning back, traveling back where they came. So is the circle of life for a body of water collected together as a unit of alliance—be it a temporary grouping or one of permanence as Joyce now hoped the three of theirs were to be.

31

Detective Sgt. Tony Rawling and partner Detective Sam Hayden were going through boxes of evidence taken from Sheriff Roy Burks home. They were working through the night on this one while the leads were fresh. As a murderer walked free out there somewhere, two Florida State Highway Patrol Homicide Detectives took this specific case very serious. A long-time law enforcement officer's life was taken, gunned down at the scene of a catastrophic car accident. Things like this didn't happen on the outskirts of small coastal towns around here, so as weary-eyed as they were, they poured through the boxes diligently.

"Hey Sam, take a listen to this name. It's got a ring of familiarity to it—Billy Jay Cader. Ring a bell?" Tony asked.

Sam answered right away. "It sure does, he's the guy that killed his boy and went missing for three or so years! When he came back—his other boy tried to kill him with a shotgun." Sam shook his head. "A hell of an outstanding family. Why? Don't tell me you got something pointing to him. Why I'd be shocked at a fine example of a family man like him bein' involved here." Sam spoke smothered in sarcasm.

"We may have our first lead. Sheriff Burks, it appears was diggin' into him." Tony held up a folder to show Sam.

"I'll check to see if he's still hanging around town these days." Sam began typing into the databases on his computer.

"Looks like this box of women's underwear we found at the

sheriff's place are being attributed to Billy Jay Cader, according to the sheriff. Note says a couple who now live where Billy Jay and his family lived before he took off, found these stashed inside a hidden wall compartment in the out-building. We're gonna wanna talk to them too." Tony picked up a note. "A Jim and Judy—Bullinger. They reference their house as the old Willy Chantilly place off Moses Road. Looks like we need to see them first thing in the morning." Tony yawned. "I'm gonna need to lay my head down a minute or two. My eyes are blurring."

"Go ahead and catch a few winks, I'm too keyed up to close my eyes. I guess it's my younger age!" Sam laughed. "Hell, I'll probably have this crime solved when you wake up! Nothing left but the arrest," Sam chuckled.

Tony whipped back, "You young pups with your wet noses to the ground think you're the shit—right up to the point you look up and bump your soggy nose on an electric fence. That's when the reality hits you square in the intestines as the pile of excrement shoots outta' your ass at eighty miles per hour. Age lends the knowledge of avoidance, and that's some valuable information. Tony laughed and headed over to the couch at the corner of the sheriff's office.

Sam smiled and shook his head. "Thanks for the lecture, gramps! You be sure to drink yourself some warm milk while I brew a young pup's pot of coal black coffee!"

After Tony laid down, Sam picked up one of the pairs of panties and studied the burnt matchstick with the alphabet letter etched in. "Interesting." Sam pulled them out one by one and laid them across the conference table, writing the letter on a piece of paper for each. He quickly noticed there were no duplicates. He shook his head. "Hmm. What the hell does it all mean?" He picked up another box and started sorting through. An hour later, his eyes too began to feel heavy. Ten minutes after and his head dropped down to his folded arms, soft snores followed close behind. Soon, Sheriff

Roy Burks office sounded like the bass horn section of an orchestra pit tuning their instruments.

32

Darrell opened the door to the church the minute he got there. Even out of breath, he felt an urgency to find Mitzi and her mom. He hoped he would find them inside. He scanned the sanctuary quickly from front to back left to right. Reverend Gabriel nodded to Gloria on the front row and then back to him.

Gloria glanced back and her eyebrows furrowed in surprise. She began sliding to the side aisle where she hurried to the back doorway where he stood. She pulled him by his arm outside and pushed the door closed. "Darrell! Honey! They let you out? We been tryin' to get hold of you. Hasn't anyone told you? Didn't Mary Lou tell you nuthin'?"

"Ms. Gloria, please don't tell me somethin's wrong with Mitzi? I can't find her or her mom?" Darrell's voice almost begged her for information. His eyes showed desperation in them.

"I'm sorry, Darrell. I don't know a thing 'bout that. But what I need…." Darrell cut her off cold.

"I gotta find 'em. I think Jay's done somethin' with 'em. They're not home, but her mom's Volvo is in the drive and…."

"Darrell! It's your momma! She…." Gloria loudly interrupted.

"My Momma, what?" Darrell asked.

"She had an accident, and your dad was apparently there, it happened here at the church. We called and let the police station know, didn't they tell you? Is that why you out?" Gloria quizzed.

"Where is she? Is she okay?" Darrell began to show signs of a panic attack. Darrell suddenly became overwhelmed. He fell to his knees and held Ms. Gloria's legs tight as he sobbed. "I don't know what to do Ms. Gloria. How bad is my mom? She's not gonna die, is she?"

Gloria got down on her knees and wrapped her arms around him and tried to comfort him. "I think she's gonna be alright now, honey. But we came real close ta losin' her, honey. The good Lord wasn't ready to take her." She gave him a squeeze. "She may be needin' some time to get back to normal, honey. She suffered a head injury."

"What is happnin'? Is God angry with me? Is this why I'm losin' everything?" Darrell looked up with tears. "Why would he punish my mom? She didn't do nothing."

"Oh, honey. You surely don't think its punishment, now do you? The Lord don't work like that. Darrell—I know you don't believe He does. You been comin' to church and hearin' Gabriel's preachin' God's Word long enough to know better." She pulled him into her body again and then patted him on his back. "You're gonna hafta help an old woman up though. My bursitis in my hip ain't gonna take much more of this. Darrell wiped his face and hopped up just as the front doors of the church opened wide. "Service is over, gonna be a crowd headin' out. Help me up, honey, please and thank ya." She held her hand out and Darrell pulled her up to her feet. Gabriel walked out and smiled at them. He stood ready to greet the congregation on their way out for dinner.

"It's a glorious day, Ms. Tomberly. Glorious indeed." Reverend Gabriel said as he held her hand in his, ready to move to the next—Good mornin' Jeb, Mary…."

***

The church crowd dispersed, then Gabriel walked over to his

wife and Darrell. "How we doin' today, Darrell? You look a bit frazzled mixed with worry, I suppose Gloria told you 'bout your momma?"

"Yes sir, I wanna go see her. Will they let me?" Darrell asked.

"Let's go find out, son." Gabriel squeezed Darrell's shoulder as a father would to give encouragement and love.

33

Tony awoke by Sam lightly poking his back. "What, what the…" He turned to Sam standing over him. "Where's the fire, Sam?"

"I found something you're gonna wanna take a look at." Sam held a list of girl's names he'd found in one of Roy Burk's folders. "Burks was on to something." Tony got up and swung his legs off the couch and stretched a minute. "Come on, follow me!" Sam said in a hurried voice.

"Hang on Sam! Is whatever you have gonna run off like a peppered dog? Because even a dog's got brains enough to stretch before they leap unless it's a squirrel or somethin' streakin' across the damned yard!" He pushed himself up with the couch arm and finished stretching.

When Tony got over to Burks' desk, he saw panties laid out in a couple of lines with some yellow Post-It notes placed on top of each pair. Sam handed him the folder which contained the names of missing girls from 1971 until 1976. "Take a look and see for yourself the correlation between the Post-Its and the names in the file." Sam waited a second while Tony acclimated himself to the task. Sam couldn't stop fidgeting and snapped up his empty cup and almost skipped over to the coffee pot for a refill.

Tony caught his jerky movements from the corner of his eye; it distracted him enough to comment. "How many damned cups of go-juice have you consumed? You're more jittery than a mess a fire-ants on sugar and cocaine!" Not waiting for Sam's response, he returned his gaze between the panty notes and the file pages.

The sudden sound of a crash sent glass breaking on the floor. "Shit!" Sam looked down as Tony whipped around and saw liquid down the front of Sam's pants and his cup in pieces on the floor.

Tony laughed as he shook his head. "Young enough to stay up all night, huh?"

"I caught a couple minutes sleep, it's all I needed." He wiped at the wet area with a fistful of napkins.

"I do see what you mean, Sam, about how these two different items conjoin rather suspiciously." He looked back down and read a letter from each matchstick and traced it to a name on the file page. "C- Camerren Ballard, K-Katy Frye, D-Dixie Dunham, M-Makenna Dupree, G-Gabby Montgomery—damn! Each matchstick letter does match a correlating name on Burks' list." He looked up at Sam with a question showing across his brow. "Now this list of missing girls is all from one place? Or scattered?"

Sam held up a print-out of a map. One of the lower halves of the U.S. east to west. There's a line drawn following Highway 10 from Jacksonville, Florida to Lafayette, Louisiana. Along the path is a blue dot with two capitalized letters, which after looking, Tony assumed were the initials of the first and last names of missing girls.

"Is this what I think it is?" Tony asked Sam.

"If you're presuming those are spots the corresponding initials would be the places those girls went missing—than you've almost caught up to speed." Sam answered.

Tony shook his head and looked at the list of names on the paper he held. "There's seven names on this list. Are you thinking these girls are tied to someone Sheriff Burks may have stumbled onto or somehow been a part of?" He asked as he glanced back at the map. "Odd these are spread out down highway 10 fairly systematically—except for the voided area between Bonifay and Tallahassee. Peculiar wouldn't you say? Almost like a safe zone or buffer area." Tony paused.

"Like possibly too close to home? Maybe the person wanted a bulwark or defense from his home area. To keep any suspicion away." Sam shared.

"But instead, it draws attention. The fact these are all along a major east and west highway for the southern distribution of food and wares—it makes me think of an over-the-road-trucker." Tony and Sam's eyes met. "Don't suppose there'd be any possible truck drivers listed on a piece of paper within all those files you been scrutinizing?" Tony asked.

Sam smiled and let out a short guffaw. "Yes sir, yes sir there is. His name appears throughout quite a bit of Sheriff Burks'—investigation, which I might add, appears to be pretty thorough." He paused to take a drink of his newly poured coffee.

"Don't suppose you're ready to divulge the name, although I already have a theory who you're gonna say." Tony smiled and they again shared eye contact. They both spoke in unison.

"Billy Jay Cader." Neither shocked at the others answer.

"Pour me a cup too, I need to wake up before we visit Mr. Cader in a bit." Tony said. "I sure hope he cooperates, if there's trouble—you may be too jittery and tired to be a lot of help!" Tony smiled.

"I'm just the guy who sacrificed to line all the ducks in a row!" Sam grinned and gulped another swallow of the "go-juice."

34

Inside the room Cat stared out through the window with an expressionless face. Darrell stepped through the doorway quietly. "Momma?"

Cat's head turned and when her eyes met her boy's eyes, an incredible smile instantly formed. In a raspy whisper she spoke. "Darrell, baby." She suddenly glowed in the brightness brought not only from the morning sunrays, but from the sight of her son. "I've missed you—terribly."

"I've missed you too, Momma." He walked over and leaned down, hugging her and kissing her cheek. "Momma, what in the world happened to you?"

Cat looked up and her smile faded into a look of question of confusion. "I—I don't know what you mean Darrell. I'm just restin', that's all. I been kinda'—kinda' tired today."

Darrell looked at Ms. Gloria and Reverend Gabriel with his brow scrunched. They hadn't really told him she didn't remember things. They just reassured him she loved him and missed him. He turned back to her. "They finally let me out, Momma. I don't know what happens from here. Sheriff Burks was holding...."

Cat's face turned flush, and her entire head flexed away at the sound of the sheriff's name.

Again, Darrell looked to the Watkins in wonder. "I'll be right back, Momma, I need to go to the bathroom. Okay?" She nodded at his question and her head turned back to the window and the sunshine."

Gabriel and Gloria followed Darrell through the room's doorway. Darrell maneuvered toward the nurse's station. The minute he reached the counter, he blurted out his question. "What's the matter with my momma, and how long before she's right again?"

The nurse looked up and asked, "What's your name and your relationship to the patient, young man?"

"I'm Darrell, Darrell Lee Cader and she's my momma, Catrina Anne Cader. She's actin' like she don't remember stuff. What happened to her?"

The nurse responded cautiously. "Let me call the on-duty doctor to answer questions, his name is Doctor Blanton. If you have a seat over there in the waiting room, I'll have him come out as soon as he's available. Is that alright, sir?"

Darrell looked to the Watkins' for assurance. They nodded. "Yes ma'am, thank you for your help. I'm sorry I acted so abrupt; I'm just now finding out my momma is in here."

"Did you come from out-of-town?" The nurse asked.

"No ma'am, I came from lock-up at the jail. Sheriff wasn't supposed to have me in there as long as he did. I woulda' been there for her if he hadn't." Darrell answered.

A moment of awkwardness hung between he and the nurse. "I see, well—I'm glad you're here for her now. The doctor shouldn't be too long." She looked and kind of nodded to the waiting room again. "I'll give him a call."

"Reverend?" Darrell looked to Gabriel. "I don't know what all you know about things that have happened..." Darrell dropped his head feeling ashamed of what he needed to talk about. "There's a lot that's happened in my life since school started. I know I haven't been around as much and I'm sure I've hurt my momma and you and Ms. Gloria..." Gloria placed her hand on his knee, he looked up and quickly smiled, but it stuttered his thoughts. "...I—I met a girl. She's real special to me. I—I'm in love with…well…I at least was in love with her." His eyes looked up and they showed pain. A pain he knew certain Reverend Gabriel could easily read.

"What do you mean, 'was in love' son? True love don't rarely end as quick as you're makin' it sound. Can you explain?"

"I'm getting' to that, sir. We were, at least until things happened recently, in love. This thing happened and then this other person told us…" Darrell started getting worked up and his normally paler skin reddened. He began feeling hot and clammy. "You see Mitzi, that's her name, and me—we—we fell in love and we—we had relations. I know we weren't supposed to and it's a sin and all, but we love each other, Reverend Gabriel." Darrell looked up at him and Ms. Gloria expecting them to shun him. When they didn't immediately, he continued. "Anyway, we were makin' all sorts of plans together for when we graduated this year. I planned to suggest you marry us! But we were tryin' to make us right with God."

"I'm not here to judge you, son. Gloria ain't neither. You're like the son we never had but more maybe even more like a grandson, I guess. Anyways, you know we both love you like our own. Sure, our blood don't match, and our colors are different pigments, but in God's eyes—we're all family—children of His. We ain't gonna stop lovin' ya 'cause you may have made some mistakes. Lord we all have! I still do." Reverend Gabriel smiled. "Good Lord knows we all gonna keep on makin' 'em too, so let it out son, so you can heal. Lay that sack of rocks down."

Darrell lifted his head higher, less ashamed to speak to the two people other than his mother, that he considered family. Darrell, stuck in the middle of explaining what happened at Mitzi's house with the sheriff, and Jay saying Sheriff Burks ended up being his real father, when the doctor interrupted. The look the Watkins gave each other became one of shock and surprise. Darrell knew they probably hadn't known the details, by the look on their faces. They sure enough did now.

***

"Hello, I'm Doctor Blanton. Are you Mr. Darrell Cader? Hello again Reverend Watkins, it's nice to see you and your wife again."

"I'm Darrell, sir, and my momma's in there. Cat Cader. I just found out she suffered some sort of accident and is here. I wasn't expectin' to see her like she is."

"Well Darrell, she suffered a blunt force trauma to the base of the skull but it's a closed head injury, meaning the object didn't penetrate the skull, which is good. There are some residual symptoms of some slight memory loss, but I think she will slowly regain a good portion with some practiced skills. Some cognitive rehabilitation will help speed up her recovery time. She's doing quite well considering she suffered an aneurysm in the lower temporal lobe." Doctor Blanton paused. "I know it's a lot to take in, bottom line, she is lucky she got brought in quickly and she does have a good prognosis of recovering back to her normal, or very near normal self—it's just going to take a little time." He reached over and touched Darrell's shoulder. "Your mom is strong, and she's a lucky lady. Is there anything I can try and explain further?"

Gabriel slipped in, "Yes Doctor, what kind of time before she can come back home? My wife and I can help with getting her around and her day-to-day needs."

"I'd like to keep her here until next Friday and then have another closer look at her progression." Replied Dr. Blanton. He then looked over at Darrell. "We have a much younger patient who'd been involved a serious car accident late Saturday night and she is in a similar circumstance as far as a temporal lobe injury. Your mom in her older age is keeping up with my other patient who looks to be more your age, Darrell."

"Is she from around here? I may know her from school." Darrell answered.

"I would like to be able to tell you, but the gentleman with her is in more serious shape and his family hasn't been notified, so I'd better not. I'm just saying your mother in comparison age-wise, is doing incredibly well." Dr. Blanton looked at the chart he held and then glanced to his wristwatch. "I have to run unless you have any further needs. I can promise we will take the best care possible of your mother, Darrell." He patted him on the arm and then headed down the hallway into another patient room.

Darrell looked at Gabriel and Gloria. "I wonder who the guy and girl were in the wreck? I hope they're okay."

***

As Darrell headed back into his mom's room, a code blue alarm rang out down the hallway. Nurses hurriedly scampered to assist. After a few minutes, the nurses and doctor quickly rolled a hospital bed with a young man's bandaged head and splinted arms and legs down the hallway towards surgery. In the mix of the conversation between busy nurses he unknowingly heard that the young man who came in from the car accident on the East Bay Bridge was the one coding. Darrell's ears perked. He'd gone many times with Kyle and Vio back and forth on that bridge toward St. George Island to hang out and swim. That thought caused his mind to jump back to Mitzi, whom he had not been able to find yet.

Panic.

35

Sgt. Rawling and Det. Hayden eased up into the quadplex drive and parked between a white Dodge van and an older Volvo. The property appeared quiet with a few windows open on the left side while the other apartment looked closed up tight. The two climbed the stairs slowly, both men moving cautiously and aware of their surroundings.

Sam eased his face to the window of the first apartment, slowly peering in. He motioned the all-clear sign to Tony. The deck boards groaned occasionally as they moved to the left towards the door around the corner. The one they'd taken notice of as they drove up to the property. There were reasons to be cautious, the two shared some hairy times when dealing with suspects on their home territory before. Downright scary incidences their wives hated hearing them recall with drinks. Drinks that calmed their nerves and reminded them they were indeed just men and not superheroes.

Tony noticed an opening in some drapes on one of the windows. He signaled Sam to halt as he listened closely to the inside through the open window. The breeze occasionally billowed the drapes, giving a brief view of what appeared to be the living room. It seemed quiet. With each blowing of the breeze, the drapes swayed inward into the room, widening Tony's view for a few seconds.

Tony leaned back from the window and stepped cautiously

away, sidestepping to Sam. He leaned close and whispered, "I need you to move to the door, it looks like there's another window open beside it just to the right. See what you can see and if it appears clear, give me the bird whistle. Count to ten and then knock, we'll see what comes to the door. I'll cover you." Tony nodded and Sam gave him the okay sign. "And Sam, be careful."

Sam winked and whispered back, "Always." He quietly moved down the railing and then disappeared around the corner. Tony moved back into his position beside the window and waited for either a bird call—or all hell to break loose.

36

Ben pushed the cracked bedroom door open. He carefully peeked around to see if Gina looked awake or not. The bed lay empty, and the sliding patio door stood wide open. He pushed on through the door checking if the bathroom door was open or closed. It was open also. Ben walked over to the patio door and saw Gina sitting with her legs crossed in front of her on the stuffed outdoor settee, covered with a sheet over her shoulders. She held a cup of coffee in both hands, up close to her mouth.

"Good morning, Gina, sweetie. Are you feeling better?" Ben asked. "I'm glad to see you up."

Gina turned and said hello without any expression and then turned back toward the bay view. The restaurant sat in her peripheral view. It felt like a big overpowering hammer just hovering, ready to be dropped onto her head. The pressures of pouring their lives into it, in such a short time after marriage. It consumed Ben and while she'd been a big part in designing the interior, she felt like a sideline and not the focus of her husband. In retrospect she could see the slow change in their relationship hadn't really been very slow. She admired how Ben poured himself totally chin deep into everything he took on. His addictions like sobriety, his faith, his motivations to move away from the city; and at one time, his relationship and attention to her. Even his attempts to save a lost soul such as Jay. All were head-on and full stride for him. His dedication to the outcome for success.

Lately, every waking minute she'd spent putting her focus on herself and her jealousy of not being the apple of her husband's eye. So, she slipped, she slid big. She made a huge mistake. One which is impossible to take back. She told herself at first it had been his fault. He'd ignored her, he'd chased her away and put her into Jay's arms. Afterall, he persuaded her to ride with Jay to pick up the artwork. But now, as she sat scrutinizing all of her recent choices and Ben's actions from an encompassing point of view, looking down, she knew he loved her endlessly. She'd become his new addiction, his new folly. Ben poured himself completely into attempting to make her world a perfect safe and beautiful place. He showered her with affection when he wasn't preparing the world he was driven to provide her with. It wasn't for himself. It never had been. He'd become the warrior with strength—fighting the good fight any other woman would kill for. *But not me, I chose to self-destruct it.*

She turned again and glanced at Ben, who stood looking out over the bay. She studied his face, so kind and loving, she looked at his eyes and they still glimmered. Resilient to whatever got dumped on him or piled in his way, blocking his path to please. Even his brother, Robert, had told her once that he was jealous of Benny's drive and fortitude on something once he became focused.

Why didn't I just end it last night like I should have? He might have felt the pain like a band-aid being pulled from a fresh wound at first, but a determined man like him would have soon healed. There were plenty of women who would consider themselves lucky to be the scab that healed his wound I would have left him with. Why am I so fucking blind and self-destructive? I'm just a living scar now, that will keep reminding him of how I've failed him.

Gina looked away again before being caught, not wanting him to see her tears and feel responsible for them, like he undoubtedly would.

"Gina..." Ben's voice sounded almost distant as if he were

calling out to her from a million miles away. "...I'm glad I found you." His words were an attempt to quell her inner demons, but out of habit she resisted to hear them in her heart. "Not just in the beginning, Gina. I'm glad I found you last night..." Her tears pushed out angrily as if they'd been forced captive underneath her eyelids. "... you couldn't really have left me, could you? I—I don't know what I would have done. There is nothing," Ben's voice seemed to project louder as if the vast distance he'd just been standing from her had quickly closed. "...there is nothing, no matter what you are telling yourself—that could ever separate my love from you."

She felt the gentle touch of his hand on her shoulder. Soft like a warm summer cloud which somehow wafted slowly back and forth until it gently landed and engulfed her in a cozy, safe, and loving touch. "Gina, you are my life, my breath, my salvation from the clutches of everything bad inside me. You helped heal me..." Gina now felt the bone warming touch of both hands gently squeezing her shoulders. "...give me the chance to help heal you, completely."

Gina let her head fall back until it rested against Ben's waist, her eyes closed but her face moving upward toward his; eyes holding puddles of tears which now spilled out and over, trailing down and soaking into the sheet she held tightly. She fought the muscles squeezing her eyes closed until they slowly opened to see the blurred outline of her husband standing over her. Through the overlay of tears and the sun's bright background of blue, Ben's silhouette looked like what she imagined Jesus would appear looking down from the heavens at her. The image alone spoke to the same miracle as the one in Ben's Bronx home as she saw the tile of GRACE on top of the unmoved Mason jar. The one which before their miracle had read KILL. She'd now been saved twice and forgiven for sin. She felt it in her heart and soul like a warm flood of overwhelming tenderness. Gina smiled up to Ben, a smile that screamed 'I need you, please forgive me'. She knew for the time being, she needn't say a word. Gina's glowing face said it all. She unfolded her legs and slowly stood up as Ben sidestepped around the settee. They pulled each other in, entwining their arms tightly and surrounded themselves in only the sounds of the bay and its cool morning breeze. The singing of seagulls, called out to each other.

__37__

A bird chirp shattered the silence in a way that didn't fit into the surroundings. Jay jumped and began to move slightly from the floor he'd apparently slept on. His lower back ached like never before. He reached behind and felt the grip of the Smith and Wesson 38, its cold steel barrel imprinted into his skin from being tucked against it all night. Jay moved around slowly, getting acclimated to why he woke in the corner on the floor of his living room. The memory didn't seem to exist how he came to be there. Ms. Cela's Book lay face up and open. The table which usually held it, lay overturned. He tried to wrap his head around everything when all the sudden a strong knock rattled his door. He looked over and as his vision passed a nearby window, he saw a large shadow behind the blowing curtain. He quickly withdrew his revolver from his waistband. Another knock but even louder with firmness, not the rap of a lady's fist.

"Billy Jay! Billy Jay Cader." Detective Sam Hayden shouted while Sgt. Tony Rawlings stood at the ready by the open window.

Jay heard the rattle of a doorknob turning—did he not lock it? He stayed in the corner apparently undetected, revolver pointed at the door and ready for it to open. He wondered how many more than the two he knew about were out there? Was he surrounded? He didn't imagine the police would fool around if they'd somehow placed him at the scene of Roy's murder. He reached into his pocket and finger counted five more bullets. *Damn!*

He smiled an odd grin and then thought to himself. *What an inconvenient time to have to take a shit. Damned regular morning schedule.* He let out a small guffaw and the door crept open, giving Jay a dead bead on the unsuspecting cop. As soon as the cop's body lent an open target, Jay squeezed the trigger twice and quickly swung his arm to the window and squeezed another shot off just behind the shadow on the window screen. Both men dropped and he waited for the rush of others to follow or a rash of gunfire hitting his house. Neither happened immediately. He glanced over to the man in his doorway, he sat doubled over groaning, his firearm slid away from his hand across the floor and closer to Jay's reach. He reached it with his foot and pulled it to his hand and picked it up. Jay then turned and crawled toward the window where he stayed low and peeked behind the drapery. He quickly spied his opponent clutching his stomach and scooting backwards trying to get to the steps in front of Joyce's front door. The cop's gun wasn't visible on the deck, he must still have it in his hand. He carefully looked outside through the other windows for cops or cop cars. He only spied the one car parked out between his van and Joyce's car.

Jay cautiously butt-slid over to the bleeding man's body in his doorway and quickly crawled over him, rounding the corner to catch the other cop before he made it to the steps. "My, my looky-loo who we got here..." Jay held the barrel of his gun pointed squarely at Tony's face. "It's all shits and giggles ain't it? At least 'til the other giggles and then shits." Jay mocked a giggle. "I had one pokin' out the barrel and you damn near shook it free by surprise, but it's back in my ass tighter than a fat coon in a skinny hollowed out log."

"Billy Jay, we need to get my partner some help. You don't wanna murder a state...."

"Are you fuckin' serious? I already murdered a worthless raping piece-a-shit sheriff last night! That's a death penalty on its own and your partner looked pert near dead already. I don't reckon the state of Florida is gonna give me a fuckin' get outta' jail free card if I let you go free to testify...."

"He's got a family, a wife and young son—give the man a chance to get some help before he bleeds out. I'm beggin' you Billy Jay." Tony looked up and into Jay's eyes, seeing nothing but crazy white circles with the devil's darkness in the middle. Jay heard a thump behind him and turned, seeing the other cop struggling to hold a small pistol up in front of his head, sighting him in. Jay fired a finishing shot to his neck. Sam's arms dropped to the deck as the palm pistol clattered on the wooden boards, Sam's head slumped over against the corner of the house.

Jay turned around to see Tony squeeze off a round hitting Jay in his left shoulder, spinning him into the side of the building. Tony squeezed another round hitting Jay in the side causing him to release his revolver, sending it tumbling over the edge of the deck as Jay's body slid down the railing.

The two sat looking at each other. One showed crazy in his vision and one thankful once again but saddened by the loss of his partner.

"You...ya...you got me...judged...convic...ted, sentenced and pun...punished...." Jay smiled and laughed a wicked cackle that faded into a gasping for air.

"You're not sentenced yet, Billy Jay, you got a long time to pay for the pain you've caused." Tony quietly rebutted as he looked down at his stomach wound.

Sirens could be heard traveling up the road. Maybe a neighbor or passerby had seen or heard the shootout and dialed 911.

"There's a shattered woman's heart now that you've stolen her future with a good man—and a small boy who will never get to play ball or hold his daddy's hand again." Tony said, holding back some tears fighting to escape into sight.

"My dad...tried...tried...to beat me with...with a

hammer…maybe—just maybe…I saved that boy some pain…pain like…like I lived." Jay sucked for the breaths he struggled to bring into his lungs, but the cold harsh smile never left his face, not even for a minute. He knew he was beat, and he knew deep down he wasn't going to die today, his escape from this world wouldn't be that easy. Jay continued, "You shoulda' shot straighter—and killed me…." Jay spit out blood onto his arm. "It's your fault your partner's dead. Why didn't you come through the door—'stead him?"

Tony looked at him with the coldest darkest glare reflected from his greyish-green eyes and spoke only six more words to him as the ambulance and police cars pulled in. "Billy Jay Cader, you're under arrest." Tony's gun still pointed at Billy Jay's head with his finger itching to finish his sentence but opting for letting him think of what he did until the day he was wired up for electrocution. He'd be certain to personally watch him fry and sizzle if it were to happen—for Sam.

38

Billy Jay Cader was taken without further resistance and loaded into an ambulance where he was driven to Wewahitchka Medical along with several cops. Sgt. Rawling got loaded up and taken to George E. Weems Memorial Hospital in Apalachicola in the passenger side of a patrol car. Det. Sam Hayden didn't make it, being pronounced dead at the scene with the murder weapon retrieved. The quad-plex was quickly taped off as a crime scene now being fully investigated.

Rumors travel fast, it didn't take long until the Cader family once again became the talk around the table, bar, and grocery check-out line in the Piggly Wiggly.

What followed next came just as predicted by an old silver-haired gentleman at the Lazy Lee's diner not long after the attempted murder of Billy Jay Cader, by his son Darrell. "We ain't seen nor heard the lasta' that damned family, no siree." And the old guy smiled as he brought the cup of coffee back up to his lips.

The news-crew vans rolled back into town. Every dang reporter trying to break the night's leads came parading back into town. It became just like a line of annoying ants on a picnic blanket, sniffing out the baked beans and Grandma's sweet peach cobbler.

The word among the locals—it would be a fast track to Billy Jay Cader being guilty with a sentence of two full minutes wired to two-thousand volts of electricity. The town's lights would dim while he fried up like a thick slab of bacon. Supposedly the second worst way of being put to death according to the town-talk. First being stoned like biblical times.

Monday morning awoke with a hum across the town and television. Apalachicola became a beehive of verbal buzzing. It seemed mixed with both kinds of drones. Honeybees waiting for the facts of the case to show how the honey comes out and of course, the killer bee types which injected their own poisonous opinions as fact, pronouncing Billy Jay as Billy the kid of the Florida panhandle.

***

Mitzi had been out in the "boonies" since Saturday night and hadn't heard anything that happened in town. She'd been too busy reeling in all her emotions of Darrell and of course the quickly growing steamy relationship of Ethan and her mom. Mitzi really wanted to support her mom's new romance, but all she could do is wonder what Cali's tie was. The younger waitress at Poppy's Net and Pasture had to be tied to Ethan, somehow. Now the three of them were riding back into town together this morning, playing the big happy family. It just seemed almost too much. And she remained clueless to the things awaiting her back in town, especially school.

***

Ethan glanced from Joyce to Mitzi in the rear-view mirror. His battle within himself this morning was debating to reveal knowledge he now held about Roy. He'd avoided it all day Sunday and the television or radio were never turned on. *Should I play dumb to the fact and let the chips roll? Or should I turn the radio on and wait for the inevitable coverage or quietly break the ice of knowledge on the ride into town?*

***

Joyce looked over at Ethan, trying to read his expression. She then turned to Mitzi and smiled before looking back to the road ahead. For some reason, the ride felt extremely awkward. Joyce couldn't seem to read either one of them. A fact which made her mind work overtime conjuring up possible scenarios within. Would Ethan treat her as an employee today with stolen winks from the intimacy they'd shared? Would he treat her as his new partner in life and business, he the pilot, her his co-pilot? *And just what would Addi think—it was all happening so fast? Would she be able to read her tell-tale eyes the moment she saw her? Jealousy or acrimonious platitudes?*

Such a wonderful weekend which now brought a plethora of problematic questions. All these worries and to then throw on top of the heap how her daughter is truly taking things. Wondering herself what the living conditions would be and where? Well—it became maddening to her. Mitzi never shared so much with Joyce until now. Even with her more adult age, how would Mitzi deal emotionally with it all? *For that matter, how would I?*

***

The time spent contemplating how to share his recent knowledge of Roy's death probably took too long. His choice of how to handle the situation now chosen for him by his inaction. He'd let his emotions for Joyce cloud his need to prepare. Not an ideal use of his courtroom talents now having to negotiate his moves from off-the-cuff. A superior attorney such as himself normally never leaves oneself vulnerable to unknown odds.

Now almost to the bridge, he wondered if there would be any signs left of what happened Saturday before they'd crossed to get to his home. Ethan also battled within, being robbed of spending the drive into town enjoying the moments he and Joyce shared in each other's arms last night. Their bodies twisted together with raging hormones and passion. The amazement of all his years spent pursuing her now coming to such breathtaking fruition. Ethan's orchestrated plans and his skillful plays to prevail in his end desires—now came together far superior to any defense he'd ever masterminded for a paying client. Ethan had taken on countless criminals who'd been obviously guilty of the crimes charged, but through his legal maneuvering and implacable engineering of testimony, brought them verdicts of innocence a myriad of times. Enough he'd become tri-state acclaimed, but none of those media-followed trials held a candle to the trophy he'd won last night which now sat next to him. Ethan felt like he could almost retire and be satisfied with his life's attainments if he could only wrangle a favorable outcome to the loose ends which still dangled. He knew the case wasn't a wrap—until the final verdict became disclosed.

The BMW made a ta-tunk as it crossed the first bridge seam and began its flight over the bridge which crossed the East Bay where it mixed waters with the Apalachicola Bay. The annoying sound of the tires crossing seams remained constant until the wheels left the last segment of the bridge.

Next stop Apalachicola High, home of the Bull Sharks.

The interior of the automobile remained as silent as a shipwrecked pirate on a lone empty island when the BMW pulled onto the high school campus parking lot.

39

Darrell flew out the door and headed to school before Ms. Gloria whipped up breakfast. His normally shared room with his momma, with nothing but quilts to divide their space, now felt painfully deserted. He'd lived close to the last four years waking up and hearing a faint snore on the other side of the cloth wall. He'd thought it a bothersome sound and he blamed many nights of lost sleep from her waking him. Last night—the silence kept him awake, not her light snores. The stillness not only reminded him his momma remained gone, but also the fact he didn't know where Mitz was. AWOL like a soldier who couldn't handle boot camp. Over the wall without so much as a good-bye. He now prayed as he cleared the porch steps, she would be at school when he got there.

***

Ben woke up and turned to see Gina's back. She lay curled tightly in the fetal position. He scooted over closer and reached out to touch her. As his fingers lightly ran down her bare soft back, she turned and smiled. "I love you, Benny." She softly spoke.

"I love you, Gina." He quickly answered.

Gina rolled onto her stomach and looked at Ben. He began again to run his fingers across her back. Tingles and goosebumps. She smiled and closed her eyes reliving their lovemaking last night. She'd felt guiltless for the first time since Jay. Her confession to Ben hurt him, she could instantly see his heart break. But Benny wasn't the guy to hold grudges. He'd forgiven her almost as soon as her painful words came out. How did she ever get lucky enough to meet him, let alone marry him? She opened her eyes and spoke softly, "I don't deserve you, Benny. I don't know why you love me, but I won't ever hurt you in that way ever again." Her eyes never blinked or looked away. She wanted to assure him of her heart and intent, the honesty they truly held.

Ben quietly shushed her and then smiled. "I forgave you last night, there's no need to think or worry about it ever again. We have both made our misjudgments, now we both know what's at stake. I believe you, Gina. I cherish you."

After several minutes of cuddling which led to another torrid session of lovemaking, Ben rolled to his side and looked over at the clock. "It's already almost seven. I need to get up and get ready. We both need to get up and get our day started." He smiled. "We only have four days until grand opening! Four days!" Ben rolled back over and kissed Gina's lips and then reached for the television remote. Giving it a click, the screen lit up and the morning news popped on. A couple of minutes went by and both Ben and Gina were dead silent, eyes glued to the screen in shock.

***

Darrell walked in the high school's front door and immediately bumped into Mr. Bingham.

"Darrell! Good morning, son. Could I have a quick word with you in my office, please?" Charley asked.

"Yes sir, I pretty much expected to be called down at some point. Might as well get it over right up front." Darrell responded. "Can I ask you something though? Is Mitzi here yet?"

"That's a part of what we need to talk about. Let's head into my office and I'll answer your questions." Charley made his way to the office with Darrell right behind. As they entered, Mr. Bingham pulled the door shut and motioned for Darrell to have a seat. He noticed the angst in Darrell's demeanor at the onset of their meeting. "Darrell, I know you have been through a lot. I don't know if all the rumors bare truth or have been blown all out of proportion, but I know you've got to be suffering."

"Yes sir, my world kinda' blew up in my face. My momma is in the hospital with a brain trauma injury, I can't find Mitzi anywhere, the man I thought all these years was my poppa—ain't. I been locked up in jail for hurtin' the man who supposedly is...."

"I know son—life can take the wind from our sails and turn us around from where we thought we were going—and all in an instant from out of nowhere. It's why I want to let you know I'm here for you. And yes, son, Mitzi is here today. I saw her about fifteen minutes ago." Darrell's face lit up with a look of anticipation. "Now Darrell, have you seen any of the news or heard of the weekend's happenings around here?" Principal Bingham asked.

"No sir, there's been too much personal stuff takin' my attention."

"Do you drink coffee Darrell? I'd be glad to get you something—there's been some things happen and I want to be the one to tell you, instead of you hearing it out there from your friends or—others." Charley gave Darrell a serious look which caused instant concern.

"No sir, I don't really drink coffee and I'm not thirsty. I'm worried now about more bad news though." Darrell said.

Charley got up from his chair and walked around behind it, grabbing the seat back, he pushed it toward Darrell and then sat back down. "I'm not sure where to start, so I'll just do the best I can. Saturday night out on the bridge over the East Bay—a horrible accident happened. The police don't know exactly what transpired, but they believe a single car traveling at a very high rate of speed, lost control." Charley Bingham stopped to take a breath before he continued. "The car rolled and flipped several times and the two people ended up being injured very badly. Son—the two kids are friends of yours. Your's and Mitzi's." Charley took another deep breath. "They're both alive at this point, but...."

"Don't tell me it's Kyle and Violet. Please, Mr. Bingham—tell me it's not...." Darrell's eyes held their stare firm but were pooling with tears which began to spill over.

"I'm sorry son, but it is. Kyle's already been through a couple of emergency surgeries. He suffered a severe spinal injury—Violet's suffered a significant traumatic brain injury. Doctors don't know what either outcome will be at this point, other than they will more than likely live." Charley reached over and cupped Darrell's shoulder with his hand. "I hate to go on Darrell, but there is more."

Darrell's head briefly dropped into the palms of his hands. He sniffed several times and then lifted his head back up to face Principal Bingham squarely. Darrell slammed his hand hard on the table. "What else could there be? Mitzi is okay, isn't she?"

"Yes, she's in with Counselor Thomas. She is being filled in about the same things right now." Charley said.

"I wanna see her, I wanna see her now, sir." Darrell said.

"We're gonna bring you two together after we talk." Mr. Bingham paused before he continued. "Sheriff Burks ended up responding to the accident and went out to help. This is where the state police are having trouble figuring out just what happened." Principal Charley Bingham hesitated in a long pause.

"Yes? What happened?" Darrell asked wondering why the principal was hesitating.

"I don't know how you feel about Roy Burks. I was just recently made aware your father, Jay, made a statement about Roy being your true birthfather..." Charley closely watched to see Darrell's reaction.

"Yes, it's what he says. When I found out it was the night everything went down and I...I beat on the sheriff. It's why they arrested me. My whole world exploded in a few short minutes. I found out Mitzi is pregnant and now she's ...I...I don't know Mr. Bingham. I guess she's my half-sister. We haven't talked since all this. I've just been in jail and right in the next cell across from my poppa...from Jay, which has been a hell all of its own." Darrell buried his face in hands.

Charley shook his head. "I'm sorry Darrell, you've been such a joy to watch and see how you've come out of your shell and shined. I'm so sorry for all this pain and drama. You'll survive this, you're a fine, strong young man. I'll do whatever I can to help. But—unfortunately I have more to this weekend's story. Sheriff Burks...well—he was killed, Darrell. Shot to death by someone and they've made an arrest." Charley hesitated again as this news would be something which would most likely effect Darrell drastically, even if he didn't acknowledge it immediately. "Darrell—two state police detectives went to Jay's house to talk to him and..." Darrell's eyes opened wide. Charley looked in them while putting his hands on each of his shoulders. "...Jay shot them both—and he got seriously wounded himself in the gunfight. One officer died on the scene, and one had to be taken to the hospital here in town and undergo surgery. Jay's been arrested and taken for surgery at the hospital in Wewahitchka. Up to now, this is all we know." He pulled Darrell into a hug. "I'm sorry about your mother, Darrell. The entire school is praying for her this morning along with praying for you and Mitzi. We all back you. All of us."

***

Principal Charley Bingham truly felt an engulfing compassion for one of his students like he'd never felt before. He knew what kind of man Sheriff Roy Burks really had been. Looking at Darrell and the suffering he'd been living all alone at this moment, made Charley take a deep long look at himself and the life he'd chosen to live. He lived his life a fraud, a self-manufactured counterfeit, a sanctimonious actor, just as Roy and Ethan both were.

The pains they'd caused to so many of the students he'd been hired to protect and teach. He now felt a stinging sensation deep in his heart and soul. Charley worked himself tirelessly from student to teacher, up the educational ladder to becoming principal of the high school he himself attended. It now suddenly felt fraudulent. Topping it off, he would more than likely be the next superintendent of the entire Franklin County school system. He instantly felt all the failures of his duties to each of them. Down to each individual student he'd ever crossed paths or conferred with or disciplined.

From the beginning days, as the young teacher he'd started out as, he'd taken advantage of the natural lure he held over his young female students. The things he'd done to some of them, the tawdry and lewd acts he'd performed. The methods he'd picked and chosen each one by their looks and susceptibility to trust. Only to betray their loyalty to leverage seduction and sexual gratifications for himself and his friends. The gawd damned beach house of Ethan's with the devil's playroom of perversions and mental befouls. His guilt suddenly ate at his gut.

Why were these inclinations of guilt suddenly overtaking him? Roy's dead and no longer a threat of revealing their past. They'd gotten away with it all. Why now? There's nothing he could do about any of it anyway. The damage long done, the unwitting participants long faded into the backgrounds of failure or inconsequentiality. None ever came forward. He couldn't find them all now and for what—what would some lame kind of apology sound like after all these years? *Hey, I'm so sorry I lured you to a house of perversions, so I could take advantage and fuck you with my friends and then discard you like yesterday's news.*

Would you please forgive me? No, that would never be an adequate solution, so Charley packed away the sudden inkling to succumb to the guilt. He stowed it deeper into his psyche. He would unpack and deal with it later after doing what he could to help with this current situation of Darrell's.

40

Ethan held Joyce in his arms. "I'm sorry, I know even though your relationship wasn't good—it's got to be difficult news to hear and absorb."

Joyce burrowed into his chest. "I hated him for what he did to Mitzi. He ignored her and I know how she hurt because of him. I saw it every holiday and birthday when we heard nothing from him." Joyce became panicked. "I need to get back to the school Ethan. I need to be there for her. I know they said the counselor is talking to her, but I need to be there beside her, protecting her."

"Of course, I'll turn around and take you right back." Ethan's BMW made a wide swath in the road and when he straightened out, the wheels screeched on the pavement as the car accelerated.

Mrs. Tammy Hatley answered the frantic Joyce Bonham. "Mrs. Bonham, Mitzi is in with the senior counselor and the principal along with Darrell Cader. As soon as they come out you can see her."

"Mrs. Hatley, is it?" Ethan questioned. "I'm an attorney representing Ms. Bonham, and I must demand we be in that room immediately. I'm certain Principal Bingham would understand Ms. Bonham's concern about her daughter."

"I'm aware who you are Mr. Kendrick along with the fact you personally know Principal Bingham and are friends." Tammy answered. "Nevertheless, Mr. Bingham, my boss, demanded they not be disturbed for anything short of the building being on fire. So, I'm not about to disturb them when I don't smell smoke!"

Ethan looked at Joyce pulling her back from the counter and leaning in, placing his lips next to her ear, and whispered something.

Joyce walked over to the wall and without hesitation, reached to the red and white fire-panic lever and pulled it. The alarm sounded and very soon after, teachers were leading students into the halls and out the front door onto the lawn. The principal, counselor, Mitzi, and Darrell soon exited into the office where Charley met Ethan and Joyce.

"I might have guessed, Ethan. You always get what you want, by the rules or not. Mrs. Hatley, call the fire dispatch and report the alarm as a student prank." Charley said.

"But Principal Bing...." Tammy started to retort.

"Mrs. Hatley, you heard what I said." Charley snapped back.

"Yes sir." Tammy answered as she raised the receiver to her ear and dialed.

Charley Bingham's look of consternation transformed into a more bilious expression when he turned from Mrs. Hatley to Ethan. "Ethan, Ethan, Ethan. I suppose you are claiming Ms. Bonham and her daughter as clients now?" Charley smiled at his old friend. "When the dust settles, Ms. Bonham and you are welcome to sit in. I'm guessing you've been hearing the breaking news in our small municipality. We're again the buzz and scuttle of our fine state."

"Being put on the map isn't all bad, Charley." Ethan winked.

The six of them, four adults and the two students sat around Charley Bingham's conference table. The four adults were very aware Darrell and Mitzi were barely hearing a word they spoke, but instead shared stolen glances to and from each other.

Counselor Debbie Thomas spoke up, "I think we need to all exit the room and give these two a chance to communicate and work out for themselves what is going on between them."

Joyce agreed, followed by Ethan and then Charley made it

unanimous. They started to get up and as they all stood, Counselor Debbie said, "If you don't mind, I'd like to have a word or two with them—privately." Charley led Ethan and Joyce back out into the office.

Debbie held her arms out, one towards each, motioning for them to all come together. She put her arms around each of their waists and continued, "I can't imagine what emotions, questions, and pain the both of you are battling. What I do know is what I've seen between you two and what it's blossomed in to." She squeezed a little tighter. "I've heard the possibility that's been thrown at you, and I just want to say—there is a blood test which may determine the truth to the accusation. I will help get one set up if you'd both like to pursue it. I can't force the outcome to be a favorable one, but it could help in determining where you two may stand on the matter." She looked at each of them eye to eye. "Treat each other with respect, please. Let me know if you'd like to set up the test." She gave each another squeeze and then left them alone as she gently closed the conference room door.

41

Ben looked over at Gina who wore an expression he couldn't seem to decipher. "Are you okay?" He asked. "I can't believe this. I don't even know what to think, let alone say." He continued.

Gina turned to Ben. "I...I'm really not surprised. I've felt the evil inside him again since the trip here." She looked back to the television. "I think his horrible deeds go back much further than this. I think he's killed women—women and young girls, lots."

"Gina? And you didn't tell me?" Ben asked.

"I don't want to say anymore. I felt it and I thought I'd let you know. It doesn't matter now—if he really did what they say—I won't ever have to worry about him ever again."

Ben watched Gina's expression as she spoke. The only thing he could read in it contained some sort of relief she wouldn't have to deal with him. He however seemed totally shocked. He received his miracle in New York and held it tightly so he wouldn't regress and have it become a wasted gift from God. He assumed Jay felt and did the same. He knew Gina did, even though she'd struggled lately.

Now Jay had just been arrested for double murders and injuring another? And Gina wasn't surprised by the news, even thinking he'd done worse? My gawd! He counted on Jay, not only for the menial tasks he'd given him but for Jay to be a part owner of the restaurant. That alone also gave Ben some tension relief. Ben never even worked in a restaurant, let alone owned and managed one.

Sharing this project with Jay meant he shared some of the worries and responsibility. Jay felt like a relief valve to him. Jay, now out of the picture—awakened a fear inside his head. Four days until the grand opening! Sure, there were his chefs and his waitresses, dishwashers and kitchen staff, but...."

***

Gina looked from the television to Ben. She could read his thoughts at times, like reading a book. She could see him drowning himself in restaurant worries. "It'll work out Benny. Our bases are still covered. Jay wasn't anything but a charity case—you do know it don't you? He used us. Think back at the tasks he did. Any of our other employees could have done them. Thank God you didn't purchase the damned fishing boat for him. Both of us know who it was for. He faked it, Benny. He played us the entire time."

"But Gina! Ms. Cela's Bible! He knew it, he recited verses at a whim!" Ben exclaimed.

"He schooled himself for the part. Like the lead role in a play. He's an excellent actor, but he owned evil intent inside. I'm not saying he wanted to be the evil man he is." Gina acted prosecuting attorney in this discussion while Ben assumed the defense's role. "He'd been trained from birth. A sad story with a sad victim, but he grew into his father's role. The kind of damage done that went even too deep for faith to undo. Satan holds the key to his soul."

"I can't believe in those terms, Gina. I've got to hold out for hope. If not—none of us would stand a chance." Ben answered.

"Benny, I love my Maker, my newfound Father. I've come close to giving up and going back to my old ways or giving up completely. I know God's got control and I feel his presence frequently. I also know to believe in God, one must accept Satan holds power also. The fact is—it all boils down to a choice in life, especially as a believer. I believe Jay made his choice and with it brought Satan's power of deception. And the power of destruction, both internal and external."

"I've not thought of it like that before Gina. Where did you get the wisdom to think things through this way? Robert didn't explain it in those concepts," Ben asked.

Gina sat up and turned toward Ben, facing him directly for effect. "Robert hasn't lived every experience personally in the world, Ben. He opens a lot of doors for a lot of people and shines a light where it's needed to get away from the dark, but…" Gina's face suddenly bore the ache of something very personal. "…has Robert ever looked out over the dark abyss of an ocean while holding a knife ready to plunge it into his heart, just because the choice was too hard to make correctly?" Gina's brow furrowed with trouble and her beautiful bright green eyes sank into her hollowed sockets. "…I have. I've been fortunate this time, Benny, because when I couldn't make the choice other than the dark one locked in my heart…," a smile started to slowly appear as her brow became smooth again. Her green eyes regained their flare and glow. "…he sent you to make my choice for me because Jesus won't force us." She reached for Ben, but he was already at her side with arms open and tears streaking down his cheeks. They pulled each other tightly into an unbreakable embrace. Their worlds recreated in one spectacular and miraculous moment.

Satan certainly felt a deep wounding blow to his darkened empty soul from the love remaining vigil even when surrounded by temptation and hate from this dark world he's tried to rule over.

42

Mitzi held her hand out to Darrell. "I've missed you. I thought I'd lost you." Mitzi carefully studied Darrell's demeanor. "I haven't, have I?" She looked down to her belly where their baby lay inside and then back up to Darrell's eyes with hope mixed with worry. "I guess I should ask if 'we've' lost you?"

Darrell reached and held her hand, pulling her closer. "No, you both still have me. I love you both. Always." They gripped each other in a tightly held hug.

Mitzi pulled back. "Did Bingham tell you about the accident?"

Darrell's smile fell into a grimness. "Yes. They don't know if Kyle will ever be able to walk again. And poor Vio may never remember anything. We need to go see them soon."

"Counselor Thomas said they were going close to a hundred miles per hour. Why? First Chubbs, and now Kyle and Vio, it's not fair. And you and I being related? Why is this happening to us? What did we do so wrong?" Mitzi asked.

"I don't know, Mitz." Darrell pulled her back into his arms and squeezed. "At least my poppa…I mean, Jay…or for that matter yours and my…" Darrell stopped. No matter what he tried to say, it somehow came out correct and incorrect at the same. "…Jay and Roy will never bother us again. It's all I meant to say. It doesn't hurt me—does this fact hurt you?"

"The only thing that hurts me is you may be my half-brother. That kills me inside and I don't know what to do," Mitzi answered.

"We could tell Ms. Thomas—to set up those tests, so we could be sure. Darrell said.

"But, what if...." Mitzi asked.

"We'll figure out the 'what if', when we get the results." Darrell pulled his head back and looked into Mitzi's eyes. "I'll never stop loving you, Mitz. I promise. Forever." They kissed each other deep. The passion still obviously there and shared.

"Me too, Darrell—forever."

43

Charley lifted his glass and swirled its caramel- colored liquid, just as he'd done so many times in the past. "I must hand it to you, Ethan—I never saw it coming, just as I'd asked. I, of course, never predicted you and his ex-wife together either." Charley shook his head displaying his ponderance of both statements before inhaling the aroma of the bourbon. He sat staunchly in the over-stuffed deck chair, now seeming more judgmental. "What other secrets do you hold?" Charley turned to try and eye Ethan. "Yes sir, you're a sly wolf in sheep's clothing. I certainly pray I never cross you." He lowered his glass to his lips and took the entire shot into his mouth, barely swirling it over his tastebuds before swallowing. It seemed that kind of day. "Oh, and how did you get out of the office without your new houseguest coming with?"

Ethan rounded the corner bringing a new bottle of bourbon he'd discovered while up in Lexington, Kentucky. The label read Pappy Van Winkle and of course a very expensive barrel run. "Charley, even if I found your usefulness less than exemplary, I would still find your friendship beyond compare. Besides, I have no one other than you to appreciate the finer distilled libations with, so I guess you're safe! As far as our mutual recent dilemma—I've yet to hear if it were performed under a blueprint or merely happenstance." Ethan unwrapped and de-corked his recent rare find. He prepared two fresh crystal highball glasses. "Let's drink this neat without ice, what do you say?" He began pouring before Charley could answer. "And as for Joyce..." Ethan cleared his throat. "...let's just say I feel very fortunate and would rather the subject never come back up again. She of course held no idea of Roy's and our past relationships in business nor the sharing of pleasures." He filled the second glass and handed one to Charley and then lifted his glass to him. "Let's drink a toast, dear friend." Charley lifted his glass.

Ethan began, "Hearts live by being wounded! Or so says Oscar Wilde, a man who obviously never knew Roy Burks." He clinked his glass together with Charley's. "I hate to say it, but I feel no wound today. I want to feel at least a sting, but...."

"Ethan, I feel a burn. I think back at the plan we concocted as young men and carried on into our adult age, and I feel the burn. Granted, Roy wasn't the brightest bulb in the light fixture, but damnit, Ethan, we should both feel the burn of hot wax for bringing this ending down on him. For that matter, the very plan from the beginning. All those young girls."

Charley put his hand over his heart momentarily. "My very soul feels like it just quaked from a huge ground fault giving way. I surely am weary now of what my friendship really meant to you all these years. My God, Ethan—have I too now sealed my fate?" Charley turned and cautiously eyed his friend of so many, many years. "If so, I suggest another—more sorrowful toast to our departed classmate. And in performing it, another gawd damned glass of this magnificent example of grain distilling!"

Ethan turned to fetch the bottle from the rolling bar-cart as he took the glass from Charley. Ethan continued talking while he opened the small drawer and without notice picked up a tiny glass vial. "Charley, you're correct to call me out. My heart's been jump-started with something I've never known, and the fact she'd been Roy's first—along with the way he mistreated her..." Ethan poured the two glasses and turned slightly away, quickly dumping the small vial of liquid into one, swirling the glass before handing it back to his good friend, Charley. "...well, it's laid a covering of frost over my heart. I see the damage in his daughter's life and the pain in Joyce's. It did make solving our likely dilemma much easier than it should have been." He held up his glass to Charley's again. "I'm so sorry Roy, I admit wanting something you had but rather be shed, Now I am reaping rewards to the fullest, while you my friend feel the heat of hell being dead." Ethan reached and quickly clinked glasses with Charley again, before he'd caught the gist. "Cheers, good on ya." Ethan winked as Charley sat quietly reminiscing with guilt—the tawdry times with Roy and the girls he himself brought to be enjoyed in ways which suddenly did not seem natural at all. He looked out across the beautiful horizon before him, the waves lollygagging up the shoreline before the high tide would come and drag them further away. He smiled to himself thinking how such a beautiful ocean scene could hide such deadly bull sharks unnoticed below the surface. Charley downed the last swallow of the expensive glass of Ethan's latest acquisition. He quietly tried to rationalize what Ethan spoke, which he couldn't decipher it's meaning when he said it. *Good on ya.*

The two friends sat in their respective chairs and enjoyed the effects of Ethan's newest discovery. Bottle number thirteen of one hundred and twenty-eight of Julian Van Winkle Jr's own recipe. One commemorated to his late father, Julian "Pappy" Van Winkle, a man who never planned to be in the whiskey business. "Good on ya, Old Rip Van Winkle Distillery. Frankfurt, Kentucky."

Ethan watched as the sparkle slowly departed his childhood friend's eyes, the sound of the surf making Charley's last gasps for air barely audible. His friend's life receded almost unnoticeable as if it mirrored the falling tide. Ethan realized the last possible betrayal of his and his friend's sordid past could no longer bare any trepidation for him. He held up his last nip in the bottom of his glass and before beginning the final task of taking care of business, Ethan stated four words before tipping his glass and swallowing.

"Good on ya, Charley."

Ethan studied the beach both the left and right down the shoreline. Seeing no one in sight, he rolled up his pant legs and shirt sleeves. He removed his shoes and socks sat them on the last step of the deck. Now would come the time he'd need to draw from his physical and mental strength the most.

With a ceremonious stare washing over his face, he lifted the handles of the heavy-laden wheel-barrel and began his trek toward the crashing waves. He would send Charley for his last swim on earth. It somehow felt fitting to him to send his friend off into the view he both loved but also feared. Charley was lucky though, fortunate not to have seen his demise coming. He left this world a man. No chance to whine or beg at saving it. *What man wouldn't rather go to the next world not knowing it was coming?*

44

Ethan called Joyce at the office and told her his meeting would go a little later than he planned. "I'll pick you two up around eight and we'll eat dinner out? Sound good?"

"Of course. It may just be you and me tonight. Mitzi is wanting to stay at the Watkins' home, to talk things out with Darrell. I think this is probably a good thing. The Watkins' seem like a great couple."

"Okay. Hey, if you could, ask Addi to help you find the Wilmnere file. I have some questions outlined on the cover page I could use your help finding answers. By the way, how is she treating you today?" Ethan asked.

"I worried about the very same thing on the ride in, but she is her normal bubbly self. No problems nor questions about us."

"Good, I'll talk to her later. And I'll see you around eight!"

Ethan gave his place a once over and after finding everything satisfactory, he gave Jimmy a quick call. "Hey Jimmy, I'm gonna need a ride later, could you pick me up and I'll take care of the bill I owe on my 'car' you took care of?" He listened to Jimmy respond. "Okay. Come get me and I'll give you a bonus for your time and fuel." Ethan listened again to Jimmy. "Yeah, sure enough. It'll be about a two-hour round trip. No problem, yeah, Vause Boat Landing up on Lake Talquin, straight up Jack Vause Landing Road. See you around 3:45." Ethan climbed into Charley's car and headed out toward a private road he knew about. It ended at the lake shore and happened to be an old camping spot for him and his friends. Things were working out like clockwork. He now held something to look forward to tonight. An uninterrupted evening with Joyce and no daughter. "Hmmmm." He hummed aloud.

An hour later Ethan Kendrick pulled the auto down the empty dirt path where it dead-ended on a ledge, twenty-some feet above the lake. He'd grown up hearing it contained the deepest waters of Lake Talquin. He and his buddies swam there all the time as kids and none of them could ever hold their breath long enough to find the bottom. Here would be the perfect final resting place for the last puzzle piece Ethan was about to put to rest. The last outstanding tie to any record of what he, Charley, and Roy concocted that summer night so long ago after graduating.

"Phuck-House ends here today. Fitting, as it began here." Ethan said as he swung the car door open and walked to the edge to look down. His mind half expected to see Roy and Charley swimming and splashing below. Ethan, as he stood lost in thought, became immediately taken back to the day so many years ago when they'd met to camp together for the first time after four years of college ended. Not kids anymore, but not adults either. Each feeling stuck somewhere in between. They all experienced the college life, each at their own school of craft and of course affordability. Now, the three of them were supposedly ready to be thrust into life and their learned careers. He himself, needed to continue in law school, but Charley would soon be becoming a high school teacher at Apalachicola High. Roy becoming a new law officer in town. They all held their aspirations set in their minds. They'd each been inseparable cronies who'd run together their entire gamut of life up until now. Kindergarten thru high school, only to be separated during their college experiences. Somehow, they would all turn away from the draw of the outside world and end up back in the small town of Apalachicola. Each drawn back home like a mouse to a cheeseball set in the trap. It felt familiar. It was comfortable.

The outside world of college had been an adventure, but each one somehow felt the pull of the forgotten coast of the Gulf. The slow and easy, the three big ducks landing back on the small pond. Each feeling as if they now owned it lock, stock, and barrel.

"Enough of this melancholy bullshit! Goodbye, Phuck-House! We dreamed it, we built it, and enjoyed the fuck out of it. It's over now, boys. Time to grow up and be respectable. Someone needed to pay the price for it before it got exposed and foreclosed. We grew up and grew apart. The one with the most money is supposed to win, right? Well, I not only have the money and the envied beach home, but I now have the woman too. You two certainly understand, don't you? I couldn't take a chance when my life's ambition actually became an attainable possibility, could I?" Ethan reached through the passenger window and pulled out the remaining bottle of his Van Winkle treasure. He then walked around and reached in through the driver's window and turned the key until Charley's 1970 Volvo slowly cranked over and started. "Charley, you gawd damned frugal bastard!" He guffawed, then walked to the ledge and poured a little of the bourbon into the lake water down below. After this ritual, he walked back to the driver's side of the Volvo and held the bottle high before he brought it down to his lips and swallowed the last shot and yelled out, "Good on ya, brothers in lust and crime!" And he chucked the bottle as far out as he could before reaching in and slapping the gearshift lever to drive, sending the Volvo over the edge, and splashing head-first into Lake Talquin.

Ethan slowly walked back to the cliff's edge and watched the automobile slowly gurgle and sink into the greenish-blue water until there was nothing but rings billowing from the center moving outward. The placid surface now looked like a whale had just breached it and then submerged. Not to be seen again. When the water became still and held no image left to see, Ethan turned and began his walk—retracing the path he'd just driven. It would take him thirty-five to forty minutes to reach Vause Boat Landing where his return ride's driver would be there waiting for the bankroll of cash he'd stowed in his left front pocket.

Nothing would be said between themselves, no explanations given. It had to be the way things were handled between them. An "I'll scratch your back, you scratch mine" kind of an arrangement. Like two attorneys hashing things out, covering each other's asses. It was business.

45

Wednesday at noon and Tammy Hatley seemed very worried. She'd been Charley's secretary for seven years and he never missed a day once without calling in. This is oddity, an extraordinarily unusual breach of his protocol. "Something's got to be wrong or have happened to him. He would be here even if he'd contracted a strain of the Mongolian death flu. He'd call me at the very least." Tammy told Mary Lou at the police station. "Could you please send an officer to his home for a well-check?"

"Yes ma'am, I will dispatch an officer out immediately. I'll call you back when I get any information, Tammy."

Tammy thought to herself. *This is exactly why I love a small town, you cut right through the bureaucratic bullshit the big cities still hang onto!*

***

By Friday morning, an all-points bulletin became issued state-wide for Principal Charley Bingham, now listed as a missing person.

"What is going on in our little town, Ethan?" Addi and Joyce both asked. They spent the morning listening to the radio and were discussing all the news of late.

"The news reported the state police sergeant pulled through surgery and would be released today! At least there is some good news." Joyce relayed. "No status on Billy Jay Cader, though, the man accused of committing such a horrendous act. I'm not sure why they waste our tax dollars saving such a monster just to put him to death after all the money spent." Joyce let her thought slip before seeing Ethan's eyes sharpen.

"Are you sure you want to be in this business of defense?" He half-smiled. "You do know we may very well be defending Mr. Cader?" Ethan stated with seriousness sprinkled with sarcasm.

"I know Ethan, everyone deserves the best defense possible. It's just hard not to separate some of the worst perpetrators from shoplifters and tax-evaders. I'm guilty as charged!" She smiled. "Are you really taking his case? I mean, I'm not shaming you—but there will be those who do."

"They've moved him to a federal medical center in Springfield, Missouri. My flight leaves out from the airport in four hours." Ethan said. "I'm sorry, but I'm going to be missing our date to the Big Apple on the Bay grand opening. I have to get to Springfield ASAP."

"Oh, Ethan. I'm sorry." Addi said.

Joyce looked over at Ethan, her puppy dog eyes staring before looking away quickly.

"Addi, why don't you and Joyce use our reservations and enjoy tonight together? I'd love to hear how the food is and what it looks like inside." Ethan asked.

"That would be wonderful, Ethan—Joyce?"

"Sure, Addi, I might actually get to see my daughter for a change too. She told me Darrell is taking her there tonight."

***

Customers began showing up for their seating at six in the evening sharp. Joyce and Addi walked in and were seated by the expansive wall of windows overlooking the bay and Battery Park.

By seven all tables were full and stayed full until closing at eleven. The conversations among the tables were all complimentary and everyone loved the food and ambiance.

Ben and Gina were exhausted as well as the entire restaurant staff. Kudos were given to each employee as well as a first small bonus check at the end of the evening for a job well-done. It appeared to be a success and now time would only tell if there would be return customers nightly. Ben and Gina carefully came up with a menu which would suit most customers; priced from family affordable to all exclusive custom prepared meals. Tonight's special sold out quickly. "New York Strips and Snapper with twice-baked potato and Brussel sprouts sauteed in olive oil and spices." The entire place was at capacity tonight, both open dining room to the three private rooms. The restaurant would also be open and accommodating to both small or large parties. They had tried to cover all the bases.

A very tired Ben and Gina fell back into their bed just after midnight. They'd finally met almost the entire town's people, now officially calling Apalachicola, Florida their home. Ben's brother Robert even flew in last minute and surprised them. He checked in at the Gibson Inn before he popped over and caught them off-guard at the reservations desk. Ben and Gina were going to meet him in the morning to spend time catching up. "I can't believe Robert showed up!" Ben smiled at Gina.

"I know. I thought he went to some sort of convention?" Gina said as she snuggled into Ben's stomach, spoon style. "I wonder if he's heard about Jay yet?"

"I don't know, but I certainly hate eating crow in front of him. It's why we don't serve it at the Apple on the Bay!" They both giggled. "We'll never hear the end about how lucky we are..." Ben tried to stop before he finished. "...I'm so sorry Gina. I know we really weren't very lucky in the end. But we're past all of it. I say we just acknowledge Jay wasn't able to maintain his faith and let it go like a helium-filled balloon."

"I'm all for it. I don't even want to watch the television anymore. I just want it all behind us." Gina rolled and twisted to face Ben. "We're good now. I'm good now. Jay is no longer tied to us in any way. We tried, right? We did what God wanted us to do. It's time to move on and do our best to the next in line. Just like Ms. Cela does, every day." She smiled and gave her husband a kiss, which even though they were both worn to the seams—became a spark that lit a fire from the friction between their bodies. The Danes house became a happy home again and they christened the place again just to seal the deal.

Gina suddenly felt a bit nauseous. The night full of tension and worry. She felt wound up tighter than a spool of thread. As she got back up from the floor in front of the toilet, she looked down at her tummy. She lifted her shirt and turned perpendicular to the mirror and studied her body. *Could it be?* She dropped Ben's shirt she wore back down and flipped the light switch off. After crawling back into bed, careful not to awaken Ben, she laid on her back and felt her stomach rumble again. Gina tried closing her eyes and willing her thoughts to recede, but to no avail. *Am I pregnant?* She gasped. *If I am, Lord—please let it be Ben's and not Jay's. Please.*

The night for Ben felt blissful and filled with deep comforting sleep. His wife's night seemed anything but....

46

Darrell and Mitzi sat patiently in the waiting room even though their nerves were tight. They looked over at Debbie Thomas, their school counselor who said she would help set up an appointment which could possibly answer their burning question. A question able to either help their love flourish or shatter their dream into pieces. They both gave blood samples to test their possible relationship to her father. Roy Burks. Were they siblings? A sample of Sheriff Burks blood was obtained from the coroner's office and would hopefully be enough to give them the answer they both now waited to hear. Ms. Thomas sat consoling and preparing them, showing them her support and comfort by being with them.

The nurse called out, "Darrell Cader and Mitzi Burks—please come to the front desk."

"Yes ma'am, I'm Darrell and this is Mitzi."

"Nurse Williams will take you to Dr. Middler's consult room. She'll take you there now, the doctor will be in to discuss your tests right away."

Darrell asked, "Is it okay if we have our friend and school counselor come in with us to see the doctor?"

The nurse answered, "Yes sir, that would be fine. As long as you and Mitzi are agreeable."

Darrell motioned for Debbie Thomas to follow, and they were led down a hallway off the front waiting room. The nurse turned a couple of corners and then opened the door to Consult Room 3. "Doctor Middler will be right in folks, make yourselves at home around the table. Please leave the one by the computer open for the doctor." The three sat down.

"I know you two are nervous. Hang in there. No matter what happens, you have people who care for you and are available to help you navigate your way through this. Including me." Assured Ms. Thomas.

"We know Ms. Thomas and we appreciate all you are already doing."

Darrell held Mitzi's hand and the two looked nervously at each other. This was a very important day. Ms. Thomas drove them here from school. From the school which everyone now worried about news of their missing principal, Charley Bingham, missing for three full days and half-way into the fourth. None of the three, especially Mitzi, felt like talking about it. It reminded her too much of when Chubbs went missing earlier in the year. His outcome must have been horrible and unexpected. She'd still suffered waking up with the night sweats imagining him fighting the sharks off before he drowned. She shivered at the thought.

Last night, Darrell and Mitzi's big date at the Big Apple on the Bay grand opening, waiting on today's news overshadowed their night. "I sure hope we have good news and if so, wish we could have gotten it before last night." Mitzi said soberly to Darrell. "I know I should have told my mom about the blood tests, but…." She'd worried about telling her what they were doing. She somehow felt she betrayed her. She didn't know why, just an intuition. She couldn't explain it.

"I hope we have good news to tell her. We just won't say anything if it's not." Darrell answered.

There came a light knock on the door before it began to slowly open. The doctor peeked in and introduced himself. "Hello folks, I'm Doctor Henry Middler, and you must be Darrell and Mitzi?

And...?"

"Yes sir, that's us, and this is our school counselor Ms. Debbie Thomas. We've invited her and she can hear anything you are gonna tell us, sir."

"Well alright folks, it's nice to meet you all. I imagine from the story you've told our nurses this test is important to you. I'm going to skip as much of the medical jargon as possible and get right down to the important information." Doctor Middler looked up over the edge of his eyeglasses which made him appear older than he more than likely was, and his cologne entered the room before he did. It smelled kind of oaky with a musky after-aroma. Mitzi imagined its scent to be more fitting on Ethan than Dr. Middler.

"Okay. This blood test is not a hundred percent proof of paternity. I need to let you know this test will not define who your birthfather is, but it can help determine a person who is not the father in some cases. DNA testing is coming along, and its results have been proving to be an accurate form of human cell testing. Unfortunately, we don't have this specific type of test available to us yet. What we do have in helping to determine sibling testing is the ABO blood-typing test." Doctor Middler cleared his raspy throat and then looked at both Darrell and Mitzi. "Are you following, or have I lost you in the mumbo jumbo?"

Darrell asked, "So will you be able to tell us if the sheriff is my father or not?"

"Darrell, this test is the only way at this point in time to determine if a father could be excluded or not, and only if the father holds AB blood type, which in this case, Roy Burks blood type is AB neg. When the father holds this type of blood type, his children will be able to have any of the other four blood types. If the child holds O type blood, the parent with AB type would not be the child's birth parent. Darrell, you have B pos, showing there is a possibility Roy could be your birthfather."

Darrell's head dropped now knowing Jay may not be his father, but worse yet there now existed a strong possibility Roy was. He felt the pain of his and Mitzi's dreams crumbling before him. He suddenly felt fury for his mom. This meant his mom probably cheated on Jay at some point; it also meant Mitzi more than likely is his stepsister. "Son-of-a-bitch!" He let it slip out before he thought and then it hit what he'd just insinuated with his statement. He looked up at Mitzi, who displayed matching wet eyes. "I'm sorry, Mitz." His head dropped back to the floor, not being able to face her.

"Now hold on just a minute before we draw conclusions. Don't assume before we release all of the facts." Doctor Middler said. "Like I stated, Roy carries the AB blood type—but Mitzi, your blood type is O. Do you remember what I said if the father holds type AB?" Doctor Middler turned to Mitzi to see if she realized.

"I...I think...think you said if the sibling had type O...then...then the father couldn't be the birth parent?" She looked confused. "But my mom told me all my life Roy is my dad?"

"Well, young lady..." Doctor Middler pulled a paper showing the blood types of each of them and pointed them out to her with his ink pen. "All I can say is the science doesn't lie. I hope this is the news you wanted to hear because it's my best diagnosis Roy Burks is not your birthfather, which means you and Darrell here are almost ninety-nine percent, not blood related. Those new ways of DNA testing I talked about is on the way and will give a much more accurate paternity diagnosis in the future, but they are not available yet."

Darrell jumped up and pulled Mitzi into his arms, tightly to his chest in a huge hug. "I don't understand it all, but..." He pulled away enough to look into Mitzi's eyes. "...I love you Mitz. With every bit of my heart and soul, I love you."

Mitzi still wore the look of shock and confusion but quickly answered back. "I love you, Darrell. Forever. I promise." She looked down to her tummy and smiled, knowing this time everything would work out right. "We have our baby, and we have each other."

47

Ethan's airplane landed at the Springfield Municipal Airport an hour late. It wasn't a problem as his scheduled meeting with Billy Jay Cader wouldn't be until 9am the next morning. A Saturday. He'd be there at least forty-five minutes early because of all the check-in rigamarole one must to go through when entering a federal prison system. He smiled to himself. There is no way Jay would ever see the light of day again, no matter how well he defended him. There's only one way a double cop killer ever left the glass house once they were convicted. In a plain black body-bag. Jay may go in a hero among the inmates for his nasty deeds, but they tend to turn on each other for as little as a cigarette. He didn't imagine a guy wired as hot as Jay would make it too long in general lock-up. He would more than likely end up with a shiv in his gut on the way back to his cell some evening for pissing off another inmate. Or of course, the longer route to hell. A ten-year battle fighting his probable date with the electric chair.

Ethan wondered exactly what kind of shape Jay would be in, physically—and mentally. He guessed he'd find out soon enough in the morning. His flight was lengthy with several transfers due to the tiny little municipal airport of this shitty southwest town in the middle of the bible-belt, hell, it was the friggin' buckle of the belt. He'd never traveled to Springfield, Missouri. Ethan wondered if there were any decent cigar bars in town. He sensed the urge for a nice bourbon or two and a good smoke in a quiet reserve setting to get him relaxed and ready for tomorrow. After checking in at the University Plaza Inn in the downtown area, the concierge gave him a couple of recommendations just a short walk from the hotel.

About a ten-minute walk downtown and left on Jefferson then right on Walnut Street, he saw the neon sign. The Alibi Room. A two-story old 1930's, black-painted brick warehouse type building. The door outlined with green neon tubing and a brown neon stogie with red and orange lights which staggered on and off in intervals at the end of the cigar. It looked interesting so he opened the door to see an immediate staircase leading to the upper floor door containing glass panes with subtle light flickering and shining through. He climbed the fifteen or twenty steps to the landing. The walnut stained door with tall multi-shades of red stained-glass sidelights on either side appeared as if it were at least a hundred years old. The brick wall surrounding the landing displayed thick dried mortar oozing out between each fabricated stone. He opened the large door with curiosity, and he stepped through, the old worn wooden floor creaked with each step. "Welcome to the Alibi Room. Would you like a table or a seat at the bar?" The thin-framed woman wore bright red lipstick which outlined her full lips and accentuated her jade-green eyes. Her beautiful milky-white skin appeared soft and sensuous against the black skirt and red cropped shirt. He couldn't help but look her over from her reddish-blonde hair down to her tall thin legs which were hoisted taut and angled by the black fuck-me pumps she wore. She looked the part of a gorgeous dame right out of the thirties. He imagined she would have been a routine customer at a speakeasy during prohibition. He liked the whole ambiance of the place. It made him feel like Melvin Purvis walking into a classy joint looking for John Dillinger. "Sooo, Mister, a table, booth or the bar? I'd share a drink with you at any of the above." She blinked her beautiful green eyes in a provocative inquiry.

Ethan smiled coyly. She knew nothing of his past. She looked only a couple of years older than the schoolgirls he and his younger buddies toyed with back at PH. In fact, she reminded him of the cute little red-headed girl who showed up once and then disappeared. Of course, her appearance got him thinking of Cali back at Poppy's. He suddenly thought of one more loop that needed closing. Cali Lea Jenkins.

She broke his lack of attention he paid to her. "You do like women, don't you?" She winked again with even more seduction. "You don't look like a 'man's man'."

Ethan winked back. "I'll take a table in a dim corner if you'll share it with me for that drink?"

She quickly took his hand and led him around a corner into the larger part of the bar. Steering him to the very back table which sat at the intersection of two large windows meeting in a bricked corner, "How's this?" She asked. A metal light fixture holding electric flickering candles hung just above head-level and centered. "This is where I take my very favorite people I meet."

Ethan looked around at the different tables with couples sitting at some and small groups of men at others, smoke billowing up into the very tall ceilings. He could smell fine ambrosial cigar smoke mixed with perfumes and colognes of people clad in their "going out on the town" garb. He pulled a chair out for the striking young lady before answering. "This is perfect. Isn't the management going to question you sharing a drink with me? I wouldn't want to—cause you any inconvenience."

She looked at him and slightly giggled. "I just clocked-out of work. I'm on my own time now—Mister...?"

"It's Burks, Charles Burks. And who might you be—Miss...?" He asked.

She smiled and touched her perfect rounded mouth with her pointing finger. Her nails were as brilliant red as the glossy painted lips she ran them across. "My name is, is something I'd like to remain a mystery for just a bit." She grinned with a sly wickedness. "I like mystery in my life sometimes, do you?" She motioned to one of her co-workers to come over to the table.

As the dark-haired waitress came over, she held a drink tray and smiled at her friend who now sat with the handsome new face in the nightclub.

Ethan's new friend said, "Jaime, I think I'll have my usual—A Gin Lime Rickey, and I'm not sure what—Charley will have. May I call you Charley?"

"If you have a Wellers 107 bourbon, I would take a double neat, and would you have a Churchill Cohiba from your humidor?" Ethan asked and then answered, "Charley would be fine, darling."

"I know we have the Churchill; I'll check on the bourbon and be right back." She smiled and winked as she left.

"So, you like being a mystery?" Ethan questioned as he let his eyes search into his new visitor's dark pupils surrounded by lush Irish-green glistening spheres of beauty. "I enjoy solving an enigma occasionally." He then asked without so much as a miniscule blink, "Should I just call you by a name I think is fitting? Because with those jade- colored eyes and your reddish hair and beautiful fair skin..." He let his gaze follow from her eyes down to those long legs. "...leads me to guess maybe you come from Irish lineage. Maybe a name such as Aisling (Ash-ling) would fit?"

"Hmm, an interesting choice..." She stared at him, looking into his greyish-green eyes. "You look and sound like maybe a baron or wealthy landowner from somewhere towards the south. Am I close?" She ran the fingers of her right hand in small circles on the tabletop. "And yes, I think I like the name, how do you spell it? Like it sounds?"

"No, It's spelled A.i.s.l.i.n.g. And no, I'm not a baron or a landowner, But I do live—towards the south. I'm a broker of sorts. Libations and other treasures of enjoyment—but here I go, spoiling my part of our mystery. I'm sorry."

"Well, Charley, That's okay. I can still be the mysterious one between the two of us."

Jaime walked up behind Ethan with his cigar and their drinks. She leaned in between them as she placed the glass down on the table, turning to Charley's ear. "Or I could be the mystery between the two of you?" Jaime winked followed by a naughty grin.

Aisling quickly interrupted. "Jaime! He's mine at the moment." She reached out and lightly slapped the top of Jaime's hand as she placed the cigar and cutter on a napkin she laid out.

Jaime looked at Ethan and giggled. "I see a fine-looking gentleman and hear the word mystery…" She giggled again. "…a girl sometimes needs to try, right?" Charley watched as she turned and walked back toward the bar. He admired the way she jiggled in all the appropriate places.

"Aisling, I have to ask, just where the hell am I? Did I walk across some invisible other-world entrance when I crossed the threshold of the old ancient door out front?" His hand rubbed his close-cut goatee. "I'm not saying I mind of course, but…."

Aisling lifted her drink to her mouth, touching her lips ever-so-softly to the glass's edge and sipped. When she pulled her lips away from the glass's rim, she'd left a bright red print of her full lips that he noticed as she set it back down on the napkin.

Charley (Ethan), swirled the ice in his glass and held it up to smell the aroma, smelling a familiar scent; he enjoyed it. Afterwards he took a drink and placed the glass down, picking up the cigar and trimmer. After inserting the tip, he snapped the trimmer down and then wet the end with his mouth before holding it up to the table lighter and flicking the flame to life. He stared into Aisling's eyes as he drew in the smoke after the flame kissed the other end. He drew several puffs and let the smoke escape his mouth upwards to the ceiling.

Aisling watched as he performed a ritual he'd obviously done often and became seasoned at.

Ethan watched the flame glimmer in the shininess of Aisling's irises. He knew he should stop this sexual charade they were playing—but his devilish side became awakened and now blended with the alcohol. The amalgamation began taking control over his common sense. He knew he must follow along and find out where this "mystery" would lead him. He wisely chose mixing his expired friends names as his own, making it truly a mystery for—Aisling. *What could go wrong?*

***

Jaime watched from across the room as her friend and the very attractive man both appeared to play back and forth with each other; as if they were encompassed in a chess game of cat and mouse. One would take a drink and then lean in toward the other and smile and laugh. Sarah (Aisling's real name) was very adept at working his male ego. She could tell her friend wanted to play tonight. When Sarah entered this level of percipience, she rarely failed at captivating her target of interest and taking him home. Jaime really wanted to be a chess piece in their game tonight. She wasn't ready to turn her king over in submission. Not just yet, Jaime smiled a naughty little grin.

***

As Ethan played along, he felt himself truly being drawn in. Allured and mesmerized. What in the hell was he doing though? He'd struck fortune to have a beautiful woman back in his home waiting for him. He'd literally spent most of his adult life pursuing her and after almost twenty years, finally succeeded. Did he really want to risk his dream come true over a young, vivacious and mysterious one-night stand? He thought about her co-worker who would obviously try to catch a glimpse of him every opportunity she saw. Could he take her suggestive banter about sharing the evening together in a three-some and move the idea forward? It would be like old times, but without Charley and Roy. What a felicitous way to celebrate the closing of this chapter of life, the recent exits of the other two-thirds of PH! And of course, quite an appropriate way to go out with their old style of sexual prowess before rolling into the new one of monogamy with Joyce. Could this be coincidence or some sort of destiny—an impromptu pre-bachelor party of sorts?

Ethan never spent a moment's time thinking about things of faith, including Jesus, or any religious thing at all. He'd been driven far away at a young age when his mother would spend hour upon hour listening to some radio charlatan begging trades of eternal life for nickels on the dollar. But tonight—he considered maybe, just maybe—he could be being shown the path! How else could one explain such an easy gift coming one's way?

Ethan milked the smoke from the twenty-dollar cigar he continued enjoying. He also appreciated his Weller 107 bourbon. After working on his second double neat, he in fact began feeling very relaxed. On the verge of being "toasted." Aisling worked her way closer and closer to him and every time Jaime came to check on him, she would smile seductively and sneak a wink to him. He looked down at his J.W. Benson watch, seeing it was almost eleven. He began to feel a little weak-kneed and knew it had been a ten-minute walk when he was sober. "So, Aisling, are you going to tell me your true name before I have to head back to my hotel? Or am I going to go to bed without solving this mystery?" Ethan smiled devilishly.

"Oh Charley!" She reached and cupped his hand in hers. "It's not even the witching hour yet! Don't tell me you turn into a pumpkin at midnight!" She grinned with a returned naughty smile. "My friend Jaime gets off at one, maybe we could go back to my place and—you know, have a nightcap or two? I know she's been dying to spend some time with us. I live in a loft just around the corner not far. I'd love to show it to you. Who knows, maybe we could solve this mystery in my bed?"

Ethan knew he shouldn't. He really needed to be ready for his meeting. But...two...beautiful...young....

"I see the wheels turning in your mind, Charley. They're like timepiece gears slowly clicking—I can almost hear them." She giggled. "I bet your gears will fit nicely with ours—Jaime's and mine. I know you wanna...."

Jaime walked up from behind and touched his shoulder as she pulled a chair beside him and sat for a moment. Her hand quickly disappeared under the table and found a spot on "Charley's" lap. She looked down where her hand rested and then looked back into his eyes. "So, Sarah...."

"Awe hah! Mystery solved!" He slowly blew smoke her way and then set the cigar down on the ashtray and picked up his glass. "Sarah and Jaime. Hmmm. Makes one curious why two—very young vivacious women—would want to share a bed together with an older libations broker from 'down south'? Have you ever done this before? Because I have—many, many times. In my distant past. In fact, two of my "friends" who used to enjoy evenings such as I imagine I'm being invited to attend, just recently left this magical world behind. It's a shame, you would have loved them. Ethan lifted his cigar and puffed the life back into it, its ashes becoming orangish-red again, as the smoke billowed. He watched and waited to see if they'd change their minds. He turned from one pair of eyes to the other. "I see the gears turning inside your minds, girls. Are they meshing or did I wedge a splinter in between?"

Sarah taking the bait, became the first to respond. "It seems the mystery is suddenly shifted upon us." She looked at Jaime with inquisition. "Jaime—I don't like walking away from a mystery until it's solved, do you?"

Jaime sat beside Charley, her hand still sitting on his lap, his male anatomy still at attention, "I just can't walk away, especially when it's hard." She smiled at Sarah and then turned and grinned at Charley vivaciously. "I've got to go finish my shift. Can I get you another Wellers?"

"Coffee, black if you want any kind of imperishable lovemaking." Ethan quipped.

Jaime gave him a little tug below and looked to Sarah again and then back. "Oh, it's not love we'll be making. It's just plain old-fashioned rumpy pumpy." She winked, giggled, and walked away, jiggling her ass, leaving Charley mesmerized. Sarah just watched the two, as Charley eyed her walking away, an insatiable lust-filled hunger on his face.

48

Joyce pulled her Volvo up the drive to Ethan's house. She looked over at her daughter who sat next to her in the passenger seat. Her face glowed and she looked happy for the first time in a month. "I guess we have the whole place to ourselves for at least tonight! I don't know about you, but I could use a walk on the beach around sunset and then stay up late on the back deck and just stare at the stars while the waves crash in?"

"Do you love him, mom? I mean…or…do…" Mitzi couldn't believe she'd just blurted it out like a lightning bolt from a normal puffy white cloud. "…or are you playing with the idea of love? I didn't mean to just spit that out, but I've never seen you with a man. I know it's surely been hard all these years. I'm just thinking I wished you'd met him before you met…you know…Roy."

"What do you mean 'just thinking'. It sounds like there may be some kind of implicating factor behind it?" Joyce asked.

"Well, I don't know how to tell you this, so I guess I'll just blurt it out too." Mitzi hesitated. "Darrell and I went and got tested…."

"Tested? For what? Did he give you an STD or something?" Joyce asked.

"Mom! Ewe, no, nothing like that. We got our blood tested for paternity purposes. You know, to see if we were really siblings."

"And?" Joyce's face became painted with concern.

"We found out we couldn't be. And while I'm thrilled about it, it…well…it…." Mitzi's sentence trailed off to nothing.

"My gawd, Mitzi! So, Roy isn't Darrell's dad? Wonderful news!" Joyce started grinning ear to ear and reaching for Mitzi before they even got out of the car.

"No, mom. That's just it. The million-dollar question—Roy IS Darrell's father." Mitzi shut the passenger door and waited for her mom to get out of the driver's side. Joyce remained seated inside without opening the door or moving, both hands on the steering wheel, silent.

The minute and a half Mitzi stood waiting must have felt like an eternity before she leaned down and tapped on her window to gain Joyce's attention. Joyce looked, but didn't move to exit. Mitzi pulled the door handle and climbed back in. "Mom? Are you okay?" She didn't know what to say now. Her mom's response broke her rhythm of the conversation. She too suddenly felt dumbstruck. They both sat quietly taking it in, eyes looking straight ahead to Ethan's front porch and door.

A breeze must have blown outside the car. Their windows were still up so neither seemed to hear it through the trees, but the porch swing began to glide in small circles. The movement seemed to draw both of their attention as if a ghost broke their gaze to cause an interaction between them.

"Mom, I know you're shocked. I…I…never knew you'd…you know…been with anybody else? I know you didn't after dad…I mean…Roy left. Or at least—I never knew about it."

Joyce turned to face Mitzi; her suntanned face sheepishly white. "Mitzi, that's just it, sweetie. I did have a high school boyfriend and we…we…um…we did the sex thing once, but it was my…the last of my junior year. I never got pregnant, but the thought of the possibility scared me back then." She looked directly at her daughter, her face stern but confused. "The only other times I had sex, were with your father, Roy. He's got to be your father. There's no other plausible answer."

"Mom, by our blood type, the doctor couldn't rule for or against

Roy being Darrell's dad, but he ruled a hundred percent Roy wasn't my biological father. Our blood types make it impossible. I can't explain it, but Doctor Middler talked like he felt certain about it. Roy isn't my dad."

Mitzi's mom sat still with a confused look, her eyes squinting as if the sun were in them, or she began searching internally for a possible explanation. She suddenly looked at Mitzi. "I can't even ask Roy how it's possible because he's dead now." She slammed her hands on the steering wheel. "What am I gonna do, baby-doll?"

Mitzi pondered a moment and then thought about bringing up a subject she wasn't sure she should. Joyce happened to look at her and saw the look of question on her furrowed brows. Mitzi saw her and her momma's look. They knew each other so well it was nearly impossible for either one to hide something from the other. It's why Mitzi didn't doubt when her mom said she'd not had sex with anyone but Roy and the boy back in high school. She would have known if her mother were lying.

"What are you thinking, Mitzi? You can tell me. You sure as hell can't tell me anything that would shock me anymore than your news about Roy."

Mitzi looked squarely at her mom. She let the sentence form inside her head for a second or two before asking it. "Is there any way you... you...could have been...raped and not known it? Either drunk or blocked it because it had been so traumatic or...."

"No. I don't really drink much, I never have. It makes me feel, kind of sick. Anything more than a glass or two of wine and...no...I don't see that happening. And I'd think I would remember something as scary and violent as a rape." Joyce just shook her head back and forth.

"Dad...I mean, Roy was a cop during your marriage, wasn't he?" Mitzi asked.

"Yes, he's been a cop since the day we met." Joyce answered.

"Could he have drugged you or something for some reason?"

Mitzi asked.

Joyce looked shocked at the question. "Why? To let another man rape me. That makes no sense at all." Joyce shook her head and opened her door. "I don't want to think about this any longer this evening. I just want to go walk on the beach, get my feet wet in the calming surf. Hell, I may even have a stiff drink tonight, sweetheart! My mind is already blown!" She half smiled to her daughter and they both got out and went inside.

49

Ethan's legs were slightly rubbery on the climb down the stairs of The Alibi Room. Once they walked through the green neon doorway of the entrance, he put an arm around the waist of each woman. He smiled and corrected his internal faux pas, *they weren't women, they were girls.* His anticipation now stronger than his will would ever be to question or halt the evening's future events from happening. He'd become intoxicated, not only with the bourbon, but the unquenchable thirst of lust he'd been spoon-fed. He'd done his best to let Joyce mentally shame his thoughts while it had all been gameplay, but now the act of the play had ceased, and they were speeding forward toward climax.

Ethan knew plays usually consisted of five acts. He'd sped through the first two. Act One, "the exposition," when he'd said goodbye to Joyce and flown into Springfield, then walked across the bar's threshold. Followed quickly by Act Two, "the rising action", sexually sparring conversation and drinks over the evening with two enticing girls. He still dominated in the middle of the second, but the Third Act, "the climax", is what kept his hunger ferocious, not questioning the next scene to be followed. Act Four, "the falling action." This scene he chose not to dwell on before it's time. This would take place after his body became spent, muscles, and skin sore from all the friction, yet having a beautiful girl on either side still begging to replay the third act again. But then of course, all great things enter the final act. Act Five, "the catastrophe," this would certainly open with the morning's first light and his coy attempt at exiting. Hopefully in the invisibility of both the girls booze induced heavy sleep. Ethan chose not to mentally consider the fifth and final act. He would deal with it when the show truly ended after all the encores.

He looked to his left and then to his right. The second act continued splendidly racing to the third. His blood pumping as if it were twenty years earlier in his life.

Back then he'd just built the beach house and the playroom hadn't yet been christened. It had been Act Two of his life, but the first time Charley knocked on his door and he went to answer, oh, it definitely became Act Three of his life's play. The way his heart raged with lust at the sight of the three or four beautiful young girls Charley convinced to come party with them. Their tight young bodies bouncing in their skimpy bikinis on his private beach. Imagining their wet perspiring skin sliding against his with friction and the satisfying saltiness of their taste against his tongue. Each vying for their spot to be mutually gratified.

Ethan (Charley) took another look at each of the girls hanging onto him. His seasoned hormones quaking back to life, his loins aching to empty his seed into both well plotted and shapely acreages. He wanted to experience every square inch of both properties as if he were planning to purchase and build on them.

Ethan became swallowed up with the devil's treasure. What he thought he owned on his own, he merely rented the deceit from a power he'd never known, ignored, or denied. He truly had been the slave but too slathered in drunkenness to know it. Gin-soaked and lust-filled. If he'd been driving, the telephone pole he'd likely have smacked into could have saved him from himself. But instead, he powered full speed being driven to the den of debauchery by two beautiful works of art he'd now become irreversibly beguiled by.

They stopped at a doorway in the middle of an old brick warehouse. Sarah pulled a key from her bra which hung on a short gold chain. It glistened of perspiration in the light of the streetlamp glowing overhead. Charley eyed her cleavage she'd pulled it from and couldn't resist leaning down and running his tongue between her breasts, tasting the salt, anticipating saltier landscapes down south. She smiled both at Jaime, the most sober, and Ethan who wore the look of the wolf. Hungry beyond control. Ready to ravage them until their muscles would move no longer.

Sarah dropped the key and as she bent over, Ethan spoke under his breath of what he planned to do to her as soon as she opened the "damned door."

When they reached the top of the stairs they met a landing. Sarah smiled, "only two more floors to my apartment. Hang in there though, I have the only door to the roof. The sky is mine and I want to share it along with my body and my friend with you. It'll be worth every step, I promise." She leaned back over to him and licked his lips while Jaime reached around and massaged his crotch, giving him the stamina to keep climbing toward the pinnacle. Ethan's heart raced. Lust filled passions were firing rockets in his brain as he'd never experienced. He began to question if bourbon had been the only thing he'd ingested. He'd drank far more in his past without feeling like he felt now. He felt like a stud horse held back from the mare, ready to kick the stall down to mount her. His sexual drive kept him climbing, stair after stair, watching each of Sarah's ass cheeks jiggling back and forth driving his imaginations to what lay ahead in that milky white flesh hidden in her skirt. *Had these girls slipped me a roofie of some sort?* This sensation was unlike any other feeling he'd ever felt, and it came on suddenly. He felt like the dominant silver ape he'd watched on television at one time or another. He wanted to pound his chest before his mates who lie stretched out in waiting.

They finally reached the top. No more stairs were visible. A large steel door with scissor bars which locked it tight as if it were a bank vault. Sarah pushed a series of numbers on a keypad, and it suddenly clicked. Sarah pulled the bar handle down, and the scissor locks glided open, the pins removed from the slots. The door opened into a room with windows at floor to ceiling level as far as his eyes could see. The beautiful stars and a small downtown skyline were sprawled out before him, an ocean of light. Just one dark tower rising above in the moonlight. It looked black as night and phallic like, with occasional windows on different floors lit up, showing no pattern throughout. He found the view spectacular. No ocean or waves were crawling up the shoreline, but it overtook his hormonal rage for an instant. When he turned around to comment, he saw something he hadn't expected but came as a very welcome sight. A strawberry-blonde girl held the hand of her dark black-haired friend standing in nothing but their glowing naked skin.

"Do you want something to drink before we go up onto the rooftop?" Sarah pushed a button, and a stocked bar lit up with the silhouette of various bottles displayed in light and mirrors.

Just who in the hell were these women? And what world have I crossed in to?

"I have a special blend I enjoy—would you like to try it, Charley warlie?" Sarah asked.

"Your castle, your call." Charley answered as he continued to look at the beautiful naked bodies before him and then around at his surroundings. The stars seemed to perform extra sparkles and the dark tower in the distance held a haunting appearance with the moon just off its shoulder. The sight vied for his attention over the milky white nakedness—briefly. "Speaking of castles, is this entire building yours or are there other tenants?"

Sarah walked back carrying a tray of three shots of a lime-green liquid that looked toxic by appearance. "My father left it to me. The first floor is all warehouse space and is full of his collection of automobiles. Do you like cars and motorbikes, Charley?" She asked as she walked leading him and Jaime to a dark brown leather pit group that sat sunken into the middle of the floor. Three steps down to enter and sit. She set the tray on the green marble slab table in the middle and then sat to one side of the sofa and patted the spot next to her.

"I do. I enjoy all the finer collectibles in life. I'd love to see them sometime." He answered. "Three glasses, so can I assume it is just the three of us for the rest of the evening?"

Jaime sat to his right, just opposite of Sarah, Charley in the middle. "Is two of us not enough?" She smiled as she leaned up and picked up one of the lime green shots, handing it to Charley, then reaching for another. She leaned across his lap to hand Sarah a glass, her breasts almost in reach of Charley's lips. She looked down and saw movement and sighed.

"So, what's in this home blend, Aisling—I mean, Sarah?" Charley asked.

Sarah smiled, "You can call me either. In fact, I rather like the name Aisling." She straightened up, lifting her shot glass to the air. The ambient light from outside lit the green liquid and it sparkled as it swirled about in the glass, appearing as if it were some magic potion. "It's my own special blend of absinthe, Midori melon for color and taste—Yohimbe and Ecstasy for pleasure. We call it, 'the green fairy' but you'll call it heaven on earth." She winked as she held the shot up where Charley and Jaime could clink glasses together. "Here's to using our bodies as your vessel of pleasure, just for you, Charley."

Clink, clink, clink. They each held their glass to their lips; Charley hesitated in thought for a moment as he watched the girls down theirs. *What the hell?* Charley swallowed the glass's contents in one gulp and waited for the rollercoaster to begin.

Ethan realized one thing. He hadn't become who he'd become, because of the end reward—the orgasm.

It felt far beyond that. He held Jaime, now bent over the railing wall of the three-story building rooftop, squirming and gyrating, as he watched commercial jets fly overhead, very low as if Sarah's warehouse home was in the flight pattern near the runway. She was obviously enjoying him by her movements and vocal sighs. In this singular moment, he'd become mentally lost in the thought that he would eventually climax, and it would all end. His brain became a quagmire of electrical impulses filled with deep understandings of the entire universe he'd suddenly become aware of. His mental orgasm became the power he held over her, not his physical one. He realized he ruled as the king of this specific moment in time. She totally dependent on what he did to his slave. If he instantly stopped, she wouldn't receive the electric pulses he manipulated her to. His head never so clear before, it felt vibrant and omniscient. Completely lucid. Could it be the concoction he'd shared with Jaime and Sarah? Or maybe he'd just experienced an epiphany. He needed more. His awakening seemed to suddenly begin a descent and vagueness. The high began waning one moment, then skyrocketing the next. Still the world around him flickered and twinkled. The sky above him filled with stars, large aircraft, and helicopters, while in front and behind him were building windows dimly lit in scattered incohesive tiles. And of course, the dark tower that stood ugly and staunch with its square head at the top, like some robotic beast staring down upon them.

His mind bounced from thought to thought with no rhyme or reason, still he remained rock hard and thrusting his body into Jaime.

Where had Sarah gone? He suddenly questioned, but it dissipated into a fleeting thought.

His mind lost track and moved on to another flash. Ethan held no idea what could be happening other than every move he made seemed filled with pleasure. He tingled as his mind became a bowl of impulses and quivers. He felt no self-control, but yet, total mastery—but he didn't care—he just wanted more sensations. Each new prickle or goose bump demanded a newer more impelling sensation. Ethan became transformed into a pleasure-consuming and giving machine. His hunger becoming unquenchable and a driven power he felt a continuing inability to control.

***

Jaime continued to push backwards, driving herself against the flesh giving her pleasure. She moaned and screamed in uncontrollable outbursts. She seemed driven only by the hedonistic gratifications her body enjoyed and unaware of anything other than self-satisfaction. She appeared a sexual zombie, a living Barbi-doll bent on one mission, climaxing. She seemed almost soulless.

***

Ethan's hands held Jaime's firm tight waist. He lifted her upward and pushed her body forward as he continued to seek each new sexual sensation. Jaime hollered and screamed in pleasure as her grip on the railing tightened with the rest of her muscles throughout her body. In one last thrust made in unison, it ended. The sensations died as if they'd both been killed in battle by the same tactical toss of the spear. They collapsed. His mind went black. The light switch flicked off.

50

Jay lay in his hospital bed waiting to find out when this famous Ethan Kendrick, defender of the—accused, would be showing up. The clock on the wall read after 9:30am. "Nurse!" He called out. His hollering caused a stabbing pain in his stomach. He lifted the sheet as best he could with his right arm and looked down at his wrapped stomach area. *Damn that cop for squeezin' off two rounds that found their home in my shoulder and stomach.* He knew it to be only the beginning of the pain he would now be feeling. He'd started out with a shit life and barely kept his head above the cesspool of daily living ever since. He'd been teased a time or two with what he imagined the lucky ones in life held, but it never lasted long. Jay resigned himself to the fact he would at the minimum, spend the rest of his days removed from that "world." At the other end of the spectrum, of course, the electric chair. Just because Jay resigned himself to one of those facts of life—it damn sure didn't mean he'd found his place deserving. He'd felt in some small way, if there truly is a God—he in fact, served Him by his deeds of judgment. *Even Ms. Cela could surely see there were sinners who need be reconciled by torture or even death.* His lifetime of suffering made him the most warranted vessel to carry out such matters. He would indeed have to face his maker in the end, ifin' so Ms. Cela were correct in her words.

Jay moved, adjusting to a comfortable position and in doing, caused a sudden tinge of pain throughout. He smiled to himself, considering it somehow must be Ms. Cela letting him know she was indeed correct in her words.

An officer barged into the group medical ward and found Jay's bed among the others. "Billy Jay...."

Jay slowly turned his gaze to the guard. "It's Jay. I don't answer to Billy."

"Well, Billy—your attorney is a no show. He didn't call either, so his name's now removed from the list. It looks like justice is beginning its toothy bite already." The guard chuckled as he turned to walk back out. "Ain't karma a bitch!? I can almost see the coal smoke billowing above Florida from here, getting ready for the power-surge to come." Another snicker followed before he left. "People like you call us pigs—yet you're the one that'll be putting off the odor of bacon. Maybe I'll get to see you out on the floor before you get put on the grill. Cop killers get a lot of attention in the glass house."

***

Jay refused to respond to the hate-filled words the guard spewed at him, but he did hear them, and they did settle into his psyche. He'd heard talk about inmates fryin' and not dyin' quickly. Some they'd have to give the juice two or three times before they were pronounced dead. Some said inmates' eyeballs popped from their heads and then dangled like sizzlin' meatballs. The thought caused Jay to shudder, trying desperately to wrestle his mind to other ideas. Ideas such as Cat. He thought about how the two of them now shared time in hospital beds, laid out, not knowing what their futures were. Maybe losing some memory may not be a bad thing. Jay closed his eyes, and when he did, his thoughts changed. He saw faces he'd not pictured for a long time. Girls faces. Faces which first contained cautious stares before he sweet-talked them into believing he looked out for their interests; when instead, he sought justice. The self-satisfying judgment only he'd be capable to deliver. It wasn't about the sexual gratification he'd felt. It was about watching their glow begin to fade from their eyes. Paying for their sins, at his hand.

Jay kept his eyes closed, and to the nurses, they saw a man sleeping. In reality, Jay wasn't asleep. Instead, he lie busy reliving moments he saw as highlights of his miserable life on this earth. Jay fancied himself a soldier of sorts, a man who was capable of ferreting out the rats of the world. His pay for doing so, the luxury of sexual play before condemning them and then extinguishing their lives and hiding their existence from the rest of the world. He felt much like an unappreciated garbage collector who took away the used and dirty debris we once found satisfying but now needed discarding from memory and sight. *I help make the world pretty and tolerable for them, and for this, they will condemn me to death.*

51

Ethan acted much differently since his return to Apalachicola from Springfield, Missouri. He held good reason too. The sights he'd seen were still haunting him along with the guilt of his actions. Was it emblazoned across his forehead like a seventeenth century criminal's crime branded across his? It certainly felt like it with every stare lasting more than a second or two.

The entire trip replayed from start to finish in hopes of finding out the reasoning and exactly what happened. Would he be found out?

All my careful planning up to this point and now I'm at the mercy from my own indiscretions. I'd let myself be played like Roy. Like Roy, the fucking idiot. He would never forget waking up and seeing Jaime's naked body as it lay lifeless bathed in a pool of blood below his view from the rooftop above the alleyway, or his inability to locate Sarah in order to find out what happened. *What the fuck had happened? Did I do this? Am I guilty?* He'd suddenly felt the need for self-preservation. He hurriedly searched Sarah's loft and gathered his things, trying to wipe away any evidence from everywhere he may have left it. *Just what the fuck happened? What have I done?*

***

Joyce noticed something out of character with Ethan the minute she saw him. She ran to his arms, taking him tightly against her bosom, but he felt empty and hollow. "A rough trip?" She asked. Ethan squeezed her, but Joyce felt something different. "You sit and relax; I'll go get a glass of your favorite bourbon. Do you mind if I share a drink with you?"

"Joyce, you don't need to ask me; this is your home now if you want it? You do still want it, don't you?"

She pulled away from him to see his soft grey eyes. "I'm sorry. I'm just a woman, and sometimes we let our intuitions take control and make us feel things which aren't necessarily there. Of course, I want it. Ethan, I want you." She smiled and covered up her inner impressions as best she could.

"And yes, I would very much like a drink and some time to unwind—with you. Maybe on the front porch this time? A change of scenery from the beach to the grove of live oaks?" He suggested in a question.

Joyce let go of Ethan's shoulders and walked towards the bar; she looked back, "It sounds wonderful. I haven't sat in a front porch swing in years."

Ethan held his glass to his lips and stalled as if he were contemplating a thought. Of course, he reeled in the unsolvable quandary he'd fled. Joyce immediately took notice of him. He shook his head subtly and then swallowed a fair amount of the glass's contents. "You know, the federal prison system is full of bullshit." His comment seemed somewhat out of context to what little conversation he and Joyce were sharing up to this point, but he attempted to steer any questions she may have of his odd mood, to something other than the truth. Like a good attorney, he began slowly and coyly laying out an alibi of sorts. Quietly, cautiously, and inconspicuously.

"In what way? Is this something that happened in Springfield?" Joyce inquired.

"Yes, yes. I overslept this morning and missed my meeting with

Billy Jay Cader...."

Joyce took a sip of her drink. "It doesn't seem like the Ethan I've gotten to know. What happened to make you oversleep?"

"I stayed up late preparing and had a lot on my mind. I went down to the hotel bar and probably drank more than I should have. The clock read midnight before I went back up to my room." Ethan took another drink. "I wasn't looking forward to representing Mr. Cader to begin with. You even questioned what it may do to the practice if I did take his case." He lifted his glass and downed the rest of its contents, not giving him time to enjoy its robust flavor.

Joyce stood up from the porch swing. They hadn't sat long enough to get the swinging action started. "Here, give me your glass, and I'll fill it up. Be right back."

She brought the bottle out in case he would be going through his drinks a little quicker tonight. She poured his glass and handed it back. "Mitzi is in town tonight at the Watkins' again; looks like we have the evening free to ourselves. Are you feeling like turning in early tonight?" She touched his shoulder and gave him a gentle squeeze. "I bet I could take some of the tension away."

Ethan held his newly filled glass to his mouth and sipped from it. This time he savored its flavor and again appeared lost in thought.

Joyce sat back down next to him, lightly pushing against the porch floor to begin the swing in its lulling movement. She decided to ignore the fact Ethan didn't seem to hear her subtle hint at making love to her. Ethan's lack of jumping on the opportunity didn't necessarily sting, but it did make Joyce wonder what happened in Springfield to kill his usual fervent appetite for sex.

Ethan sat and wondered if there were any markings left on his body Joyce might notice. He felt no pains or irritations, just the fog inside his brain. He thought back to the evening before and how the two girls were rough with him and prodded him to reciprocate. He left in such a hurry he hadn't really checked his body out for any signs of his—adventure. *I should have stayed a day or two more to investigate. What could Sarah be into and where did she go? Did she know enough about me to implicate me?*

52

James T. Bollard heard word from Ben Dane that apparently, Ethan Kendricks showed an interest in representing Billy Jay Cader. The news perplexed him. Ethan never in his entire career defended someone charged in a double homicide of two law enforcement officers. Ethan had talent, but he questioned his angle on this case.

The evidence the Florida state attorney supposedly held in their possession would appear to make this a slam-dunk case for the DA. Why would Ethan want to diminish his career attributes with such a dead-end case? James raised his eyeglasses, resting them above his forehead and rubbed his eyes. "What the hell have you got cooking in the kettle, Ethan?" He spoke aloud. "And why did Ben seem to have changed his heart about Billy Jay?" Questions James was very interested in finding answers to; after all, Ben spent a bit of a bankroll with him to defend Jay only several months back. He decided to set up an interview with Billy Jay Cader over in Springfield to try to dig answers up from the story's backside before attacking from the front.

***

A week and a half later, James Bollard headed out in his Silver Mercedes-Benz 300 DT toward Springfield, preferring almost any transportation mode other than flying. Plus, he'd get to view the different landscapes they never got to see since his practice became well-known. James couldn't remember the last vacation he and his wife were able to take together. He looked to his right and smiled at Doris. "Before we head back, we'll drive south of Springfield to Branson and see a show or two."

On Friday, two long days after he and his wife left Tallahassee, they reached Springfield, Missouri. It was a long drive, but so much more relaxing to James than soaring forty thousand feet above the earth at four hundred knots. *God didn't intend us to fly, or he'd have created us with wings.* Besides, in his older age, even if he did have wings, he'd grown far too heavy to want his arms to be responsible for dragging his big white, flabby ass through the clouds. He laughed and shook his head as he pictured the sight to himself, his rather voluptuous wife tethered to his belt as he flapped his way through a flock of geese. *No—my Mercedes is a much more practical choice.*

James Bollard, in all his years, never became comfortable going through the enormous electronic prison door. The sound it made as it closed—the boom as it snapped shut. It's designed for effect, and it worked. The Springfield Federal Medical Center was no different. Yes, it held a hospital, but first and foremost its purpose is a prison. A facility to house some of the most heinous inmates. There were medical wards and mental wards and cameras everywhere. James saw the bank of video screens in front of the guard as the door slammed shut. In order for the front door, into the facility to open, the other needed to shut solid and they both made a resounding slam so you knew there would be no escaping. There must have been thirty video screens being monitored at this guard station alone. There wasn't any question why the inmates called prison these days "glass houses." It's exactly what they were. Watched twenty-four seven from every angle possible, and this facility is considered "easy time" compared to others. The Birdman from Alcatraz spent time housed here years back along with persons committing treason and espionage. Mafia crime bosses and murderers of the most heinous type were the normal inmates. The facility held all kinds in its past and present. A current guest, Larry Flynt, a seedy publisher of Hustler Magazine, had been charged with a string of obscenities in the state of Ohio.

"Good afternoon, Mr. Cader." James Bollard greeted Jay, who turned his head towards his visitor.

"I'll be damned. It's the man of my hour! You come here to save me again?" Jay said with sarcasm.

James let a grin sneak from the corner of his mouth. "Saving you this time, will be merely a level of perspective, Jay. You've really gotten yourself into quite a predicament..." Moving in closer so he could talk quieter, away from the guard who stood near, he stated, "You can't expect to be charged with the murder of two law enforcement officers and wounding another—and expect to be saved? You might need to look to the Lord to answer your request."

"How is the other—shall we say, gentleman, which found a bullet or two of mine?" Jay wore a smirk when he asked the question.

"He seems very determined to see your demise, Jay. He is busy finding other improprieties of yours. I can't really talk openly here, but I would advise you to let me see what kind of a deal I can come up with to save you from a gruesome visit to the chair."

"Oh, I expect to sit in that chair. There'd be no way of denying my presence at the crime scene..." Jay grinned. "...bein' how it happened to be my home where they invaded me—but I did wear their bullets in my body and there is no repudiating that fact. I'm certain those pieces of lead sit in a small jar with a label attached that holds my name scribed upon that label, locked away in some evidence room...."

"I would suggest you let me do the talking and you try being more on the silent side...." James replied.

"I'll not be silenced! I'll not just disappear into the night!"

"Sgt. Rawlings holds a list of some missing girls, Jay. He and the detective you shot and killed found a box of evidence which could tie you to these missing girls. Do you know what I'm referring to? He's dead set on sending you to the chair and bringing your blood to a boil. I could possibly reduce it to life with no chance of parole—but you'd have to promise to cooperate. Do you understand now the seriousness of this?"

Jay turned his head away from the attorney and said nothing further despite Mr. Bollard's attempt to get a response.

Mr. Bollard started to walk away but a question burned in his thoughts, and he wanted to know the answer. "Jay—I have one question—why did you turn Ethan Kendricks away for your defense?"

Jay turned back to face James again, pausing as if mulling his words over before speaking. "I never asked for his help..." Jay's face faked a puzzled look before stating, "...don't even know the man." He'd lied. A sneer began to form in his gaze. "...he invited his own damn self to see me here...."

"Oh, he did?" James interrupted and questioned as he rubbed his chin.

"...guards told me he's supposed to be comin', but the son-of-a-bitch never showed up for our meeting." Jay looked at James squarely. "So, what's in this for you? I ain't got no money to pay?"

Mr. Bollard walked back and looked toward the guard, motioning if it was okay for him to approach Jay. The guard nodded with approval and James leaned in for a closer quiet word with him. "Billy Jay—I don't want your money. What you can provide me is far more beneficial, along with keeping you alive instead of letting a valuable commodity fry up like bacon on the griddle. Once you kill the pig and eat the bacon—there ain't any value to the farmer, but if you feed the pig in the pen—the pig becomes close to the other farm animals. Are you getting what I'm saying to you?"

"I'm no fuckin' snitch, if that's what you're implying." Jay said immediately.

"But you can get me in touch with those in the know of things I might need to know in the future. It's all built on an 'I scratch your back, you scratch mine' kind of a setup." James smiled. "I might be able to provide you with things you can't get on the inside, while you may be able to provide me such things not easily available on the outside." He winked and turned to start walking. He took two sauntering steps and turned back, "Just think about it, I'm available. The time you may have to consider this offer could be very short, so don't take too long, Billy Jay." James winked and walked past the guard and then to the door. As he waited to be buzzed out, he gave a short wave and then disappeared out of the room.

53

Ethan locked the bathroom door before he got ready to shower, something he'd never done before. He stood in front of his mirror searching closely for any scratches or marks which may still be visible from his evening of madness. He turned and checked his back out, holding a mirror to catch the rear reflection from the wall mirror. He couldn't see any and he looked as closely as possible.

The doorknob jiggled, followed by, "Ethan? Are you okay in there?"

"Um, yeah, I just have some stomach issues. I'm going to shower after I finish up and then I'll be out. Sorry, Joyce."

"You don't have to apologize, sweetie. I hope you feel better. I'm worried about you; you haven't been the same since your trip."

"I must have picked up a bug or something. I'll be fine." He flushed the toilet to help end the conversation through the door, then turned the shower on. "I'll be out in a few." Ethan felt relief he hadn't found any signs of his indiscretions. The guilt became another story. He knew Joyce wanted to make love tonight. He'd ignored her hint, but he'd heard it. His mind still a mess of trying to figure out what happened, but also wrestling with the fact at how easy he fell prey. He thought he'd buried all the sexual craziness and desires from his past. *And just what the hell happened? Jaime turned up dead and Sarah missing. How?*

54

The smell of patchouli oil overwhelmed his senses. Her thin curvy white body laid out on the vinyl car seat before him, one leg swung over the seat back and the other on the floorboard rested against the steering wheel. Dimmed light broke through the dirty caged windows which sat perched ten to fifteen feet above head level and cast eerie shadows across the tops of the various cars parked front to back. There were darkened tight paths between the different car models which appeared to be from separate eras in time. Some from the thirties or earlier and on through to more current vehicles, all in pristine shape, minus the dust covering the tops of their surfaces.

Her moans of wanting to be pleasured again caused his attention to be drawn away from the gloomy car filled warehouse. He lifted his hands from the top of the roof and maneuvered his body closer until his flesh met hers and she gently helped him inside her again. Ethan inhaled the scent of Sarah's patchouli oil perfume once more through his nose. He found it very arousing, like the scent of salty sweat mixed with the musky smell of a woman's pleasure parts. It simply smelled like sex. He couldn't remember just how many times he'd orgasmed tonight between the two young ladies. Feeling spent, his genitals felt nearly rubbed raw, yet his body couldn't fight the urge to become erect again. The "green fairy" potion obviously worked like a charm, he'd lost all self-control and began again to pleasure Sarah. Her red hair spread out wildly and spilling off the car seat. She occasionally lifted her head enabling her to watch his expressions as she enjoyed his rhythmic movements.

"Put your hands around my throat..." Sarah whispered. "I want you to be rough with me. Dominate me, baby."

Roughness never evolved in Ethan's urges. He'd always questioned who could have those desires like Roy seemed to have. When they were in the playroom back at his beach house and Roy would start to get rough, it always killed Ethan's mood. Instead, he wanted to pleasure his partners, never scare them or treat them roughly. Maybe those kinds of actions brought the realism of what he and his friends were truly doing to these girls. At least Roy didn't hide what his expectations were. They were always drugged or drunk and deep down both Charley and he knew it to be wrong. Treating women rough for them seemed an abominable character trait. But in the end, their ways weren't any kinder, they still dehumanized and degraded the young girls that were persuaded there. But it always ended up Roy who seemed to steer toward the rough way at some point in their "sexual adventures," and Ethan felt it always repulsed him the most. It would become a mental challenge inside his mind to even maintain his erection upon seeing the more dominant actions against the girls.

Hearing Sarah ask again for him to slightly choke her felt no different. He reluctantly placed his hands lightly around her throat and mentally battled himself in his mind to continue. He felt himself becoming flaccid and it wounded his ego for some bizarre reason.

He closed his eyes and accidentally pictured Joyce's face instead of Sarah's and instantly he began to slide towards the warehouse floor to his knees. He couldn't go on any longer and he began to sob. "I can't...I can't do this...it's not me..."

"Don't stop, Charley...don't leave me in begging like this...don't...be a pussy...." Sarah vocally stabbed at him along with a disappointing stare.

Ethan looked up from his knees and could only see Sarah's head lifted and looked down at him. Her legs spread apart; she began to laugh. Not just a passing guffaw, but pointedly hurtful laughter.

He rose quickly and pushed her legs further apart until she screamed from pain, before shoving her head back down to the car seat with one hand, then reached for her throat..., "This is what you want?" He screamed as he squeezed tighter and aimed his erection where she'd wanted it.

Joyce suddenly gasped for air and pushed against Ethan desperately. "Eth...Ethan...I...can't...brea...breathe." She took her free hands and began to fight intensely to get free by flailing and punching the body which lay on top of her, waking her from a sleep with him choking her and his aroused manhood pushing against her flesh, trying to penetrate her....

Ethan suddenly released his grip and rolled off the body he'd been on top of. He yelled out, "I'm sorry Aisling...I'm sorry." He then looked over and realized he was at home with Joyce and had been dreaming or reliving the night before. His eyes were open as wide as possible, showing dark specks surrounded by whiteness and he stared back into matching eyes filled with shock and fear.

What have I done? "My gawd, Joyce—I'm so sorry...I...I was...having...a nightmare...I'm sorry...Are you...okay?"

Joyce quickly moved back against the headboard and as far away from Ethan as possible, the sheets pulled up tightly to her chest, hiding her nearly naked body and shivering in horror. Her tightened throat speechless and unable to answer. As Ethan tried to scoot closer, Joyce backed further down the king-sized headboard until she ran out of mattress and tumbled to the floor.

"Joyce—I'm so sorry! I...it...was...I was dreaming...I didn't...mean to...."

Joyce scampered to her feet still clinging to the sheet until it pulled from her grip as she ran to the bathroom, quickly locking the door.

As Ethan got up and wrapped himself into the sheet he finished pulling from the bed, all he could hear from the bathroom were frightened moans and sobs.

***

Joyce didn't know what to think. Ethan had been so soft and loving last night when they made love. How could he have changed into such a violent monster? What could he have been dreaming? She knew she didn't know him all that well, less than six or so months since she and Mitzi moved down here after accepting his job offer. He'd been so kind, and Addi, his administrator, adored him. *Was this just a fluke? Am I over analyzing this?* Joyce suddenly for the first time, did not know what to do. She knew she couldn't stay locked in the bathroom forever. Ethan sounded very apologetic. The sobs continued as did Ethan's pleas for forgiveness and to come out and talk this through. She'd always been the supportive friend who never held grudges. The only grudge she'd never let go of entirely was the one she held over Roy. And this because of the constant reminder of how he continued to hurt their daughter day after day, year after year.

"I want to come out—but I'm frightened, Ethan."

Ethan softly rested his forehead against the bathroom door. "I know Joyce, and I'm absolutely sick about what happened. I don't know why I am having such horrible dreams or—or why I acted out like this from them. I've been under pressure, and I guess it all came to a head from my trip? I just don't know—or understand. I love you, though. You have to know how I feel by now?"

Joyce wiped away the tears from her eyes. She stood up and saw herself naked in the mirror reflection. She stepped closer and studied her neck, seeing red fingerprints on one side and a single thumb print on the opposite. "I thought I knew, I want to think you do, but—my God, Ethan, your fingerprints are bright red marks on my throat! I couldn't breathe and I thought I was going to die." She broke into loud sobs again and felt suddenly very vulnerable standing there naked. She went to the storage closet and found Ethan's robe hanging on the back of the door and quickly threw it on, covering her nudity. As she leaned back to her left her nose brushed up against the cloth collar of the robe and she smelled Ethan's scent. His cologne. The smell of his skin. She felt weak all of a sudden. Her mind swirled making the room feel as if it were beginning to spin. Her world started collapsing around her, imploding within itself. Joyce's eyes began to roll up inside her head and she grasped for anything to hang on to. Fingers slid down the wall as she fell backwards into a pile on the floor, her robe slid open as her arms spread out on the tile.

Ethan heard her gasp and then the sliding thud which quickly became dead silence. In a panic, he hit the door with his shoulder and it broke free from the center locking mechanism. He pushed slowly but the weight of Joyce's body blocked it from freely opening.

"Joyce! Baby…are you okay? Joyce…."

55

The months slipped by, and Darrell and Mitzi continued to go to school. Life began to take some resemblance of normalcy again. Mitzi convinced her mom to let her stay through the week at the Watkins' home. They had an unused spare room next to their bedroom which had been a shared study for Gabriel and sowing room for Gloria. They explained there were house rules they expected both Darrell and Mitzi to follow, not that it really mattered now. The baby started to show on little Mitzi's body. Mitzi took the spare room beside the Watkins' bedroom and Darrell slept in his old, shared bedroom. On weekends the two would come to the beach house and stay, making her mom feel more comfortable. Joyce never shared with her daughter about the night of Ethan's dream, instead she buried it deep, pretending it never happened and squelching any thoughts of what could have caused it. Ethan spent several days cautiously walking softly around her and spoiling her with whatever she asked. A few weeks passed and she began to feel comfortable again, but the feeling of choking never truly left her consciousness.

Darrell and Mitzi finally got to visit both Kyle and Violet in the hospital. It felt difficult to see Kyle wheel out in his wheelchair to the visitors waiting room the first time, but Kyle kept a good attitude. It appeared as if Violet's chance of a full recovery remained good. There were some speech and motor skills that needed to be re-learned, but the doctors and therapists all held positive hopes. It appeared time would do some healing.

The camera crews once again slipped away and on to another story in another town, certain to return as soon as Billy Jay Cader returned for his trial.

Cat remained in an assisted rehab facility with an outlook which wasn't as favorable as Violet's. Her brain bleed still not totally under control, continued to cause some regress. Darrell visited regularly and continued to be the only person she seemed to recognize. Her smile lit up at the sound of his voice or the sight of his precious face.

Sgt. Tony Rawlings continued to pour over every bit of evidence from Sheriff Roy Burks home. He held hopes of solving the missing girls' cases in a substantial avenue pointing to added charges against Billy Jay. The prosecuting attorney and Tony Rawlings talked about any deals which may be offered up by Billy Jay Cader's attorney, who continued fighting to drop the death penalty from the table. "When the hell will DNA be available to use?" Tony asked the prosecuting attorney, Mason Dyer.

"I would like to nail this SOB for the murder of these seven girls plus maybe more. But we'll have to do it without DNA evidence because it's at least a couple of years away, even though I'm sure his DNA is all over those panties. We're more than likely going to have to make the death penalty go away if we want to resolve any of these cases out there. Is Bollard telling you Jay will offer us body locations on the girls?"

Tony laughed out loud. "I think that crazy bastard is actually looking forward to the chair. Jay still claims he doesn't know anything about missing girls." Tony shrugged his shoulders. "It'll be a ten-year fight before he gets to the chair, maybe we should leave the death penalty on the jurors and solve the cases when DNA is available, then try to deal for locations?"

"Keep drilling down on whatever you can on the girl's cases. I wanna make an example out of this guy. I wanna order a psychological exam too. I don't want this scumbag pleading insanity when the trial starts. I want this son-of-a-bitch back here where we can keep our eyes on him too." Mason said.

56

The day finally came. The Franklin County Jail in Eastpoint, just across the East Bay from Apalachicola, would be getting its most infamous murder suspect to date. This time Jay wouldn't be held in the Apalachicola jail at the police headquarters, considered not adequate for such a suspect. Jay would spend his time here as his new home until his trial was scheduled to take place. As the van carrying him slowly drove across the bridge toward Eastpoint, Jay saw the scrape marks and chunks missing from the guard walls where his current troubles began. He looked over at the exact spot he'd gotten retribution from Sheriff Roy Burks for the rape of his wife, Cat. He replayed each shot he'd taken at Roy as he sat against the overturned Chevelle SS begging for help in retrieving Kyle and Violet's bodies in bloody brokenness as if he were a hero. He'd been certain anyone in that twisted car would probably be near dead if not already when he happened upon them. Roy sure as hell weren't no damned hero and he wasn't about to let him con his way out of judgment.

Jay later heard the two both survived but were by no means back to their normal teenage lives. He certainly wasn't assured himself of his particular outcome in the distant future at this point either. That's how life is, the shake of the Mason jar, the unpredictability of the punishment tile that drops out. Jay's expectations were a final meeting at the head of the table of death. The main chair of importance is how he chose to think of it. He would have spectators seated, mostly in anxious anticipation of watching him twist and jump in agony as the buttons got pushed, releasing seventeen hundred and fifty volts of electricity instantly throughout his body. An electrical burst so strong as to lift his seated torso in contortion from the chair to which he would be so tightly held and then dropped back down like a bag of scorched dirt, smoke spilling from the metal plate strapped to the top of his head.

To some, it would be as if they'd killed the devil himself. They surely would revel in his being vanquished from their happy little town. Very few would pity the man who called himself the judge, jury and executioner over other's sins.

Cat would probably be there mixed with emotions of love and hate. Pain churned with jubilation for the re-payment of my killing of our son, not the thankful death I gave the rapist who stole from her poor unnurtured garden—even though the son-of-a-bitch had planted the seed of the only son she had left to hold.

But before that day would be fulfilled, there would of course be the closed-circuit watchful eyes of every move made in Jay's long stay in the glass house. Lawyers and pleas, denials, and setbacks. Interviews with more psychiatrists and newspaper journalists. And then the day would come to the countdown. Suddenly removed from the other inmates as if a contagious scourge was within his body. He'd get to have a final steak dinner to enjoy before he'd take the shaky walk of death and finally resolve the matter of meeting his maker.

If'n of course there is a master creator. Or maybe I am just a fluke of some cosmic explosion in the universe that rained down onto this temporary home called Earth. Maybe in fact, I am the intended form of justice to rule as I see fit to those I seek out? The Adams and Eves kicked from the beautiful garden for their sins.

The thoughts rattled in his head as he passed where Roy's final breath was taken, but then he seemed to disappear into a brain-fog as the sound of the bridge segments played their never-changing tune once again.

Ta-tunk. Ta-tunk. Ta-tunk....

About the Author

Eli Pope lives with his family and two dogs in the heart of the Ozarks. He is currently working on several writing projects that includes upcoming additions to The Mason Jar Series.

His love of writing is his escape from the everyday grind of working full-time in the real world of paying the bills and providing for his family.

This is his passion along with painting and creating. Pope is a proud member of the *Springfield Writers Guild.*

(Author's Note) Thank you for taking time to read 'The Glass House'. I hope you enjoyed it.

Please leave a reader review with amazon.com, goodreads.com, barnesandnoble.com and other online retailers. I would greatly appreciate it.

Eli

COMING SOON by ELI POPE

BOOK 4 - THE MASON JAR SERIES
THE RECLAMATION

NOW AVAILABLE

THE MASON JAR SERIES

BOOK 1
THE JUDGEMENT DAY
BOOK 2
THE SPARK OF WRATH

also
THE CLIMB
BY Kendra Nicholson

THE WANING CRESCENT
By Steven G Bassett

Visit *elipope.com* to keep up with upcoming books and projects. Occasionally, Eli makes available to purchase paintings and artistic creations. He lists them on his website.

3 dogsBarking Media LLC strives to bring you quality entertainment. Please let us know if part of our product is not up to your level of satisfaction as a loyal customer.

Contact us at:
3dogsbarkingmediallc@gmail.com

Made in the USA
Columbia, SC
18 July 2024